MARII

By M.L. Bullock

THE BONES OF MARIETTA

Marietta Series
Book One
By M.L. Bullock

MARIETTA

M.L. BULLOCK

Dedication

For Stella, Jesse and Ryan.

MARIETTA

Table of Contents

Immortal Beloved

My angel, my very self...

Why this profound sorrow when necessity speaks?

Can our love endure without sacrifices,

Without our demanding everything from one another;

Can you alter the fact that you are not wholly mine,

That I am not wholly yours?

Dear God, look at Nature in all her beauty

And set your heart at rest about what must be

Love demands all, and rightly so...

No doubt we shall meet soon;

And today also time fails me to tell you of the thoughts

Which during these last few days I have been revolving about my life

If our hearts were always closely united,

I would certainly entertain no such thoughts.

My heart overflows with a longing to tell you so many things

Oh—there are moments when I find that speech is quite inadequate!

Be cheerful—and be forever my faithful, my only sweetheart, my all, as I am yours.

The gods must send us everything else, whatever must and shall be our fate—your faithful Ludwig.

Even when I am in bed my thoughts rush to you,

My immortal beloved, now and then joyfully, then again sadly,

Waiting to know whether Fate will hear our prayer

To face life, I must live altogether with you or never see you...

Oh God, why must one be separated from her who is so dear.

Yet my life in Vienna at present is a miserable life

Your love has made me both the happiest and unhappiest of mortals...

Ludwig Von Beethoven

MARIETTA

July 7, 1812

Prologue—Mary Fairbanks

1848

I stepped out of the chilly coach and descended into the freezing darkness. My worn boot crackled as it touched the packed snow. My destination appeared as unimpressive as my departure point, Summit, West Virginia. Although it had an exotic name, Biloxi, Mississippi, lacked urban sophistication too. Wooden sidewalks, rickety facades nailed to the front of poorly built buildings. I had an eye for this sort of thing, as my father had been a master carpenter. Sadly, this place was nothing more than a clump of wilderness with poor lighting and all the unpleasant smells that accompanied unwashed humanity. Did they slosh urine in the streets here too? I cast a watchful eye above me, but the building behind me was shrouded in shadow.

The other travelers departed without any goodbyes. We had not so much as exchanged pleasantries during our trip, so I had no idea what their names were. That was simply fine with me—easier to keep a low profile and avoid questions that may expose me later. Managing light conversation had never been my strong suit. I preferred discourses on interesting subjects, not idle chitchat.

Instead of exchanging pleasantries with absolute strangers, I spent the hours memorizing all the details I could remember about Mary Fairbanks. I could not fail in my recollection. I had stolen her future, taken it for my own. I chewed on my fingernail, a worrying habit of mine, and ignored the disapproving looks of the only other woman in our party. Eventually I met her stare with one of my own, and after a brief eye roll, she turned her attention to the opposite window.

My plan was to hide my accent, as best I could, and assume the identity that I had stolen without being discovered. Mary Fairbanks was not an Irishwoman, but in my letters, I never spoke about my heritage—or more precisely, Mary's heritage. It would be difficult, but I would explain it if pressed. I should not like to be found out as a criminal. At least until I was wed. That was the goal here, to marry John Lancaster. I had fallen in love with him, you see. I do not know how such a thing could be possible, but it was a fact.

The strangest thing was how accidental it all had been—from the first letter to his proposal. Yes. What I had done was nothing less than criminal, but I felt little remorse for seizing the opportunity.

Just as he promised, John Lamar Lancaster sent a coach ticket and spending money for the journey. This would not be the longest journey I had made, but it would still be many days, depending on the weather. Whatever the cost, I would be Mrs. John Lancaster.

Yes, I had every intention of marrying that fine man. I would have a happy life. Funny to think that my former employer, Mary Fairbanks, thought she would snare him, rob him blind, no doubt. No woman like her could ever become a good wife. Thankfully, she had a short attention span and did not like to write. After the third letter John sent, she didn't even bother reading them. Mary was content to let me "run a game" on the unsuspecting Mr. Lancaster, but it was not a game to me. He and I were meant to be together. He was my path to happiness.

My prose, my answers intrigued him. He had fallen in love with me, he declared finally. Mary thought the whole thing was very funny in a crude sort of way. If I had allowed her to follow through, she would have shamed him. He would have had a whore for a wife.

I was no whore.

By the time I slid the ticket into my dress pocket and walked down that first flight of steps, I was resolved to this course of action. Mary Fairbanks was a drunkard, an unashamed fool—a blemish on society. No two people were more dissimilar than the two of us.

Bad things happened to women like me in Summit. Eventually, I would have no choice; Mary made that clear. She expected me to join her in her ill reputes, to follow in her high-heeled boots and become one of the many cast-off prostitutes that littered the streets of Summit. It did not take long for the dirty hands of the coal miners to stain a woman. I had seen many pretty young women come to Summit and never leave.

Except in a hearse. The bloody stains the women left behind would last far longer than any remembrance of them. The most pitiful of them, the least fair, the weak-eyed or toothless serviced the poorest of the coal miners. They disappeared into those pits and never reemerged. I shuddered at the thought. Not only would they die, but their souls would be stained forever. I believed we had a soul. Mine was not perfect, but I wanted to keep it as clean as possible.

The fight to keep my virtue had been truly dreadful, but I was coming to John Lancaster a virgin. Thankfully, I excelled at drinking games. Raised on rye whiskey, I could defeat even the thirstiest drunkard.

For as long as I can remember, I have been small of stature. Smaller than most. Even at eighteen, I measured slightly over four feet tall and had no mature feminine attributes. I looked more like a doll, like the paper dolls I loved to cut and snip. The oldest of five children, I never grew tall and spindly like my brothers. My mother often joked that I was a changeling born of the fairy folks, traded at birth for the real Vienna Fitzgerald, who was no doubt as fair and as tall as my siblings. I was never offended by my mother's attempts at humor. I thought my brothers were great fools, although of a better sort than these greedy, lascivious Americans. *You are better than that, Vienna.*

Forget that name! You are Mary Fairbanks, and this is your one chance for happiness. Finally, you'll have your lucky break!

Although I am small of frame, I do have many good qualities, I reminded myself as I rode for hours in the rickety coach. I reviewed each one of them so I would know what to say if things turned bad and I had to make a case for clemency.

Yes, I am clever, resilient and hardworking; these were attributes that have helped me in the past. However, like most young women, there were times when I would have traded all those attributes for corn silk hair, an ample bosom and luminous blue eyes.

Rather than spend my life sulking over my short stature and general lack of beauty, I chose to enjoy the obscurity my height offered me. People tended to overlook me, to speak of things that they should not, all because I was small and rather childlike. For reasons beyond me, adults tended to talk about the most atrocious things in the presence of children. Or childlike people. That was me, an eternal child.

"Some men," Mary Fairbanks would whisper in the darkness, "would give a gold mine to spend the night with someone like you, Vienna." Meaning childlike, I assumed. Inexperienced. Helpless. She always appeared green with envy while telling me this information. The thought of lying with any man repulsed me.

I would do so only out of necessity. Only if I married. This man, this John Lamar Lancaster, he would expect such intimacies. But for marriage, to a good man, it seemed a fair trade. I have never been a slave to my emotions or physical impulses, and I would not start now. However, the real Mary Fairbanks cared nothing about her self-respect or dignity. She was for all intents and purposes a whore and not a particularly good one. She got ripped off often and beaten on occasion, and she drank so much that she was easily robbed after her work.

I met her almost a year before I coldly robbed her myself, taking her ticket to her new life with me. I betrayed her too. It was freeing to leave that life behind.

"Vienna, dear, be a lamb and roll me a cigarette or two. Your little fingers roll the tightest cigarettes," she would always say. I did that every day between washing her clothes and cooking her meals. "Think about how rich we would be if you helped out." To her, "helping out" meant giving my life to prostitution. When she was sober, I politely refused. Later, when she was completely sotted, she would smack me with her hand or hit me with her hairbrush, but nothing would convince me to take up her profession. Not even the threat of poverty or homelessness. No matter how hard she beat me, I would never do that. My poor dead mother would roll over in her grave.

Besides, it all seemed so foolish. And from what I had witnessed, coupling with a man looked uncomfortable and unpleasant. I had no desire to end up disease-ridden or pregnant or worse—dead. Despite my disdain for Mary's occupation, she was why I survived that first winter here in Summit, West Virginia. I had been promised work, coming to Summit by way of a newspaper advertisement. A store needed "willing hands," but by the time I arrived, there was no job for me. The store burned to the ground a week before I arrived. I applied for other positions, but it was always the same.

"Go home. You are too small for this kind of work. How can you possibly sew with those tiny fingers? You are absolutely grimy. I can see the grime from here." The woman had been rude beyond words. I was cleaner than most, my nails and hands impeccable, but there was no persuading her. I left heartbroken, disappointed and hungry. So very hungry.

And then I met Mary.

She had been patient at first, but her expectations were becoming more aggressive. I would not be able to say no to her forever, hence my need for a hasty departure. And then it all came together. The idea, then a plan and then the opportunity.

Yes, it did seem as if fate once again smiled upon me! I had to take the bull by the horns. Make fortune work for me. Yes. Fortune would continue to lead me to the happy life I dreamed of so long ago in Ireland. It was the luck of the Irish that I trusted in, that and my ability to persevere.

Snow began to fall as I stood clutching my black bag. The others were gone. I was all alone. I tucked my hat down over my ears and waited. Surely whoever expected me would arrive soon.

Where are you, John Lancaster? Where are you? You cannot leave me here. Please, let this be real. Let this all be real. I have risked everything. Everything! What else is there for me?

But no one stepped out of the darkness to claim me. A flickering lamp above the sidewalk did not offer me much light, but it was enough to see that I was by myself.

"John Lancaster? Mr. Lancaster?" I whispered into the crisp air. The only answer was a heavy falling of snow.

All the world grew silent.

Chapter One—Ashland

Present Day

Today was the day. I could not wait to see our child. A son or daughter. I could not begin to guess which it would be. Did I care? Okay, maybe a little. To have a little Carrie Jo running around, it seemed only right. What would my mother think about this? She would have loved every minute of it. I missed her lately, missed her a lot. Even though she had never met my son or even my wife, I sometimes sensed her around me. Felt her touch on my shoulder when I was in between awake and asleep. I often smelled her familiar perfume around Seven Sisters, a place she loved more than me. At least that's what I believed when I was a young boy.

When I was a child, we always came back to this place. Mother knew there were ghosts at Seven Sisters. She wanted to contact the spirits that roamed there, but I had been the one to see them. She wanted to see the ghosts, but I witnessed the apparition.

I had been the one to meet the beautiful yet snakelike Isla Beaumont, and so my life of seeing ghosts began. I had only been a child, but the ghost of Isla did not have any qualms about seducing a child. It did not happen, thankfully. I sensed the evil behind her lovely face. She blew her sweet breath in my face; I could smell lemonade and honey, but there was also a sour note of death. Funny that I should know what death smelled like. I had not experienced it before, or at least had not witnessed it for myself. But my soul knew, and it screamed the alarm bell.

At least now Seven Sisters was empty of all those spirits, or more accurately empty of anything dark and evil. It was a shame that they *all* left, the good and the bad.

Yes, I found myself missing my mother quite a bit lately. Sadly, for all the ghosts I did see, I never saw hers. Carrie Jo had a vision of her a few years ago, but me? Nothing. I wished I could. I wished that with all my heart. But wishing would not make it happen. I used to wander the gardens thinking about her, hoping to catch a glimpse of Mother's gleaming blonde and white hair. Hoping to see her elegant smile and smart dress, with her favorite string of pearls around her neck. It did not happen often.

Why so glum, Ashland? You have a beautiful, growing family.

"Are you sure you want to do this, Lily Bean?" I asked hopefully. "It might seem kind of strange for someone your age."

"My age? Why? It's just technology, Uncle Ash."

I did not know how to counter that argument. Instead, I offered a sigh of retreat. I agreed with Carrie Jo that it was important to include Lily in our family's expansion, as much as Lily was comfortable with. Maybe I *was* treating her like a baby. I never wanted my niece to feel like she was unimportant to us because she wasn't our biological child. We didn't want her to get the idea that the baby would take her place in our hearts. I really didn't think we had much to worry about in that regard because Lily knew we loved her like she was our own. We had adopted her, after all.

"Okay, you guys. I'm not a baby. It's not like I am going to watch you give birth, Aunt CJ. It's just an ultrasound."

Carrie Jo and I glanced at each other. Lily was just barely a teenager, but she had a full-blown teenager attitude. It was not so long ago that I had those same angsty feelings. And of all of us, she deserved to be quite angry with the world. But she usually wasn't this sarcastic. Carrie Jo was right. Despite all of Lily's big talk, something was going on inside that head of hers.

The technician led the three of us back to the dimly lit room. It had been a long time since I witnessed an ultrasound. I knew what to expect, but I was so excited to have another child. It was always a bit surreal until you got to hold the baby. Would it be a her or a him? I did not care anymore. Not really. Did I? Why was I so nervous?

"Okay, Mrs. Stuart, climb up on the table and get comfy. We will get this session started. You guys can sit in those seats. You will have a great view."

I squeezed Lily's hand briefly as we took our seats. Carrie Jo smiled at us, and I grinned back. The technician prepared Carrie Jo's stomach for the ultrasound while the nurse chitchatted with her. She asked her how she was feeling and whether she had felt any movement. Was she singing or talking to the baby? The setup seemed to take forever even though it was actually only a few minutes. I impatiently waited for the first look at our new baby. What a miracle! Babies were nothing less than little miracles.

I wished AJ could be here, but he was too little to appreciate any of it. He would not enjoy sitting still even for a few minutes. My son was the busiest kid in Mobile, Alabama.

Wow! This was really happening. And as much as I wanted to be a dad again, I did not feel ready. Carrie Jo was right. I hadn't really thought this through. Late-night bottles, diaper changes, doctor's appointments. Sleeplessness. Endless sleeplessness.

Oh, crap. Weird how that worked. Too late now. The baby would be here soon.

The technician turned up the volume and slid the wand over Carrie Jo's gel-covered belly. We immediately began to hear the baby's quick heartbeat.

Lily squealed like the child she truly was and gave Carrie Jo two thumbs up. "Oh my God! That is so cool! That's the baby, right? Look at that! I see eyes and...is that a finger? How sweet!" So much for being cool, calm and distant.

"Yes, and he or she sounds great. I hear the baby's heartbeat!" The technician tinkered with the machine. "Here, you can listen too." We sat in awe as the sound of the baby's heartbeat echoed back to us. "Oh, the baby sounds perfect! Time to look around. Looks like this little one has his or her back turned and does not want to give us a peek."

Lily whispered impatiently, "Turn around, baby! I want to see." She patted her jeans with her hands.

"Don't worry. Babies are never still for long. What do you think, big sister? Is it a boy or a girl?"

Nobody bothered to correct her, although I could not help but see that quick glimpse of hurt flash across Lily's face. It was a common mistake, and I knew the tech did not intend to cause harm. How was she supposed to know our family situation?

"I say...boy," Lily said with some hesitation. "I mean, I'm okay with either, but I bet it's a boy."

"What about you, Dad?" the nurse asked me as she continued to move the wand over Carrie Jo's stomach.

"I go back and forth. Either one, but I think it is probably a girl. We have AJ and Lily, so we're happy either way." I hugged my niece briefly.

The tech smiled and talked to the machine a minute. She was doing her best to get the little one to turn and reveal his or her identity. "Mom? What do you think?"

"No predictions, but the suspense is killing me. Oof! That was a big kick—or something. Either she's a ballerina or he's a football player."

The technician, I already forgot her name, cheered. "The baby moved, and look! It is a girl. She is healthy and fat and wonderful. I love my job!"

Katie! That's her name. "A girl? Are you sure?" I asked as I stared at the screen. I had no idea what I was looking at.

"Pretty sure," she said with a laugh.

I could not tell what in the Sam Hill I was looking at, but it was nothing less than miraculous. I immediately hugged Lily again and held Carrie Jo's hand and kissed it. Somehow or another, my hand got into the goop, but I did not even care. At least I did not get a mouthful of it. I could not stop staring at the screen.

The technician began snapping and printing photos for us. "Now for her face. Would you all like a picture of that?"

"Yes, please," Carrie Jo whispered without taking her eyes off the monitor. She was smiling too.

Wow! Had I really wanted a girl so badly? I don't know, but I was feeling emotional. Strangely enough, Carrie Jo was the calm and cool one for this pregnancy—so far. I was crying at the drop of a hat.

Then I noticed Carrie Jo had gone as pale as a ghost. Yeah, she looked white, like something was wrong. "Are you feeling okay, CJ?"

She squeezed my fingers and released them. "Yeah, just a little weak, babe. I shouldn't have skipped breakfast."

The technician completed printing off the pictures and handed her some paper towels. "Well, let's get you cleaned up so you can grab some lunch. I'll forward these to your doctor, but everything looks great. She is a beautiful baby girl. If you do not mind me saying so, I think she looks like you." Her comment to Lily produced a beaming smile.

"Yeah, I can see it," our niece said cheerfully.

Carrie Jo added, "She's right, Lily. She does look like you, and she's definitely moving around. She must be hungry too. Let's go find something to eat. Oof. I'm dizzy."

"No more skipping meals, Mrs. Stuart. We don't need you fainting."

I helped CJ sit up and held her briefly as she clung to me. It was an urgent cling, not a joyful hug. My wife had something on her mind, but unfortunately, mind-reading was not one of my skills.

I would not push her. She would share with me eventually. This may not be a conversation we should have in front of Lily. I hoped and prayed that her distress had nothing to do with Marietta, with this weekend's adventure to the historic home. A recent hurricane revealed a disturbing secret—bones were found, an incomplete skeleton, bits and pieces of someone who died long ago. Since the storm blew through and uncovered the partial remains, paranormal activity had kicked up at Marietta. Hence the phone call for help.

Deep inside, I already knew what was happening.

The ghosts of Marietta knew Carrie Jo was coming. She knew it too.

Chapter Two—Carrie Jo

I dreamed about Marietta last night. Upon waking, my wet cheeks surprised me, but the tears had nothing to do with my new child. It had nothing to do with that at all. It had everything to do with Marietta and the spirits that surrounded it. When the idea first came to me to embrace my dream catching abilities as an actual business, Ashland was a little leery. But I made my case, and he agreed without much argument.

I am a dream catcher—just like my mother and many of the other women in my family. I love being a historian and researcher, but at the core of my being, I am a dreamer.

"I am embracing my gift, Ashland. I will not advertise the service; it will only be by word of mouth. We will be selective about which cases I take—I mean, we take. We can still run the restoration business; I know it pays the bills. But I want to do this. Okay?" Who was I trying to convince? Me or him? I hadn't felt this unsure when I was rehearsing this speech. "It makes me happy. Really happy. Sometimes it is scary—as scary as anything—but what about the others?" Surely, he knew what others I was talking about.

All the dead.

All the lost.

All the living who needed my help.

To his credit, Ashland did not argue with me. He knew what I meant. There was certainly something magical about coming to a location on assignment and discovering that there were mysteries to be uncovered. Yes, very magical, but was it necessary? Why not go into each situation with our eyes open and not hide the fact that we work with the dead, Ashland with his ghostly sight and me with my dream catching skills?

This had all been Rachel's idea. Why not come at this in a positive way? That had been her suggestion. Why not come at it like it is my job, what I do for a living? Yes, I loved the restoration and the research and all the things that we had to do to get these historic places in shape—to put the spirits to rest—but people knew what we did here. They knew we were different. Why not just make it official?

That had been one odd conversation, but it got me thinking. I joked and asked Rachel how I would do that. *Buy black business cards? Put a black cat marquee out front of Seven Sisters?*

I guess there was a small part of me that still cared about what people thought. I shouldn't, not after all we've been through, but what can I say? You cannot beat out what was born into you. It was not long before we received a discreet phone call from the owner of Marietta, a beautiful Greek revival located not far from home in Biloxi.

Like with Seven Sisters, it was a miracle that the place was still standing. The historic home had managed to survive Hurricane Katrina and other major storms, but there was quite a bit of damage and the remodeling was not going as easily as the current homeowner had hoped. The most recent hurricane left more than sand and shells in its wake, more than broken trees and a damaged roof and cracked windows. The bluster of Hurricane Angel had uncovered old human bones inside the property line, and no one knew where they came from. Now that they had been uncovered, something disturbing had been awakened.

According to Heather, who was rather skimpy on the details, the situation was dire; no contractor wanted to touch the place. Marietta already had a reputation as a place of tragedies—Heather's description, not mine—but she made it sound profoundly foreboding. I shivered thinking about our many phone conversations.

"I always knew this place had a reputation. I am a local. Marietta always interested me, even as a child, and I knew stories about the Lancaster family. But this...I do not know. What I feel here is so different since the storm. I cannot explain it. I heard good things about you, Carrie Jo. I would rather you come see for yourself. I would not bother you if this were merely my imagination."

The pull to Marietta was unmistakable. I had no choice—I had to see for myself.

I was only four months pregnant, and thankfully the morning queasiness had passed. Ashland sounded a bit hurt when I insisted on running solo, but I pointed out that he needed to devote his time to podcasting. He loved the work and had quite the fan following, which proved to pay very well. But all that was only until we landed another restoration job. An official one, anyway. No, my husband would not come with me on this trip, but I would be fine. If I got there and the place put off bad vibes, I would be honest. Besides, someone had to watch the kids. Ashland could podcast from his home office. And the good thing was, I would only be an hour and a half away. I could drive home if need be, but I wanted to dream again. I wanted to get back into the swing of things.

Speaking of which, I was almost there. I tapped on my swanky dashboard and called my husband. I loved this wireless Bluetooth thingy.

Shoot. Went to voicemail.

"Ashland? It's me, babe. I am almost at Marietta, about to turn off Beach Boulevard. Traffic isn't too bad. I'll call you after I get settled in. Love you. Kiss the kids for me." I sighed as I tapped on the dashboard again. That was much safer than texting and driving. I never did that. Too dang dangerous.

I was glad I went ahead and made the ride to Marietta. Turning the leather-covered wheel, I held my breath. Wow, this place was amazing. The homeowner seemed like a lovely lady with a lot of anxiety about the gruesome discovery of bones after the hurricane. If we could put those bones—and the restless spirits—to rest, I will have done my job.

MARIETTA

The plan was that I would stay at Marietta this weekend. Heather refused to stay in the house. I liked it that way. I was a bit of a loner and unafraid, at least according to Ashland. He would have preferred it if I had a bit more fear, but he accepted me for who I was. I mentioned my dream the other night, a dream related to Marietta, but we had not had a chance to really talk about the details. Life ran fast and furious at Seven Sisters. Lily had endless hobbies, and AJ was always go-go-go.

Oh, yes. Marietta was an impressive place. At some point in recent history, the house had been raised and placed on a platform, probably to protect it from storm surge. I read somewhere that this had not been the original location for Marietta and that it had been moved here about 100 years ago. I wasn't sure, but I knew that Rachel and I would get to the bottom of that story. We excelled at that.

Like Seven Sisters, the front of the one-story Creole-style home was flanked by columns and wide porches. It was a reflection of a more graceful yet brutal time. Strange how the elites back in those days were so obsessed with luxury that they were willing to inflict immeasurable human suffering on others at any cost. I shuddered at that thought. We cannot rewrite history, but we don't have to exploit it either. Whatever I discovered, whoever haunted Marietta, I would not pretty it up.

That was one of the reasons Ashland and I were so committed to maintaining the slave quarters at the Seven Sisters complex. It was important to both of us that the true history of the families be told every day. As I got out of the car, I experienced a strange sort of solemnity, like the kind you feel when you walk into a cemetery or even some churches.

I'd viewed pictures of Marietta online, but my gifts weren't at their best with just images. I had done it before, back when I searched for Calpurnia Cottonwood. However, my abilities worked better in person. I enjoyed feeling and sensing and listening to the history all around us, and history was always around. Thankfully, Seven Sisters, our family home, was a historical landmark in Mobile. Alabama. It used to be full of ghosts, but it had been cleared of most of the paranormal activity. Yes, things were quiet around our place...but here?

"Hi, Heather. Yeah, it's me in the driveway." I put the car in park and waved at the woman on the porch. "I'm ready to get started." I smiled and got out of the car, locking it behind me. I would bring my overnight bag inside in a bit, but for now, I needed to greet the client.

Electricity buzzed around me. This did not feel right at all. Usually, when a dream portal opened, I saw the world through a sepia-colored filter. A honey hue, an invitation to see into that other world.

And see, I would...

Chapter Three—Mary

Perhaps I should have paid more attention to the letter's address before I set out on this journey, but I was in the thick of it now and would make the best of it. Without much ado, the coach hurried away toward a dark destination down the street, which I assumed was a livery stable. I suppose I could follow it, seek out the unhappy driver and ask for further directions. That is when I saw the man. He was standing on the other side of the street, his hat in his hands. His bright white hair fluttered about his face as he stood motionlessly, watching me.

Watching me like an owl sizing up a plump field mouse. I shivered at that thought but refused to slink away in fear. I lifted my chin and stared back.

"Miss Mary Fairbanks? Forgive me for staring, but you are not quite what I expected. I hope your trip was pleasant."

I walked to the edge of the sidewalk, my shoes thumping loudly on the damp wood. I kept my face a mask even though my hands nervously clutched my black bag. I was sure he could see the pale skin beneath my gloves. The flush always gave away my true feelings. What if this encounter ended badly? It was truly a brazen act, wasn't it? Everything depended on these next few moments.

"The trip was pleasant enough, Mr. Lancaster. I am grateful for your kindness and have been looking forward to this moment." I said nothing about his expectations and chose instead to feign confidence in myself. What good would it do to say otherwise? No, I was not the prettiest woman in the world. Not the cleverest. But I was honest—most of the time—and faithful. I would be a faithful wife, a steady rock on which he could rest all his cares and worries. I smiled and gently tilted my head.

"There is no reason to be so formal with me, Miss Fairbanks. We are to be married; I think that means we can use informal names with one another. Shall I call you Mary?" To my surprise, he laughed and joined me on the walkway. Oh, he was a handsome man, with a pleasant face and hair that practically glowed beneath his black silk hat. "You may call me John or John Lamar, as my mother does."

"I think I like John." My Irish tongue revealed my accent a bit.

"Mary...you are going to be my wedded wife." Then after a moment he added, "You are Irish? I did not know that. You have a few mysteries, don't you? I like that; I am a man who appreciates a bit of mystery, but please only a few, Mary. As you have probably gathered from my letters, I have my reputation to think of. And a good name goes a long way here in Biloxi, Mississippi."

I lowered my head and said solemnly, "I understand." What a strange thing for him to say, but I knew he meant it.

"My mother will be pleased to hear that you come from the Land of Green Hills. She shares your ancestry. You will have much to talk about."

I quietly scolded myself. The real Mary had no accent at all. Maybe that would not be an issue since it was impossible to determine accents on paper. But what if she came to Marietta?

I wasn't sure I had done the deed. I wasn't actually sure. *Oh, God! What have I done?*

Mary was mildly attractive except for the scars on her face from an unfortunate bout of chicken pox. If she had been foolish enough to send a painting or portrait of herself, I would certainly be tossed into jail, but I would never imagine her going to all that trouble. No, I knew better than that.

Mary Fairbanks never planned to get married. She'd found a rube, a mark, a man who had believed her pretty lies, and she'd answered his ad with a perfectly worded reply. My reply, actually. Was this man a fool? He did not seem halt or unusual, except for his bright white hair that crowned a youthful face. From the tone of the letters, I assumed that the two had never met in person although he tried.

"What should we say to one another? Should we declare our love? Speak sweet words that we can share with our children in years to come?" John's soft voice sounded both playful and serious. I did not know him well enough to discern his level of sincerity. I remained speechless while John kept his peace as he approached me. "Fair enough. There is time for all that later. I am happy to meet you at last, Mary. Let us seek shelter from the weather. We will stay in town tonight and then travel to Marietta in the morning. Where are your bags?" he asked with concern as he extended his elbow to me. I slid my skinny arm through his, but I looked like a child compared to his frame.

Despite his bright white hair, I could see that John was still a young man. Some young men did go white early. It was a rare thing but not unattractive. Yes, I found John Lancaster to be extremely attractive indeed. "Just the one bag, John. I do not have much."

"And your servant. Didn't she travel with you?"

"Vienna decided to stay behind, and I am sad to say that evidently some of my bags did too. I never took her for a thief, but I am happy to be here with you, John. I do not need much. I am content."

"Nonsense. We should file a report with the sheriff. It is not right that your servant should steal from you. All your clothing, Mary?"

With John's arm through mine, we walked slowly down the sidewalk and headed down the darkened street with a few poorly lit lamps flickering against the snow. If I were a romantic, I would certainly find this moment memorable.

I hurried to match his long strides as effortlessly as possible. I in no way wanted to be deemed unworthy of him. I did not know as much as I would like about John Lancaster, but he was a wealthy man and had an eye to marry. But why go outside his social circle? Why advertise for a wife in the newspaper, and a newspaper as far away as Summit? Could it be true that Mr. John Lamar Lancaster had his own secrets to hide?

Yes, why settle on Mary Fairbanks? That is a question that troubled me. Why would such a man resort to marrying a prostitute? Did he know what she was? And if he did, what did he expect of me?

I bit my lip in fear as I stepped into a freshly painted parlor. I could smell the paint. John closed the door behind us, and the clerk at the desk greeted us with guarded politeness. People were always surprised to find that I was not a child but a woman. I paid no attention to his unspoken questions.

"Two rooms, please. Mr. John Lancaster is my name. And if it is not too much trouble, Miss Fairbanks and I would like an early breakfast. We plan to leave right after sunrise."

"Yes, sir. Would you like to have your breakfast upstairs, or would you care to dine in the dining room? There is plenty of light, and Madge will have a newspaper at your table."

"The dining room, please," I answered in a polite yet challenging tone. No way would I wish to be mistaken for a lady of the night. I had worked too hard, endured too much to lose my reputation and self-respect at this juncture. It was unfortunate that I came here under the name Mary Fairbanks. Hopefully, my former mistress' past would not follow me. I would make sure that everything was properly done from here forward. I would tolerate no gossip.

"Your key, ma'am. You will be in room eighteen. And you, sir, will be in room twenty. I will send my wife up to wake you for breakfast. Six in the morning. Do you require anything else?"

"Nothing. Thank you. Come, Miss Fairbanks." I was thankful he used my formal name.

Together, we walked upstairs keeping our hands to ourselves, both of us behaving with proper manners as I walked toward the room with the key in my hand. I paused to thank Mr. Lancaster for picking me up from the coach. I considered offering some other pleasantries before turning in for the night, but to my surprise he was not there.

I paused in the hallway, looking up and down. Could he have retreated into his room that quickly? I leaned over the rail to look down, but I did not see him. This was odd. Yes, very odd. I had a disturbed feeling in the pit of my stomach that I could not explain.

As I stepped into my room, I discovered the fireplace had been lit and the room was moderately warm. Had they expected us after all? I breathed a sigh of relief. I placed my bag on the bed and sat down as I removed my gloves and then my shoes and my hat. I sighed from sheer exhaustion. *What now? What do I do now? Rejoice or creep away in the night?* Despite months of planning, this all felt like a hasty move. Hasty moves were never smart moves.

I preferred chess to checkers, careful calculations to impetuosity. But I was here now. As I began to remove my traveling clothing, I noticed the adjoining door, the one between Mr. Lancaster's room and mine. By the light of the fireplace, I walked to the door and reached for the handle. If there was a lock, I did not see it. That troubled me. I did not like being at the mercy of a stranger or being in a strange place. How would I sleep knowing that anyone could enter my room? I did not get a bad feeling from Mr. Lancaster, but as he may have knowingly brought a prostitute here, what might he expect from me?

I decided to act.

I found a wooden chair by the window and slid it under the doorknob as quietly as possible, hoping not to draw attention to my preventative measures. What if Mr. Lancaster, who behaved as a gentleman in public, decided to succumb to his basest desires after the sun went down? I had seen that more than once at the Golden Nugget Saloon. That was where I learned this trick, on nights when

Mary Fairbanks was drunk or not open for business. Sometimes her tricks, as she called them, came to my room by mistake. Or not.

Well, it was too late to change my mind. This was my idea—my impulse. Whatever happened, I would live with the consequences. I decided not to completely undress, just to be on the safe side. I added a log to the fire and readied my bed. My wild Irish hair would be a complete mess in the morning, but I would do my best to look presentable.

As I closed my eyes and hovered on the edge of sleep, I heard a light tapping. Not once but twice. My eyes fluttered open, and I peered at the doorknob. No, it was not the bedroom door I heard jiggling but the one that led to the adjoining room. Was Mr. Lancaster trying to covertly enter my room? What would I do? What should I do? I became completely still, like a statue. I did not even breathe loudly. I did not move a muscle in case he made it in. *And then what will you do?* I closed my eyes and pretended to sleep. There would be no sense in screaming and fighting. But the chair kept sturdy. I breathed a sigh of relief.

There were no more knocks, nothing else at all. This John Lancaster truly may have a dark side and not-so-noble intentions. It was entirely possible. Now that I thought about it, what kind of man would search for a wife in the newspaper? He was wealthy and relatively handsome and owned his own home, or so he said in his letters. Maybe I had stepped into a spider web?

Wouldn't that be ironic? One spider trapping another. The door handle shook a few more times and then nothing. I did not hear his footsteps or anything else.

Well, to the victor go the spoils!

John Lamar Lancaster had better be careful not to cross me. I had already done the unthinkable to get here. Yes, unthinkable. But I would do it again if I had to. I would do whatever it took to become a lady, to avoid a harlot's future. I would rather die than do that.

MARIETTA

After some tossing and turning, I fell asleep.
I slept like the dead.

Chapter Four—Carrie Jo

"Hey, honey. It's me," I said as I watched Heather's car leave the driveway. She was coming back with dinner soon. I only had a short amount of time to speak with him. What was I going to say? *Please come over. I need you.* Or maybe, *Hey, remember how you wanted to come? I changed my mind about going alone, Ash. Get your behind over here!*

"Hey! How was your drive?"

"Drive was great, traffic was crazy, but this place is active. I barely got out of the car when I met the first unhappy spirit. Her name is Mary Fairbanks. I had a tough time explaining to Heather that I was not a kook, just in a trance. I am calling because you..."

"You know I'll come."

I twisted my curly hair with my finger as I pondered what to say. *Here I am, trying to be Miss Independent, and I am afraid. That's right. Me, Carrie Jo Stuart, stone-cold scared. And I don't even know why. Mary Fairbanks wasn't scary, not really. But there is an evil here. An evil presence. Might as well be honest about it.*

"I need you here, Ashland. I know it's a huge inconvenience because you have your podcasts, but I do think this is going to take both of us. Maybe it's a confidence thing—maybe I am wrong, but Rachel will watch the kids for us. If not her, then Jan. She loves when the kids come over. There is a cemetery here, Ashland. I didn't know that. How did I miss that? You were right, babe. We should do this together. I'm sorry."

"No reason to worry. Of course I'll come. I'll be there as soon as I can. The podcasts can wait. How is Heather? Do you find her credible?"

I wandered around the front room as I thought about his question. "Yes, I like her. She's telling the truth, but I've hardly been here long enough to know what all she has experienced. It's strange; she reminds me of Detra Ann."

"In what way? Is Heather a human lie detector?" Ashland said, poking fun at my comparison.

"No, I mean she is a tall, beautiful blonde. Really put together, but there's more to it than that. I don't know exactly. Heather is a little more nervous than Detra Ann. She has seen an apparition; I think I've seen her too. She calls this apparition the Red Lady—kind of like a banshee. Have you ever heard of the Red Lady of Marietta?"

Ashland paused, and I could hear him breathing. "No, but now I'm anxious to get to you. Give me a few hours. Promise me you won't dream walk until I am with you. You can control it, Carrie Jo. I have faith in you."

"Roger that. I will do my best. It's a beautiful place, Ashland. Deathly beautiful." My own words triggered a tsunami of apprehension that washed over me not once but twice.

Why? Why did I feel this way? The furniture here was exquisite, teak and cedar, overstuffed cushions, with lots of green plants. It was a welcoming place, a nice mix of old and new. I found the photographs especially fascinating. Generations of families watched me from their gilded frames, and the strange thing was, most of them were smiling. It was rare to see turn-of-the-century photographs where the subjects were smiling. They were not showing teeth, but they seemed happy.

No. Not happy. Something else. Were they posed? Yes, they appeared like dolls.

I paused in front of a photograph of a young boy sitting with a black Lab. It was a heartwarming photo, but even it seemed off. I just could not put my finger on it. The boy was not looking directly at the camera; there was a hint of a smile on his face, but he was watching someone or something far away. Something just out of my view. But with all my heart, I wanted to see. I touched the glass and quickly withdrew my fingers.

"I will. I almost took a second dream walk in the cottage; it is right out front. Marietta is beautiful, but it has that disturbed feeling. Something isn't right. I cannot put my finger on it, and that surprises me. Since there are apparitions, I thought you might be able to help me see who is here. I had a dream about this place, Ashland, but like I told you before, I cannot remember the details. So far, all I have are more questions than answers." I plunked down on the comfy chair and continued my visual survey of the front parlor. I caught my breath as I felt baby butterflies in my tummy. This was not nerves; it was definitely the baby. She was still small but already quite active.

"Oof..."

"What is it?"

"Baby girl is pirouetting in Mommy's belly again; it is almost lunch time. That's probably why. She doesn't like missing a meal." The whirring of the ceiling fan above me drew my attention. Marietta did not have the creaks and pops that our home did. Seven Sisters made lots of noise, but here...it was too still. Very still. I heard nothing except for the clock and the fan.

"Should I bring you something?"

I shook my head as if he could see me. "No, I'm okay. Heather went to pick up supplies for dinner. She should be back soon, and I do not want to alarm her. Hey, when you come, would you bring my phone charger? Believe it or not, I forgot to pack it. Also, do not let Lily talk you into bringing her along. I don't want to put her in harm's way. She's tough, but this place is eerie."

I did not want to sound like an alarmist, but it was true. Lily had a gift, but she wasn't ready to step into this realm yet—or maybe I wasn't ready for that. Not fully. Not like this. Dang it! Had I made the right decision? Maybe I should not have opened this dream catching business in the first place.

"You got it. See you in a couple of hours. Oh, and Carrie Jo?"

"Yes?" I said as I continued to listen to the clock tick and the fan blades click above me.

"Remember, no dream walking without me."

I smiled and closed my eyes. Just hearing his voice made me feel better. "I heard you the first time. See you soon. I love you." I hung up the phone and breathed a sigh of relief. Ashland was on his way, and we would sort this out together. So much the better. Yes, this was the right thing to do. I did not need to be here by myself. I was off balance, spiritually speaking. A worrying fear crept up within me, a fear that warned me all was not as it appeared here at Marietta.

After a few minutes of nothing but the sounds of the clock and the fan, I whispered, "Hello? Anyone here with me?"

I did another survey of the portraits around me and then decided to walk the house alone. Heather had given me a rushed walk-through before announcing she needed to pick up the grocery order. However, I got the feeling that she did not want to be here at Marietta, even for a few minutes. What was happening here?

I walked back to the front door. Of course, the house had lovely wood floors. Despite having endured Hurricane Angel, the house didn't seem to have any interior damage. Coming into Marietta through the oversized front door, guests would enter a large open room. It would have been called a parlor back in the day. It was elegantly decorated with a lovely oil painting of a dark-haired woman in a deep red dress, which hung over a dark wooden buffet. Certainly, she had been the lady of the manor. Was this Marietta? It was a real possibility. I got the feeling that this was a showroom, a room where any guest would immediately understand that Marietta was a place worthy of respect. It held a quiet solemnity. No, there would be no frivolous conversations in this room. The formality of the straight-backed chairs and marble-top table did not invite comfort.

Only elegance, a cold and unwelcoming elegance.

Through open doors on either side of the painting, I saw two bedrooms. There was more red in one room—expensive deep red curtains were pulled back with gold tasseled cords, but the room was bright and sunny nonetheless. I spotted a lovely sleigh bed with an overstuffed mattress and a red canopy. Each bedroom's entrance was flanked by freshly painted woodwork. I loved the columns. Atop the round marble-top table rested a green glass vase filled with red roses. Yes, red appeared to be a popular color in this home. The walls were interesting too: light tan paint with touches of sage green and white panels which gave clues as to this time capsule's not-so-humble beginnings.

Marietta began as a beautiful residence, and today it was a haunting museum.

Haunting. Interesting word, Carrie Jo.

Off to the left I spotted a kitchen, but I wasn't drawn to that area. I would certainly check it out later. My stomach rumbled to remind me that eventually I'd need food. Beyond that I could see a fine dining room. So formal yet also interesting. Strange brass statues perched atop the mantelpiece. *What were those? Gargoyles? Yuck.* If I owned this place, those things would have to go. Who decorated a home like this with demon statues? On the long table there was a white linen table runner with crescent moon cutouts. There were no place settings, but the china cabinet against the far wall displayed exceptional examples of antique cutlery and dishware. The historian in me wanted to handle and examine them all, but I kept myself in check.

"Hello? My name is Carrie Jo. Are you here? I came to help you. Are you scaring people?"

Nothing. Just the ticking of the clock; even in here I could hear it. I decided to stroll through the bedrooms. There were three in all. Strange that such a lovely place would have only nine rooms. I found the master bedroom, and I was in love. It was richly decorated with opulent furniture and a hidden door that led to a small study, where the scent of tobacco lingered. Wood absorbed smoke. You could smell pipe tobacco for years after the last pipe had been lit. The front parlor, study and dining room had airy ten-foot ceilings, but the bedrooms were more like nine feet high.

There was a garage that I had not explored and two porches that invited visitors to come sit a spell. Everything about this place appeared charming but not inviting. As my husband often says, "You can't believe everything your eyes tell you."

I did not have the eyes needed to see the ghosts that were here, not without stepping into the dream world, and I'd promised Ashland I would wait for him. To be honest, I was not sure I wanted to dream walk.

Oh, who am I kidding? I wanted to step through the door. I knew which door it would be, too. There were many dream doors here at Marietta; I had encountered two already. But more than that, even stronger than any door, was a female spirit. She sensed me, as I sensed her. I felt she didn't want me here, didn't want me poking around.

The woman named Mary Fairbanks, or so she wanted everyone to believe, had much to tell. Mary had more secrets to share. I did not want to be her confidante, but it would be impossible to avoid her.

She wanted to keep her secrets to herself. She would fight me tooth and nail. Who knew how far it would go? That had certainly proven to be the case before. Isla Beaumont fought to keep her treasure to herself at all costs. She had been a murderess in life, and death did not deter her. Even after she was dead, Isla Beaumont had been a dangerous soul.

I prayed that Mary Fairbanks was nothing like Isla, the stone-cold killer with the cherubic face. How desperate had Mary been? The woman I saw in my dreams had robbed her so-called friend of her ticket, but what else had she done? And was she the female presence I sensed here.

"Mary? Mary Fairbanks? Is that you I feel? Are you trying to keep your secrets to yourself, Mary? What did you do?"

No response. Not even a sigh or shiver. I continued reaching out.

"My name is Carrie Jo. I am here to listen to you. Was it your bones we found, Mary?" I did not have to wait long to receive an answer. The last question barely fell off my lips when a piercing scream filled the house.

But it was not a female, not an adult. It sounded like the scream of a child.

I collapsed shaking in a nearby chair.

Chapter Five—Lily

I was really kind of surprised in the beginning when my aunt and uncle were acting all weird about the baby. I hadn't even thought about being upset or threatened by a new addition to our family. But then again, I am distant from how I really feel. My counselor says it's a coping mechanism. Dissociation or something like that. But honestly, I am not so childish as to hate the idea of a new baby. I like kids. Having other kids around is way better than being an only child.

But I've found myself questioning a lot of things. What if they decide I'm extra weight? Extra baggage. Normal kids wouldn't think like this, but I am anything but a normal kid.

Nothing about me is normal. Never has been.

I try not to think about my parents too much. Also a tip from my counselor—do not romanticize your parents. "They are gone, and they loved you in their own way; the best way they knew how." *Really, Doctor? My mom was scared to death of me, and Dad could not figure out if he loved or hated me. No worries about me romanticizing them.* Not at all. Chance and May had not been remotely good parents. In fact, they were psychos, in my eyes.

Life had changed so much for me in the past couple of years. Not in bad ways. Well, mostly not bad ways, but I didn't like change. Who really does? I find that people crave stability. Kids need stability more than anyone, and even though I am not technically a kid anymore—I am a young teenager—I don't like things to change. But it always happens.

Never in a million years would my aunt and uncle send me away or do anything crazy like that, but how much room can a person have in their heart? How much room did they have for me? So now, when I least expect it, I find myself feeling concerned. Is that the word? Yes, let's go with that. My English teacher would be so proud.

I was excellent at vocabulary; it was a kind of pride thing. Tossing around those big words with my schoolmates, words they didn't understand, made me feel superior. That was also an observation from my counselor. As I explained, everyone needs to feel good about something. If my special skill was vocabulary, so be it.

Uncle Ash was in his office talking to his microphone about the good ol' football days, and AJ was with the Devecheauxs. Aunt Carrie Jo left for Biloxi. No one wanted to talk about what she was doing, but it's not like I needed to ask.

I dreamed about my aunt from time to time—I could see what she was doing if I wanted to. She was probably working with the dead, no doubt trying to bring peace to another family. I didn't intentionally spy on my aunt, but we did have this weird family connection. We were both dream catchers. My ability to turn off my gift had gotten stronger, but it still got the best of me occasionally. I didn't mean to step into her dreams, but it happened at times. Luckily, not recently, not since she got pregnant. I couldn't figure out why, and I didn't have the heart to ask her about it.

See there, the baby is already coming between you. Ugh. Where did that thought come from? Surely it was not my own? I momentarily paused what I was doing. Must be my imagination.

Whack, whack, whack.

I smacked the tennis ball on the concrete again and again. Hmm...maybe I could talk Uncle Ash into taking me to the tennis court at the park. I needed the practice if I was going to join the team. I wasn't sure I was going to try out, but clearly, some part of me wanted to do it.

Whack, whack, whack.

I had an eye for the ball, according to Uncle Ash. That was important for tennis. You always had to keep your eye on the ball. No matter what. And you had to hit it accurately. That was not always so easy.

Whack, whack, whack.

I sighed. I was not doing myself any favors standing here bouncing this ball. I needed actual racket time to strengthen my wrists and get better on my feet. Yeah, that could be a problem. I had two left feet, but as Aunt CJ always says, "Practice makes perfect." I hoped she was right.

What am I thinking? There was no way I would excel at tennis. I would not make the cut, and then what? I did not have a bunch of friends, except Katrina Valentine, and she was kind of wishy-washy. One day we were best buds, the next we were acquaintances. I could not stand her moodiness.

I squeezed the bright yellow tennis ball in my sweaty hands. *No. I am not doing it. I don't care what that stupid counselor said. He can take his advice and put it where the sun don't shine, to quote Detra Ann.* I sighed again, feeling terribly defeated. I couldn't say why. One minute, I was excited about the challenge, and the next I was terrified. Man, I am not usually scared about anything. Maybe team sports just weren't for me.

With all my might, I pitched the ball, and it caught air and landed somewhere in the Moonlight Garden.

Whack!

I stared in wonder as the ball returned. It bounced in front of me and came to a stop at my feet. Before I could ponder what happened, I heard whistling coming from the Moonlight Garden. I glanced around but saw no evidence that the gardening staff was here today. They only came on the weekends, unless there was a special occasion like a big party. I glanced back at the house, but I didn't see anyone. The housekeeper would be in the kitchen toiling away at freezing casseroles. I did not like the new housekeeper very much, and I believed the feeling was mutual. Some people did not like kids. Uncle Ash hadn't emerged from his office yet, so he was probably still yakking away about football.

Then I heard the whistling. A goofy tune, one I did not know. It was coming from about where the ball launched from. I had to check it out. I had to see for myself who this trespasser was and what he or she was doing here. I was not a kid anymore. I could handle this by myself. But just in case, I patted my back pocket. Yeah, my phone was there, a gift from my family for my most recent birthday. If I needed to call for help, I could. Picking up the tennis ball, I tossed it in the air and caught it once before stalking toward the maze's entrance. Time to get to the bottom of this strange visit.

"Where are you headed to, champ?" My uncle's voice surprised me, and I spun around on the toe pads of my worn tennis shoes. I clutched the tennis ball tightly, wondering what to say. The whistling conveniently stopped, and for a moment I cocked my head hoping to catch the sound one more time. I cannot say why, but I said nothing about it to Uncle Ashland.

"Don't call me that—but I guess it is better than Lily Bean. I'm just hanging around, waiting for you to get finished. I thought..." I glanced at the hedge again and thought better of it. "What time are we supposed to pick up AJ?" I walked back up to the porch and began bouncing the ball. *Keep your eye on the ball. Keep your eye on the ball.* I was intensely curious about the whistler, but I wanted to investigate on my own. My independent streak was coming out again. I got that from my aunt, or at least that's what Uncle Ashland always tells me.

"I noticed you changed the subject, champ, but I'm going to have to ask for a rain check. CJ called a few minutes ago. She needs my help on her case after all, so I'm going to..."

"Ditch me? Pawn me off to a babysitter? Take me to the orphanage?"

Uncle Ashland's sunny face darkened. *Oops. I went too far with that last comment.* I did not intend to sound so mean, but I felt crabby. Very crabby. It was happening more and more recently, unexpected crabbiness, sharp words and a bad attitude. I did not apologize but tossed him the tennis ball. That was kind of an apology.

He briefly held it, looked at it and then looked at me. Uncle Ash didn't smile but tossed it back to me, which meant he forgave me. "None of that will ever happen. However, boot camp is not out of the question. I have to go to Biloxi. Rachel will stay over with you tonight. I've already called her, and she's planning on bringing pizza and some movie called *Twilight*."

Uncle Ashland knew full well that *Twilight* was not a movie my aunt wanted me to see, but I got the idea it was a sort of peace offering, and it was one I was going to accept. I did not have the heart to tell him I had been watching clips of it on YouTube. I mean, I pretty much knew how the story went, but to see the whole thing all at once? That would be so cool.

"That sounds perfect. What about AJ? Is he coming home? I can take care of him, you know. He is my little brother. I am sure I can keep him alive for a few days."

Uncle Ashland hugged me briefly. "I know that, but he wants to stay with Chloe. It is nothing personal, but for some reason he likes her bossy little ways. I tell you what, I will make it up to you. When I get back, we will head over to Cottage Hill Park and play a few games of tennis. That reminds me, you know who's really good at tennis?"

"Detra Ann?" I answered, sounding snippy without meaning to.

"Yes. How did you know?"

"Because Detra Ann is good at everything. I will settle for Aunt Carrie Jo as a practice partner. She's as bad as I am."

To that he gave a hearty laugh. "True story. Okay. Come help me locate your aunt's phone charger. She said she left it behind. I'm going to pack an overnight bag."

"It's okay, Uncle Ashland. I am sure I will survive. But I do not understand. Lots of girls my age babysit their brothers and sisters.

They even make money babysitting. I am thirteen. I can't be trusted to babysit a family member?"

His blue eyes softened. "In all honesty, it is not about you, Lily. It is about the house. It is about Seven Sisters. I trust you. We both do. It is just...I am never quite sure this place is...settled. I would feel better knowing someone else, someone who has dealt with the paranormal, came to stay. Just in case anything happens."

"Uncle Ashland, like I haven't? Nothing has happened. Not since Gulf Coast Paranormal came. A few strays, but they haven't stayed."

"Please trust me; it is not about you. I wish you would believe me. I really do." He sighed and looked down, a clear sign he was not up to fighting about it.

"Go on then, Uncle Ashland. Go be Ghostbusters. Who you gonna call?" I began singing the tune, and in true Uncle Ashland fashion, he reached over and tousled my curls.

I pushed his hand away playfully. "Dude! What is wrong with you? My hair is a hot mess already." I tossed the ball up in the air. Uncle Ashland caught it and went into the house with it. "Hey, that's mine!" I trailed behind him. When I reached the door, I paused for a moment and whistled softly hoping someone, whoever was in the Moonlight Garden, would hear me and whistle back.

Nope. Nothing.

This was not over. Not by a long shot. "I'll be back," I yelled threateningly before I closed the door behind me.

I would keep my promise. And sooner rather than later. Probably tonight. If I could get away from Rachel's watchful eye.

Chapter Six—Ashland

I made a few phone calls. It was easy enough to postpone a podcast or two. I'd recorded one already today. Why hadn't I thought of this? I should have insisted that I come with Carrie Jo, but I wanted to be a supportive husband. And now there was a chance she was in danger. This was on me.

I could tell Lily was not happy about this turn of events, but she said she understood. When I called Detra Ann, I could practically feel her eyes rolling over the phone, but she didn't argue with me or discourage Carrie Jo and me. From what Henri let slip, they had their own paranormal situation happening at their antiques store. Detra Ann might as well face it, the paranormal was all up in our lives, not just Carrie Jo's and mine. The four of us—five if you include Rachel—were like some sort of paranormal fight club. Even as I shoved clothes, phone chargers and toiletries into my bag, I could feel oppression drawing closer.

The dead at Marietta were gathering against me. To this day, I do not understand how it all works. I could compare it to a game we used to play as children using two cups and a piece of string. I don't know that it actually worked, but as kids we totally believed we were communicating. Sometimes you could hear well, other times not so well, depending on the length of the string. At least that is what we schoolkids surmised long before cell phones.

That is what it is like with the dead. They have their own sort of grapevine. How else would the dead at Marietta know that I was on the way from Mobile, Alabama? Maybe they overheard my conversation with Carrie Jo? Who knows? It was a mystery to me, but I could not deny the feeling that things were not right. Lily did not want to spend a lot of time saying goodbye, which was fortunate because I felt very compelled to get on the road.

I barely remembered my drive to Biloxi, but the closer I got, the worse I felt. I have never thought much about what kind of medium I am, although Carrie Jo has continually encouraged me to learn more about my abilities. According to her, physical mediums feel physical things, physical impressions shared by the dead. Mental mediums hear the voices of the dead, while psychic knowers just know things.

I don't know what I am. All I know is I see ghosts. And to this day, I am still afraid.

I'm afraid to see them, yet at the same time I cannot help myself. Like my wife, I knew it was in my blood. Marietta was easy to find, directly off Beach Boulevard. I could see my wife's car in front of the house but no other. Could it be that Heather had not made it back yet? What was going on here? I spotted the cottage to the left, the one that Carrie Jo described.

I saw no ghosts. Not a single soul, living or dead.

I pulled my car beside my wife's, but before I could reach for my bag, the ground began to tremble. Were we having an earthquake? We did not have earthquakes on the Gulf Coast. And as soon as the trembling began, it ended.

What in the world?

Still clutching the overnight bag, I looked up to see the front door slowly opening. Only it was not my wife coming to greet me. I did not see a soul. The fine hair on my arms rose high.

Marietta's oversized front door yawned open like a hungry mouth. Even though it was bright and sunny out, all I could see was the darkness within. Yes, this place was very dark and very unhappy.

I could hear the voices of the dead, many dead, but they were not inside the house. Oh, no. There was only one mistress here—one dominant spirit, at least that was my initial prognosis. Carrie Jo was inside with her. I had to face the music. Crap! I couldn't see the negative presence, not yet, but I could feel her hatred. Invisible daggers of anger flew toward me, wounding me emotionally. That's how the evil dead do it, Rachel told me recently. "They flip your emotions around on you. They use your fear and anxiety."

Yes, visualization! I immediately switched it up and visualized a blue light shielding me from psychic attack. This woman had been an immensely powerful person while alive, and her power remained even in death. What was she capable of?

I got out of the car and slammed the door, hoping that the loud noise would engulf whatever stood against me. "Carrie Jo!" I called out but not too loudly. I did not want to make a scene or anything. If the owner was here, I did not want to come off as a lunatic, but I was sincerely worried for my wife.

And Carrie Jo was inside Marietta with the ominous being. I could not delay. *Who are you? I do not mean you any harm.* She said nothing but only spewed more hateful feelings my way. *Where are you? Show yourself.* Yes, this woman had been and still was incredibly powerful. What was she capable of?

As I walked toward the front porch, I noticed a darkness hovering in the threshold of the doorway. It seemed at first to be a smoky thing, an ethereal mass doing its dead level best to become something other than that. But then it was different. As the mist rose, it began to buzz and flies appeared. Many flies. What was I seeing? This strange manifestation could be nothing short of evil. The flies morphed into humanoid shape, at least the upper torso. Man or woman I could not discern, but my sixth sense led me to believe that it was the spirit of a woman—a woman who did not want me here.

I see you. I am coming in, and you cannot stop me.

"Ashland?" The door swung open wider. I could see my wife coming down the hall, and the flies fluttered but maintained their position. It was as if Carrie Jo did not see them; she did not panic or show any fear whatsoever. Was it possible that I was seeing the manifestation and she was not aware of the danger?

"Carrie Jo! Stay right there!" I could see my wife speaking but I could not hear her any longer because the droning of the flies drowned her out. I saw no fear, just a big, Carrie Jo smile. I was not sure how she could not tell that anything weird was happening. At least she saw me, but would she heed my warning? I could not believe it. One moment CJ was there, walking through the flies undeterred, and the next she had disappeared. I yelled for her to stop, but it was too late. I watched in horror as the flies vanished like smoke—and with them, my wife.

No! Stay out!

The voice of the woman rang in my mind. Her intention was clear. She did not want me inside her home. There was only one mistress here, but she commanded many other spirits. The stagnant air shimmered with muffled voices. Perhaps it was her bones that had been found at Marietta? Too early to tell. It was wise not to assume anything.

I couldn't shake the vision of Carrie Jo's petite frame vanishing behind a wall of flies. One second, she was there, innocently walking through this weird manifestation. And the next, she and the flies were gone.

Had she gone on a dream walk or something else?

Whatever the case, Carrie Jo was gone. Maybe forever.

Chapter Seven—Mary

John Lancaster and I did not speak much on the journey. I was glad for that but also a little disappointed. Glad he did not notice my Irish brogue but sad because we traveled the bumpy roads as strangers and not as two people who had fallen in love through pen and paper. Riding with him in the open carriage, I realized that I had fallen in love with a stranger. He hardly seemed like the man who had written me those wonderfully affectionate letters.

I carried a few of them in my purse even though they did not truly belong to me. Yes, I had written every single one and he had written back to me. The things we had said to one another, the promises we made, to love and be loved, to kiss and to hold and to be true. These things meant the world to me. Yet here I was with a man who barely glanced in my direction.

I knew that I would love John Lamar Lancaster no matter what he looked like or how he behaved. Only a man who could write such beautiful words was suitable for me. I'd had a fine Catholic education back home but had never been given the opportunity to put it to good use. By writing John all these months, I recalled bits of forgotten literature I once cherished. It was like revisiting my childhood. Strange that a poor girl from County Cork, Ireland, would know so much about such things, but my mother had always been very progressive when it came to education. My brothers had been nowhere near as intelligent as I was, with no interest in anything except brawling, mostly with one another.

I glanced at John Lancaster from the corner of my eye. I needed to be patient. Writing to one another was quite different than spending every day together. Now life would be different for me. I could believe again. I would be happy with him. Surely, I would be.

That is, if my past did not follow me. I shivered at the thought. John held his arms out to me so that I might safely depart from the carriage. As he did, he held me briefly and chastely, then whispered in my ear, "I never imagined you so slight."

"I hope you're not disappointed?" To ask such a question with servants collecting our luggage and leading us up the stairs was inappropriate, but I had to know his thoughts. Maybe this was a horrible mistake. Maybe this was the wrong thing to do. In my eyes, he was far handsomer and more interesting than anything or anyone I had ever imagined. I was as dark as he was light. We were quite opposites, but I found him incredibly attractive. That didn't answer any of my questions, though.

I stood poised at the bottom of the steps waiting to hear something, some affirmation that I was not a disappointment to him.

If you could give me just the slightest encouragement, my soul would be happy. It would've all been worth it. All the lies, all the stolen letters. That horrible fight. The blood...

No, I won't think about that. I won't. I cannot ruin this moment.

Everything hung in the balance. Now, this was my defining moment.

He reached his hand down and smiled at me. "I am not unhappy. Come inside, Mary. I must introduce you to Mother. She is eager to meet you, as is everyone else."

Not unhappy? What did that mean?

"Everyone else?" I took his hand and enjoyed feeling the smallness of mine in the largeness of his. His skin was warm and alive. How long until we married? How long until...

The door to the house opened, and there standing a few feet from it was the grandest lady I had ever seen. This could only be Marietta, the woman herself. I had not thought much about my potential mother-in-law other than I was certain she would understand and appreciate that I was a hard worker, willing to do whatever it took to keep the house in order. Living here would be far easier then living at the Golden Nugget Saloon. Surely Marietta would not be as difficult a mistress as Mary Fairbanks. She would not demand that I do filthy deeds.

But I, Vienna Fitzgerald, soon to be Mrs. John Lancaster, must remain calm and keep my wits about me for a little while longer. I was not married yet.

John's mother stood as still as any statue. Although her gown was slightly out of style and rather old-fashioned (compared to the clothing of the half-dressed saloon girls I had been acquainted with recently), everything about her spoke elegance. From the pearls sewn into her hair to her dangling, glittering earrings, to the starched whiteness of the lace that hung from the hem of her skirt, she was elegant. Was all this finery for my benefit? Oh, dear, she would surely be disappointed with me. I was a small, dark and untidy thing. I had chosen to wear black and suddenly regretted my decision. Perhaps I too should have dressed for a more elegant meeting. That would've been wise, but it was too late now. My hand instinctively flew to my hair to tidy it, and I saw a small smile creep across her face. Oh, she liked this. She liked feeling superior. That was fine with me. I knew how to appease people who bullied me. Humbling myself never bothered me.

Whether she consciously revealed this about herself or just wanted me to know it, I could sense that she enjoyed making people uncomfortable.

"Dear Miss Fairbanks. We finally get to meet you after having heard such wonderful things. I trust your trip was uneventful." Her eyes glittered as she spoke, and she glanced at both of us. I knew exactly what she wanted to know. It wasn't really a question, but her polite pause caused me to stammer an answer.

"There was no trouble at all. I am happy to meet you too, Mrs. Lancaster." My heart sank as I knew full well that I sounded very

Irish, very foreign. If she was surprised by that, it did not seem to shake her.

And then John was there taking my hand. "Mother, which room have you prepared for Miss Fairbanks? It is rather late, and I'm sure she would like to rest. And as we have not paused for dinner, we are famished."

"Portia will take her to the room beside mine and bring up a light meal." Mrs. Lancaster's eyes surveyed me, but she saved a polite smile for her son. "In the morning, your housemaid will wake you with coffee. Breakfast is at seven every day of the week. Welcome to my home, welcome to Marietta. I look forward to planning your wedding day." Before I could thank her for her politeness, she added, "I hope the stars are in your favor." With that, she disappeared into another room, taking a candle with her.

Only one candle was left behind. I glanced at John, struggling for some assurance that I had done well with my first meeting. What did she mean by that? The question was on the tip of my tongue, but a manservant approached, one with whom John was friendly. They quickly exchanged greetings, and I was forgotten about. That disappointed me, but I was quite certain he was as tired as I was. Even my bones were tired. That was something my mother liked to say after a long day of cutting the grass, making hay for the sheep.

"Miss? If you will follow me. It is this way." Portia's husky voice surprised me. She had dark, sultry eyes too. Yes, despite her severe bun and plain apparel, she was stunningly beautiful. Dark and fierce like a stormy night. What did I see in her face? Curiosity? Dislike? I was so out of sorts that it was difficult to read her, but read her I would eventually.

For now, I just wanted to survive.

On the way to my new bedroom, I pinched myself several times just to make sure I was not dreaming. No, I was awake, and I was finally here. But where was here? In the middle of nowhere in a grand house with people I did not know who did not know me. What could possibly go wrong?

Portia led me to my room and lit candles. It was such an airy, pleasant space. My one bag arrived and was opened on the floor. Portia offered to beat out my dresses and hang them up properly. I had no other dresses save one, a raggedy gingham frock, very plain and common. A blue-and-white dress with an unimpressive skirt. It had seemed a grand thing to have that fabric in my possession, but compared to Mrs. Lancaster, I was a pauper.

Despite the obstacles in my way, I was determined to marry John Lancaster. I kindly declined her offer, and she promised she would be back with something to eat. I did not feel any warmth from the servant, but I wasn't looking for any. The first order of business here was to figure out who I could trust. It was always good to have an ally. I would take my time, though. The door opened again, and to my surprise Mrs. Lancaster came into my room as quietly as a velvet ribbon falling to the floor. Even though her voluminous skirts billowed around her, she made little sound. With her hands clasped, she nodded at me, and I stared back unsure what protocol to follow. Clearly, she had something to say. I would listen, for now at least. Portia closed the door behind her, and Mrs. Lancaster waved her hand to instruct me to sit on the bed. She sat in the chair across from the bed near the window. What was this about?

"Finally, we meet, Mary Fairbanks. I predict you will not find this conversation at all enjoyable. But as a woman, a soon-to-be-married woman, you should learn this lesson now."

"What lesson is that?" I asked, surprised by her opening statement. Was she looking for a fight? Was she unhappy about her son's selection for a wife? I braced myself for the worst.

"You have come a long way to marry my son, but it is important that you know the truth. It is only right, I think, one woman to another. Not that you have many other options, but I think it is right that the two of us get off on the right foot. I am not a cruel woman, Mary. I do not tell you this for harm's sake but for your own information."

Honestly baffled by this strange conversation, I remained still but not too comfortable on the soft mattress. Mrs. Lancaster waited for my reply. "I am listening," I said.

"I wrote the letters. All of them."

What do I say to that? I could hardly believe my ears. This was all impossible! What did this mean?

"I don't believe you," was the only response I could muster. I was quite shocked by her words. She assumed a lot of things. How was this possible? I had to have answers. "You wrote me? Why would you do such a thing?"

Her response was merely a shrug, a true sign of cold indifference. But it was not going to be enough for me. I was not who she thought I was. I was good—as good as any woman could be living without the protection of a husband or father.

"I think I deserve an answer. I *have* come a long way, Mrs. Lancaster. A very far distance indeed. I intend on marrying your son. He loves me, of that I am sure. I do not believe you wrote those letters. To what end? It was John. Surely, it was John!"

My future mother-in-law had nothing to say to me, which infuriated me. I was good enough for her son in the letters—why reject me now? If she truly had written the letters, why not write me and deter me from coming? Why wait until I arrived to make such an announcement? Something was not adding up.

Then a possible reason occurred to me. My reputation preceded me. Or rather the reputation of the real Mary Fairbanks. It would be easy enough to hire someone to investigate such a person, but to prolong the pretense? No, I did not believe her. Those letters were not from her but from John. He may have known nothing about the true Mary Fairbanks, but his mother certainly did. The only thing I could do was assure her, share with her what I had done, what I had achieved to bring myself to this place, to this moment in time. To throw myself on the fire, so to speak. I must have a lick of a chance, or else she would not have continued with this charade. Surely not.

"Mrs. Lancaster. I am not who you think I am."

"Of that I am certain," she snorted with haughty derision.

"My name...my name is Vienna Fitzgerald."

She turned slightly in her chair to face me but did not leave the room. Neither did she slap me, and that had to be a good thing. It proved she was willing to listen. I held my breath and continued to bare my soul.

"I was Mary Fairbanks' servant for nearly a year, but that is all. I came to this country with the promise of a job, but before I arrived at the factory, it closed and I was left destitute. I had no money, no prospects and nowhere to go."

She continued to watch me like an unhappy cat. One that considered pouncing on the fool mouse that entertained her. *Oh, do not let me be the mouse.*

I licked my dry lips and continued, "This Mary Fairbanks, although not a virtuous woman, took pity on me and allowed me to stay in her closet. I cleaned for her, cooked her meals and, when necessary, helped bring her home after her long nights of debauchery. I have never known her to read the ads, but one day, she bade me respond to one, to answer Mr. Lancaster's advertisement. She never wrote a single letter herself. After the first letter, she didn't even bother to read them. I thought she lost interest until she discovered the ticket. By then it was too late, for I had fallen in love with him. I, Vienna Fitzgerald, not Mary Fairbanks."

"You expect me to believe this nonsense? How could you possibly have fallen in love with my son after a few letters? Fallen in love with his fortune, more's the truth. Your chance to come clean is in the past. You lied to him, and to me. You pretended to be something you are not. I cannot for the life of me understand why he would advertise for a wife in the newspaper. Why?"

I had the same question, but I had not dared to ask John for an answer. I was not sure I wanted to know. Light rain tapped against the windowpanes. The peaceful sound did nothing to still my troubled heart. It was now or never. Mrs. Lancaster remained here, so she must be curious about me.

I wiped a tear from my cheek. It did not soften her stare. "Until his most recent letters, I knew nothing about Marietta, nothing about this place or any kind of fortune. If you wrote the letters, as you say, then you know that is true." Of course, I did not believe Mrs. Lancaster would lower herself to write love letters to a stranger.

I continued, "Please, give me a chance. If you knew what I have endured to meet your son, if you had half an imagination, you would know that I have risked everything, even my freedom, to come here. I am not Mary Fairbanks, it's true. But think of it this way, Mrs. Lancaster: I am willing to become whoever you wish me to be. That I can do. I am teachable and trainable. I only want to be a good wife to your son. Who can say that? It is true that I am a stranger here, but that may not be a bad thing. Obviously, John—I mean, Mr. Lancaster—wanted to marry outside his social circle. There must be a reason. Please, say you'll think about it. Don't send me away without giving me a chance."

Then I saw her eyes light up. I had the oddest sensation, a rare sensation my mother called a rabbit running over your grave. A moment of sour destiny. With my pledge of obedience to this woman, to this powerful woman who had nothing but dislike for me, I had sealed my destiny. That rabbit's presence was proof that the otherworld knew all about it. Her smile revealed that she liked the idea and that she would most likely accept my proposal, but it would cost me something. Had I merely traded my soul for one sad situation rather than another? It was true that I was no longer Mary

Fairbanks' plaything, but I had too easily placed myself in the hands of Mrs. Lancaster. And for what?

She left without formal agreement and only said, "Then I will see you at breakfast, and preferably you will not be wearing black. Portia will provide you with the appropriate garments."

Portia returned and deposited a tray, then followed behind her mistress. Her dark eyes glittered as she closed the door. I sagged on the bed, alone at last, too tired to cry and too relieved to pray. I glanced at the plate. The warm bread smelled delicious. I did not bother buttering it. I took a few bites before falling asleep with my dirty boots on.

At last, I had made it.

Chapter Eight—Carrie Jo

"Come back to me, Carrie Jo! It's me! Please, snap out of it!"

I was deep into the dream and had completely forgotten who I was—such a strange experience. One minute, I had been greeting Ashland in the doorway, and the next, I was someone else. I had been Mary Fairbanks, the fake Mary Fairbanks. She fascinated me, but I had only begun to scratch the surface of what had happened here at Marietta.

"Ashland?" I smiled as I put my arms around his neck. I breathed a sigh of relief knowing that I was not alone here. Standing behind him was Heather with an armload of groceries. She looks startled not by Ashland's arrival but probably because I was lying on the floor. I quickly assessed myself, and there were no bruises or other injuries. Strange, that. Often when I found myself waking up from these dreams or dream walks, I rarely had injuries. It was as if someone on the other side was looking after me, always protecting me. Maybe Muncie? Or maybe my mother? It'd been so long since I'd seen them. At the moment, I didn't have the time to ponder my family's past.

"Heather? I am fine. It is not what it looks like. Help me up, Ash. We can help with the groceries. This is my husband, Ashland. I invited him here because I thought he would be useful in this investigation. He has special skills too."

"Did you fall? Is everything okay?" I noticed that Heather was glancing around as if she suspected someone else was here. Perhaps someone who had pushed me to the floor or abused me? I could not be sure. It was difficult getting information from her about this place. But I could clearly see that she was afraid.

I dusted my clothes off unnecessarily. The floors were spotless. Everything here was neat and tidy, at least on the physical plane. I knew for a fact that the dead were not at rest. Ashland and I helped Heather bring in the rest of the groceries and supplies. Wow, how long did she intend for us to stay? The three of us chitchatted in the kitchen as we put things away, and her tone changed. She and Ashland hit it off right away. He was a friendly person and usually gets along with everyone. While he talked, it gave me a chance to tune in to the room, to see what else I might pick up on. I settled my soul, reminding myself that I didn't need to dream walk. I wasn't up to doing that again. Not until I had a chance to talk to Ashland.

"I'm so glad that you're coming to stay with Carrie Jo. I was not comfortable with the idea of anyone being here by themselves. I sure would not do it. Tell me, your house, Seven Sisters...was it really like this one? I mean, I've heard rumors." Her cheeks turned pink. I guess she was embarrassed to talk about our paranormal past, but we were quite used to it.

I sat at the kitchen table, and Ashland got busy making a pot of coffee. It was late in the afternoon, and as he rightly suspected, this investigation was going late into the night. We were not going to have to wait long to see what we came to see.

The ghosts of Marietta were speaking, and we had to listen.

"Seven Sisters has had its share of ghosts, but I think a lot of old places and even some new places are haunted. Either by memories or by strong bursts of emotion."

Heather interrupted me, "Like a murder? Do you think that's why the activity picked up? Now that we found the bones? Do you think someone was murdered?"

"No, but violent acts are known to release a burst of energy, like a lot of joy or a lot of sorrow. These can leave imprints, a kind of residual type of energy. You've probably heard that phrase used a lot today in the paranormal communities. I don't know if you know anything about the paranormal, but residual energy often happens at the same time every day or on a certain day of the week. It has no real rhyme or reason to it; it just repeats."

"That's interesting."

"Residual energy is harmless, usually. It might startle the person who walks up on it, but it is harmless. However, there are other types of paranormal activity known as poltergeists—those are dangerous if they are not kept in check. These ghosts are activated by living humans. They may already be there, but they are more active because a living person in their proximity is giving them energy and strength. Does that make sense?"

"Oh, I find this fascinating. Please continue." Heather's pretty brows furrowed slightly as she thought about this new information.

"We've discovered that there are also intelligent haunts. Not only are these ghosts aware that they're dead, but they also interact with the living in unusual ways. They want to continue pursuing their goals, the goals they had in life, and they don't mind destroying whoever gets in the way. Those were the kinds of spirits we dealt with at Seven Sisters, but there were also good ones, family ones, too. I got to know people I never knew before because people on the other side tried to protect us. Just like you, Heather. Your family members are trying to protect you; they are watching over you. They want you to be safe. So, what Ashland and I are going to do is find out who is haunting the place. Then we will verify if it's related to the discovery of those bones. We might be able to present you a proposal for a plan of action to possibly put the spirits to rest. But that's not always the case. Sometimes these things remain a mystery. We can't guarantee that we can fix anything; I told you that on the phone, remember. Do you understand?"

Heather tapped on the round wooden dining room table with her fingers. It was a thoughtful gesture. "Yes, I do. I appreciate your honesty. Let me be completely honest with you. I don't want Marietta anymore. But I don't have it in me to dump it off on someone else while shadows are appearing and construction people are getting scared away. And I want to make sure her bones receive a proper burial."

Ashland sat down at the table with three cups of coffee. He had not even bothered to ask if we wanted them. I guess he knew we did.

I said, "You keep saying 'her.' Has it been verified that those bones belong to a female? Did you get information that we haven't received yet?" Ashland and I watched Heather's face crumple a bit.

"I do not know why I said that, why I keep saying that. I guess because the house is named after a woman named Marietta." Heather sipped her black coffee nonchalantly and continue to tap her fingers on the table as she stared out the window behind me trancelike. "It's just a feeling I get." Suddenly her phone began to beep. "I have to take this. If you will excuse me. I'll be right back." As she left the kitchen, I caught a glimpse of something in the hallway mirror.

I did not see Heather's pleasant smile looking back at me. I could hear her chattering on the phone, but it wasn't her reflection in the mirror. I grasped Ashland's hand and felt him tense behind me. Looking back at us for a few seconds was a shriveled black face with a wild umbrella of hair swirling about her. Her mouth opened in a silent scream, but I heard nothing. Only felt it deep within my soul.

As quickly as I witnessed it, the entity vanished. All that was left behind were a few flies, which appeared to follow Heather down the hall. Then all fell quiet. Too quiet.

"That is a threat, Ashland. We must get her out of here. Heather is in the crosshairs of whoever remains behind. I do not think we've begun to scratch the surface. There is so much more to the haunting here at Marietta. First things first, though, I'm going to check in with Rachel to see if there's any news about the bones. We need to start with that, I think. Tonight is going to be a long night."

Ashland agreed and went down the hallway after Heather; I could hear them talking. He would make sure she was safely off the property. I dialed Rachel's phone number, and it only rang once. She didn't even bother saying hello.

"You are never going to believe this!"

And so it began. By the time I hung up the phone, my mind was reeling with this new information. Time to find Ashland, time to tell him what I knew.

Chapter Nine—Lily

Rachel was wrapped up in her studies and not as interested in watching *Twilight* as I'd hoped. The truth was I had seen most of the movie on YouTube already. Now that I was watching it for real, I wasn't nearly as excited as I thought I would be. The house creaked and popped around us. I felt uneasy, unsettled.

"I'm going for a walk. Want to come outside?" I asked hopefully. Rachel barely looked up from her textbook. I guessed that was going to be a big fat no.

"I wish I could, Lil, but I really need to focus on this. Why don't we do it tomorrow? It's going to be dark out soon."

"Never mind," I said without bothering to hide my disappointment. Man, I sounded like a whiner.

"The pizza will be here in a little while too," Rachel mentioned as she put her pen down and turned to pay attention to me, but I had lost interest in hanging out with her.

"Ugh, I am so over pizza. Anyway, I'm going for a walk."

Her shoulders sagged a little. "I'll come with you. I can spare a few minutes."

I sighed sadly like I'd heard my Aunt Carrie Jo do a thousand times when AJ threatened to jump off something or climb something he shouldn't. "No. You study, Rachel. I'm sorry I'm so cranky. I am going to stretch my legs. I'll be back in time for pizza."

Rachel smiled thankfully and turned her attention back to her thick textbook. I hated studying. I liked reading but hated studying. Test anxiety was a real thing.

I could not take my mind off the stranger I'd heard whistling in the maze, but I did not mention it to Rachel. She would probably just dismiss it out of hand anyway. For someone who believed in the unseen, she was consistently pretending that there was nothing there. People did that with kids—and young teenagers.

No, there are no such things as monsters. No, ghosts are not real. Well, duh. Of course they're real.

I knew that ghosts were around. They were not coming in the house yet—the barriers the paranormal team put up were holding—but they were milling around outside.

And when one got in, they all came in.

It's like someone flipped a big old light switch and all the moths came. They couldn't resist the light.

Impulsively, I hugged Rachel, and I meant it. I loved her like she was a big sister. Although we were separated by at least a decade, I felt like she thought the same way about me. Even though she tried to pretend we lived in a normal world, I felt that she understood me.

Like my immediate family, she was a little weird too. Only Rachel was more studious. She wanted to understand things—she had this deep need to study things. I knew for a fact that Uncle Ashland did not trust the Brotherhood, a paranormal club or something like that. They had granted Rachel a scholarship for a particular field of study...para-something or another. I did not understand all of it, nor did I try to, but I looked up to Rachel. I think she liked paper and pens almost as much as I did, which was quite a lot. Speaking of which, I had been neglecting my journals and needed to catch up on recent events. Maybe I would do that tonight, instead of just vegging out in front of the TV. But what about the Whistler?

Maybe the Whistler was merely a gardener or some other living person. I would search for him by myself. I was perfectly capable of finding and communicating with ghosts on my own, so why not? Uncle Ash and Aunt Carrie Jo were off doing their thing. I might as well do mine.

I went outside and quietly closed the door behind me. *Ooh, I am cold. When did it get so windy out here?* There was that old familiar chill, an extra knowing—an awareness that came only when dealing with ghosts.

I would keep my word and just look around for thirty minutes or so before coming back for pizza. I did not want to admit it, but I was excited about the pizza even though I whined about it.

Yep, I did a lot of complaining lately, and I did not understand why. Why was I so dang crabby? My stomach hurt; my body felt sore. Ugh, I must be coming down with something.

Tossing the ball in my hand, I walked down the steps and toward the hedge. This was the opening of the maze, the infamous Moonlight Garden. It was a fun place to play and hide, and there were treasures to be found. However, things were not as they seemed. One time I was staring at a huge oak tree, and the next minute it was merely a sapling. It was as if time shifted here in the Moonlight Garden; it changed completely. I mentioned this to Aunt CJ once.

I didn't want to scare my aunt, but I was dream walking quite a bit now without any intention of doing it. It just kind of happened—it was both exciting and terrifying.

I stood at the entrance of the hedge tossing the ball up a few times, then I let out a loud whistle like I was calling a dog. I did not hear a thing, which was disappointing, so I walked into the maze. I knew the route to take, knew it with my eyes closed. I knew it from one side to the other, but I purposefully avoided the usual route.

Any intruders to this place would not know the way. I breathed in the faint fragrance of magnolia and an assortment of other flowers that I could not yet identify. It might be easier to catch the intruder if I canvassed the entire thing, but that might take me more than thirty minutes. As my stomach growled, I hoped I could keep my promise to Rachel.

"Are you there? Hey, Mr. Whistler! Want to play ball?" As I did earlier, I tossed the ball into the maze, expecting it to come back. It did not. Instead, it landed in a pile of dry leaves. I could hear them crunching. That was a bit aggravating. I went to go find the ball while whistling a different tune. The air around me held that creepy factor. It was the feeling you got when someone besides you paused to listen to the world around them. That was what I was experiencing. I was not alone in the Moonlight Garden.

I made the first few turns into the hedge. First to the right and then to the left and then another left. There was a pattern to it, a kind of symbol to unlock the many secrets of this place. For certain, all the treasures had been dug up long ago, long before I came here. But there were certain corners of this place that almost whispered my name.

It wasn't like me to be romantic.

I was more of a down-to-earth kind of girl, but walking these soft green paths and touching the heads of flowers just with my fingertips, I couldn't help but think of all of those who'd come before us who had taken such joy in this beautiful place.

What was that like? To be in love? To hold someone's hand. To kiss a boy.

That's when I saw him—he was in front of me, not twenty feet away. A teenager, around my age, maybe a little taller than me. And I knew from the moment I saw him that he was not alive. He did not look creepy, not like some kind of zombie or a creature you would imagine in a movie. Dead people presented themselves in weird ways. The dead move differently. They act differently, but explaining the differences to anyone who had not seen the dead for themselves was not easy.

How would this one act? Would he charge me? Morph into a hideous creature?

"You're in the wrong place. How did you get in here?" I could not think of anything else to say, but we could not just stand there staring at one another. Breaking the ice was not my strong suit, but this would have to do. He waved at the hedge behind him. I glanced back politely, knowing full well that there was no entrance in that direction.

"There's no way you came in from that direction. Want to try again?"

I spotted the tennis ball and tossed it up again. I had not quite committed to having this conversation yet, but I was curious about the ghost boy in the Moonlight Garden. How could I not be curious? The intruder stared back at me, leaving me plenty of time to study his face.

He had reddish-brown hair and a light dusting of red freckles across the bridge of his nose, which was a little too large for his face. Maybe he would grow into it. I hear grown-ups say that all the time about kids with big ears or feet or noses. *Oh, wait. He will never grow into that nose. He's dead, isn't he?* He had thoughtful brown eyes and a bottom lip that poked out stubbornly. Yeah, I could feel his stubbornness. It was emanating from him like a kind of pheromone haze. *What do you know? I managed to use one of this week's vocabulary words in a sentence. Not out loud, but at least I put it together in my head.*

"Are you deaf? I asked you a question. How did you get in here?"

"You invited me," he said in an unusually deep voice. The way he sounded, he might as well have been real. He was kind of baby-faced but had a manly voice, which led me to ask my next question.

"No, I didn't. How old are you?" The better question probably would have been, "What's your name?" but that was how my mind worked. Anyway, if he was really a kid, I wouldn't be afraid. But if he was something else... He just stared at me, and I got kind of sick and woozy.

He smiled this time, like he knew it, and I found it strangely comforting. No, I didn't think this guy was dangerous, but I didn't have a lot of experience with boys. *Move cautiously, Lily Rose.*

"My name is Mitchell. I do not know how old I am. How is it that you do not remember me?"

Chapter Ten—Ashland

My wife closed the door and leaned against it as she breathed a sigh of relief. "I'm glad you managed to get her out of here. Heather is connected to this place in a way we do not quite understand. She admits that she is a local but says she has no connection to this house other than growing up in the area, seeing it neglected and being curious about how it looked inside. She told me she could not understand why the community was not utilizing it. Whatever is happening here, it is so powerful that it has affected her profoundly. Maybe she is a sensitive."

"The bigger question is what happened to you? I watched with my own two eyes, Carrie Jo. You disappeared right in front of me. No matter how many times I see it, I can never get used to it. But this time was a little different. You did not just vanish—there was a figure in front of you, and you seemed not to notice."

Carrie Jo and I went to the parlor and sat together on the overstuffed couch. "Figure? What kind of figure?" she asked.

"Shadowy. No—kind of dark and misty, but it morphed into a cluster of flies. They took on a humanoid shape. I heard a female voice say, 'Stay out,' or 'Don't come in.' I can't remember. Something like that, and then you were gone. You didn't see anything?"

She shook her head, her soft brown curls bouncing slightly. "No, Ashland, nothing at all. Rachel emailed us a packet of information. Let's dig in. I'll grab my laptop."

We diligently pored over the old records from the Lancaster family. Mrs. Lancaster, wife of the original homeowner, was known as Marietta, although that was not her actual name. The house was named after her, and everyone knew it. Some records listed the matriarch's name as Mary Ellen, but most people referred to her as Marietta. Her husband died soon after building the home. They had two sons, John Lamar and Oscar Lancaster. The documents showed that John married in 1848, but there was no record of how many children he had with his wife, Mary.

Oscar married soon after his brother, but Rachel could find no record of Oscar's wife's name. It was not unusual to have so many holes in the history for an old place like this, but these holes felt odd. Oh, yeah. There was a story here. An awful story. Oftentimes we found that when information was missing, it was to cover up something like a mental illness or mysterious death. I would not put those out of the realm of possibility, but the big question was whether the escalating hauntings were connected to the bones that were found here.

"First order of business, Ashland—we need to go see the location where they found the bones, since I didn't get a chance to get a good walk-through earlier. Heather was really in a hurry to get out of here. What do you think?" She closed the computer and twisted her hair up in a messy bun.

"That sounds good to me. I bought a digital voice recorder with me to keep a record of any impressions I get during our walk. I don't know how accurate they'll be, but this was something Midas suggested, so I figured I would give it a try."

She grinned at me and kissed my cheek. "I like it. I think having a recording will come in handy. We should go while we still have light."

Marietta was not as large as Seven Sisters, but it was still an impressive showpiece of Southern architecture. Like so many houses along the Gulf Coast, it was built up off the ground. Carrie Jo pointed out to me that it was raised off the ground after the first flood that the homeowners experienced here. Hmm...could the house's being moved have played a role in the hauntings?

Yes, Marietta was reminiscent of a fine old Caribbean home but with a bit of stuffiness. There was a large fan in each of the rooms, the kind that were operated by slaves. Most historic homes had the decency to replace those fans with ceiling fans or took them down altogether. My heart ached a little seeing them. Of course, one couldn't hide the fact that places like this had been run on the sweat and blood of the innocent. Things like this were heart-wrenching. We stepped outside and closed the door behind us, then stood on the porch for a minute to get our bearings.

From the front lawn, we could see the beach and the long, gray seashore. The ocean moved in lazy waves today. How did it go from bright and sunny to cloudy so quickly? As they say, if you don't like the weather on the Gulf Coast, just wait a few minutes—it'll change. Locals always kept an umbrella and rain jacket in the car all year long.

The recorder quickly picked up the voice of an angry woman. I couldn't understand what she was saying, but oh, yes, she was so angry.

"CJ, I'm just going to start talking because I am getting some information."

"Go for it," my wife whispered beside me as she led me to the side of the house where the femur and arm bones had been found. No, it wasn't out of the realm of possibility that those bones had washed up out of the cemetery in the back. According to the City of Biloxi, nothing was amiss. They said none of those graves had been disturbed, but it was entirely possible that there were graves back there that no one knew about. No, not impossible in an old place like this. People had been buried out here for centuries.

"Marietta? Was that you I saw earlier? My name is Ashland. I can see you if you want to step out from hiding. And I'm not here to harm you. I want to help, but I need to know what it is you want."

I heard laughter, soft female laughter. Not the sweet, comforting kind, either. This was evil. Evil and menacing. Was this thing even human?

"Carrie Jo? Did you hear that?" I looked down at her, and she nodded but kept quiet. We stood by the dirt patch where the bones were suspected to have emerged from and poked around the dirt a little, but only superficially. I wasn't about to start digging up the yard. That would be counterproductive for sure. I'd just told this woman I wanted to help her.

Why wasn't law enforcement making this investigation a priority? Surely it warranted further searching. The police were certain that they had gathered all the remains from this location, but there may be more remains around the property. Why had no cadaver dogs been brought in? *I think that's a question I will ask Heather ASAP.*

I heard the low, menacing laughter again. Female? Male? An entirely different thing?

"Why are you laughing at us? Are we going the wrong way? We only want to help you. We want to help you find your way back home. Did we find your bones? Are these your bones, Marietta?"

I had barely gotten the words out of my mouth when a stinging slap struck my face. With a loud cry of pain, I fell to the ground and Carrie Jo scampered up beside me. I clutched my chin for a few seconds, surprised by the blow. But there was no one there. I swore under my breath but refused to run away.

"Ashland? Are you okay? Good God, what happened?"

I moved my hand, grateful there was no blood.

"That's a handprint! You got slapped?" Before I could say anything, she was on her feet with her fists clenched. "Okay. That is not allowed. No touching us. Stop it!" Carrie Jo shuffled her feet and spun around as if she would spot Marietta—and then kick her behind.

But the danger was not over, and I knew we should quickly go back inside the house, if not off the property altogether. No, we couldn't do that. We had to stick with this but be more careful. How? How could we do that? My surveillance of the cemetery would have to wait. Marietta—I was certain it was her—did not like my questions.

I touched my wife's shoulder gently, ignoring the burning sensation on my face. "Let's go inside, Carrie Jo. I think I've pissed her off. We are walking on her grave." My own words caused me to shiver, but I meant every word of it. Can't say why I felt that way.

As we began to walk back to Marietta, the mumbling on the recording grew louder. It was unintelligible at first, but then the words began to make sense. I clicked the recorder off and slid it in my blue jeans pocket.

Carrie Jo glanced back at me but did not seem to hear a thing. Thank goodness. I did not want her to feel guilty for inviting me to come; I needed to be here. It wasn't safe for her—not for anyone. Not even me.

But there was nothing for it now. We had to continue on. The mumbling grew louder until there was no mistaking what I was hearing.

John. John. John. John. I am going to kill you, John.
Kill you...

Chapter Eleven—Mary

The days were odd. I rarely saw John, only at breakfast, and then his greetings were polite but not at all what I expected. No loving embrace, and all the kisses I had been promised were not delivered. Where was the affection? Had Marietta told me the truth? Had she been the one to write those letters? Had I been trapped by my own dishonest endeavors?

"John? I thought we would take a walk this morning. I have been here two weeks, and I rarely see you. We are getting married soon enough; I would like to spend this morning with you. There is so much to talk about."

Then a strange thing happened. I heard Portia catch her breath, and John glanced at her. The look that passed between them made me uncomfortable, to say the least. Mrs. Lancaster did not seem to notice. She continued to eat her breakfast carefully with a knife and fork. I had never seen anyone enjoy their food so elegantly.

John rose from his chair, either to invite me to a walk or to leave. I was not sure, but I held out hope that John would want to spend time with me. Why wouldn't he? Why was he being so aloof toward me? Why bring me here to ignore me? How could he marry someone he obviously did not have feelings for?

"My brother, Oscar, is coming in today. I am headed to the station to collect him. We will have time this evening, I promise, dear. Mother, I take my leave."

Putting down her silverware, she patted her mouth delicately with a napkin. "Very well, son. I will see you for dinner. Maybe then you will have time for your fiancée. She is right, you are to be married. You should spend more time together."

I glanced down at my plate, feeling dejected. I could not even look them in the eye anymore. Out of the corner of my eye, I saw the small smile on Portia's face. She left the room with a stack of empty plates.

What have I done? Why did I come here?

John left without a goodbye but with a sorrowful expression. *Why? Was he not pleased to marry me?* I had so many questions, none of which would be answered anytime soon. But I was determined to marry him, regardless of the situation. Surely, I was wrong about him. He did love me. He must!

"Come now, Mary. You will have your whole lives together. Don't pout. Your wedding dress will arrive today. You will have to endure a fitting, and we have other details to discuss. There's no need for John to get involved with these minor things."

With Portia out of the room, I decided to plead my case with Mrs. Lancaster. I had to know if she had been telling the truth. Had she written the letters after all?

"Mrs. Lancaster," I began with determination.

"Eat your breakfast, Mary. You don't eat enough to keep a bird alive. I know you are a small woman, but you must keep your strength up. Marietta will be a whirlwind of activities today. You must remember yourself." I knew what she meant—I must remember who I was supposed to be. Mrs. Lancaster had been drilling me for days on end. "Later this afternoon, a few of my friends will visit, and you must look your best. Let Portia arrange your hair. She is simply the best with a hot iron."

I frowned at her. My Irish anger welled up inside me like a punishing storm, one that would not relent until it had its due. The kind that used to wash across the Irish coastline and lash everything in sight. "Mrs. Lancaster, what is going on here? Why is John behaving so distantly? It's as if he doesn't want to marry me, and your maid, Portia..."

"Watch what you say, Mary Fairbanks." Her eyes gleamed angrily, and her lips tightened. "Remember yourself. This marriage is a gift."

I flew to my feet and slapped the napkin on the plate of food before me. "Remember myself? That's what I am doing, madam. I have a difficult time believing that your son really wants to marry me. I have a difficult time with all of this. I have been here for weeks, and John refuses to so much as look in my direction. What is going on, Mrs. Lancaster? Why did you bring me here? For what purpose? To be mocked by your maid? I am leaving Marietta. I refuse to be treated like this."

The truth was I could feel an invisible noose tightening around my neck. I felt a bit like a fly in a hungry spider's web. I could not fathom what was happening, and I had a good imagination. My time with my former benefactor had taught me many things, including to always expect the unexpected.

I had become relaxed these days at Marietta, too trusting here in these beautiful surroundings. The pampering I'd received, the new dresses and the etiquette lessons, had softened me. Yes, I had gotten careless. It occurred to me suddenly that not all criminals were poor prostitutes. Criminals could take all shapes and sizes. A corrupt thing was happening here, a secret of obscene proportions. Why did this revelation surprise me so? It took my breath away. A keen sense of urgency made me want to run, run far away, but to where? Where would I go? I had no money, no prospects. The area was so unfamiliar to me, I did not have confidence that I would find the road, much less a town or a sympathetic ear.

"Did you think it would be easy? Are you weak in the knees, Mary Fairbanks?"

"You know that is not my name. I am Vienna Fitzgerald. I regret coming here. I am not going to stay, for I do not trust your intentions, Mrs. Lancaster. I am going to change my clothes and take only my own garments. I would ask for the kindness of a ride to town. If that is unsuitable to you, I will walk. Either way, I am leaving this sad situation."

"Go, then. It will be easy to replace you, but where will you go?" We stared at one another, but I wasn't persuaded to converse with her further. Her voice sounded hard and flat—and threatening. Oh, yes, very much threatening, even without having said anything specific at all. Not yet. "You haven't answered me. Where will you go? Do you know?"

"No, but I am not afraid to leave Marietta." I did not share my growing fear; that did not make my fears less valid. I would not give her the satisfaction of admitting I felt like a cornered animal and wanted to run.

"Tell me, Mary Fairbanks..." She said the words as if she were mocking me. Maybe she was because that wasn't my name, and she knew it. "Have you been baptized?"

"What?"

"It is a simple enough question, Mary. Did your proper Irish mother have you baptized?" Mrs. Lancaster rose from her chair elegantly; her neat and tidy hair did not move at all. Today's hairstyle was littered with pearl pins, as if she were the bride-to-be. Portia's handiwork, no doubt. I refused to let that woman do my hair. Ever. I wore the same boring back bun I always wore. I even used the same pins I came with. Nothing fancy for me, and nothing had been offered, either.

"I think so. I would have been an infant, but I am sure I have been baptized. Why do you ask? Is that important?"

"Maybe. Maybe not." Mrs. Lancaster smiled brightly. That was the first time she had truly smiled at me, and the sight of it caused me great worry.

"My mother was a good woman. She would have had all of us little ones baptized," I said confidently, but there was a worrying memory in my mind. A half-forgotten story, one I had not mulled over for years. Something had indeed happened, an event that had delayed my baptism. What had it been? A storm? A flood? I could not recall, but now Mrs. Lancaster's insinuation that I had not been properly baptized disturbed me no end. What could be the meaning of this questioning? I feared I was about to find out. Boldly I said to her, "Speak your mind, Mrs. Lancaster. Let us not toy with one another. Why would you ask such a thing?" And my unspoken question was, how could she know? The hair on my arms rose even higher as I pondered these questions myself. What was this about?

She walked toward me, her hands folded in front of her peacefully like a true lady. But I had seen the sharper side of her in these past weeks. A lady? I doubted that very much.

"Before you run away with your tail between your legs, Mary Fairbanks, I would like to show you something."

"What is it?" I asked without a hint of politeness. I was not much of a game player, and it was obvious to me that my fiancé's mother enjoyed her torturous games. Oh, yes, she enjoyed making me uncomfortable. Some women were like that—including Mary Fairbanks, my former employer. Those kinds of women weren't satisfied unless they crushed others beneath their boots. Or in Mrs. Lancaster's case, beneath her high-heeled slippers.

Still, even with the threat of being bested by her in some sort of way, I felt as if I had no choice but to entertain her. A small part of me was curious about what she was going to show me. I noticed that Portia stepped behind her and Mrs. Lancaster walked out of the dining room, but she did not go into the parlor as I expected. I decided to trail behind her, and the three of us went outside. As always, the unhappy help tended to their menial labors. She walked amongst them with her head held high, as if she were the Queen of England—as my mother would have said before spitting on the ground.

MARIETTA

The skies were light gray, and rain threatened to come in off the waters eventually. I noticed that sometimes the rain lingered off the coast and never actually arrived. Before I knew it, we were traveling down a worn path at the back of the property. A few steps in, and no one would be able to see us. The woods here were thick and the ground covered with soft green grass. I had no idea where we were going, but I could not stop now.

I had come too far, too far to run away from the likes of Mrs. Lancaster. I shoved my hand in my skirt pocket. I always carried a folded blade, a survival trick I learned early on during my stay in Summit. I would never be without it. Whatever these two had planned, if they tried to overtake me, they would find no mercy. I would not hesitate to do what I must.

I had done it once already. Instead of being ashamed or sad about it, I felt a kind of empowerment. A satisfied sort of knowing that I would survive, no matter what.

Yes, I am a survivor. If someone were to die today, it wouldn't be me. I would be no one's victim.

Never again.

Chapter Twelve—Lily

"I knew you would come. What took you so long? I have been sitting here forever." I waved at him as he edged closer. He moved kind of cautiously, unlike before. There was no laughing and running today. I got the impression that we weren't children anymore. Technically speaking, Mitch had not been a child for an awfully long time. And even more technically, I was no longer a kid either. I was thirteen, and aside from the perk of telling everyone I was thirteen, I saw no real benefit from it.

"This will be the last time, Lily. The magic is fading. I will be stuck if I come back." Mitch's sad expression broke my heart.

"Is that why I cannot remember you when I am awake? Because the magic is fading? What can we do?" I reached for him, but he did not take my hand or answer my question. Maybe he did not know the answer.

"I have to go. I am glad to have known you, Lily. I will never forget you. Even if you forget me, I won't forget you. In that way, a little piece of us will still be alive."

"What does that mean? We have been friends for a long time, Mitch. I like meeting you here. We are not doing anything wrong."

"But you can't remember me. That means it is time for me to go. What happens if you do not remember me tomorrow? I think I will disappear. That will be the end of me, Lily. I only live if you remember me. If I stay, it will be too dangerous. Even now I want nothing more than to...I can't say it. I won't do it, so it doesn't matter."

I shook my head and took a step toward him. "I don't understand. That can't be true. You would never hurt me. I know that. Nothing you say will convince me otherwise." A wave of nausea threatened to pull me out of my dream and back to reality. I fought against it, sobbing and clutching my stomach. Even in my sleep I had a cramp. Even in my dreams I felt ill, crabby, emotional. Completely unlike me. All of this was unlike me. What was happening?

"Whether you understand or not, it must be this way. You are alive, Lily. You need to live. Look at my fingers. It has begun."

I couldn't believe it, but he was fading, like a blown chalk painting that had lost some of its color. Was he going to disappear completely? Was it my fault? How? How had any of this happened? Even now, I could not remember when we first met. It was impossible to remember. My brain would not allow me to remember.

Mitch and I were in the maze. The sun shone bright above us. It was only the two of us, but there were other things like butterflies and birds...only I could not see them anymore. The whole place felt a bit empty. Emptier, yes. That's the word. As if it heard me, the dream sun went kind of hazy and sepia-colored. Today's dream had an ominous feel to it.

It was true. This would be the last time. Somehow, I knew that. And I did not want that. I loved my friend. I loved Mitch. I was in love with a ghost, and now I had to let him go.

This was so unfair.

"Try not to think about it. I am glad you remember me right now, in this moment."

He towered over me, a full foot taller. Mitch had never so much as held my hand or kissed me, but I loved him with all my heart. It was wrong to love the dead—I felt that in my soul. It was true, but Mitch was so different. More often than not, the dead will use that love for their own benefit. They could not help it. Mitch told me that once. He said he would leave before that happened.

It's how ghosts are, Lily. They reach for life because they do not have it. Set them free. Let them go. One day, you will have to let me go too.

And now that day had come. I had to let Mitch go, and he wanted to go. If I waited too long, if I delayed, he would not be strong enough to resist attaching to me forever. He would hate me eventually. He would hate me because he could not rest. Why couldn't he just come and go, like always? What was changing between us?

"Mitch, take my hand. Please, just once."

"No, Lily. You must know…I want you to know…I love you, Lily. I will miss you."

"Just take my hand. Please. Whatever this is, whatever is happening, we can face it together. This can't be the end, Mitchell."

"Goodbye, Lily." He smiled as he stepped away from me.

No! I wasn't going to let him go. A flood of memories returned—all the good times. All the dreams, the times we'd rested in the garden and watched the stars sail over us. His life had been so interesting, but he had been killed. His life had been stolen. I felt sorry for him that he did not get to eat good food like macaroni and cheese and hamburgers. Mitch never got to play ball or watch television. And he never kissed a girl.

"Please, Mitch. Don't leave yet. Not yet. Stay with me. There has to be a way. I cannot lose you. Where will I go to find you? If not my dreams, where? How will I see you again?"

He smiled sweetly and shook his head, a tousle of reddish-brown hair falling in his eyes. "You won't, but I will see you. You won't remember me, you can't. It's not allowed. It has to be like this. I must go, Lily. They are coming, and I don't want them to find you."

I heard the hedges shaking, and trees were moving at the edge of the maze. What was that? I heard a swarm of whispering voices, talking softly at first, then loudly. Some voices sounded pitiful, others friendly, others not so friendly. My arm hair rose on end. I felt someone watching me. I turned in my dream to look back at Seven Sisters. Baby Boy! I thought he had stayed with Detra Ann! How was he here? However it happened, he was definitely here, and he was watching me. I could see his sad face even from here. I could not leave him. He was like my brother. My own little brother.

"See? You cannot leave him. Not for me, Lily. I cannot have that on my conscience. You must live for you and him and the new one that is coming. You three are meant to be together."

"Mitchell?" I whispered as hazy tears clouded my vision. He was disappearing before me; the chalk dust effect continued as his image vanished slowly. A strong cramp hit me, and I fell to my knees. I did not bother hiding my tears anymore. Mitchell had to go. But I had not been prepared. I had not believed this day would truly come. My dream time with Mitchell had been so important to me even though my waking self had forgotten all about him.

Yes, Lily. Forget all about me.

"I can't," I argued with him as I suddenly woke up in the dark. My stomach was killing me, so much so that I had to get up. I felt strange, really strange. Hot, thirsty and crampy. Most of all, sad. Extremely sad and I couldn't remember why.

Someone, someone I loved, had left me. *Oh, but I felt so terrible.*

As I slid out of my rumpled bed, I glanced behind me. My purple sheets were in a tangle, and in the center, I spotted a small puddle of blood. I glanced down at my nightgown and gulped at the sight of bright red blood against my starched white gown. I knew what this was. Aunt Carrie Jo made sure she prepared me for this, but it was still freaky.

I scurried off to the bathroom to tidy up. I woke up Aunt Rachel, and she helped me change my sheets and did her best to give me a pep talk about periods. I assured her I was okay, just cramping and emotional.

Eventually I went back to sleep, but I tossed and turned for a while. Well, this was weird. I cried, but I wasn't sure why. Not until I fell back into my dream and walked the maze alone.

I remembered Mitchell and missed my friend. Try as I might, no matter how hard I searched, I couldn't find him. I woke up well after dawn with tears in my eyes. I found Rachel and cried on her shoulder with breathless sobs. I couldn't explain to her why, but I knew.

Mitch had been wrong—I remembered him. I always would. He had been my first love.

I cried even harder.

Chapter Thirteen—Mary

"Portia, remain here while Mary and I take a stroll," Mrs. Lancaster said. Portia's pouty expression displayed her unhappiness about this turn of events, but she remained on the path's edge and cast a watchful eye over us as I followed Mrs. Lancaster. I felt relieved that for the moment I was not lumped into a category with all the other servants. It had begun to feel that way since I arrived at Marietta. I was often overlooked, in fact ignored by most of the residents here, including the servants, and by anyone who came to visit.

My first few days at Marietta, several people came to introduce themselves. Mrs. Lancaster remained aloof, but she performed her social duties with her eyes clamped on me. I half suspected she thought me capable of stealing the silver. The visits stopped soon after they began. I was quite certain that the wedding would involve more such activities. I was content to remain in the shadows until that day arrived.

Today, Mrs. Lancaster and I walked down the sandy path, side by side, our skirts swishing against one another occasionally. She was considerably taller than me; most people were, though. The path was mostly smooth, but there were a few knotty spots that could potentially trip a lady. I mimicked her moves, keeping my hands folded carefully in front of me, my back straight, my head high. No, I was no lady. I was fooling no one. I had the feeling that Mrs. Lancaster knew that.

The trees were slender and young with bright green leaves. My skills as an arborist were lacking, but I was confident that those were slender oaks mixed in with the pines. What a strange place. The farther we traveled, the dizzier I felt. What a bizarre experience. I hadn't had sensations like this since—

"You and I need to come together, Mary Fairbanks. I think it is very sweet that you imagine yourself in love with my son. There was a time when I was young and foolish, but you cannot imagine what is expected of you." To my surprise, Mrs. Lancaster slid her arm through mine as if we were old friends. She led me to a wooden bench that was hidden from immediate view. "Come sit with me. You look pale, Mary. We haven't walked far; I hope you aren't coming down with something."

"No, ma'am," I answered without thinking much about it. I was intrigued about what she could possibly have to say to me. Some speech about breeding and etiquette, no doubt. I wasn't sure how I would assure her of my ability to fit in. I certainly was not sure that John loved me, not anymore. Before I arrived, yes, but to believe that Mrs. Lancaster wrote those letters...why? No, it had to be a lie of the darkest kind.

"You are capable of breeding, aren't you? I had not considered the possibility that you might be barren. That would be a pity, after all I have endured to bring you here."

My earbobs dangled against my neck as I jerked my head toward her. "Why would you ask me that? What an inappropriate question." A part of me warned my heart to leap off this bench and storm back to the house, but then what? Not to mention that I did not feel quite myself. My eyes had difficulty focusing, my heart raced, and my palms were sweaty. It would do no good to argue or fight about this or any topic right now. I had yet to figure out why Mrs. Lancaster allowed me to remain at Marietta, but I had a feeling I was about to find out.

My former employer used to warn me, "I am holding all the cards, Vienna." And Mrs. Lancaster was holding all the cards now, for certain. I must be patient and listen. It was always better to listen than to speak. Even when angry.

"We do not have much time, Mary Fairbanks. It will do you no good to make me your enemy. I have something else in mind altogether. Now please, are you capable of having children?"

I pulled my arm away slowly, but she appeared to not mind. "As far as I know," I answered honestly. How could one predict such things? Being as I was still intact, I had no way of knowing how fertile my loins were.

She let out a long sigh as her sloped shoulders slumped slightly. I had never seen Mrs. Lancaster appear anything but on top of her game, always erect and kind of stiff-looking. Now she gave the impression of a woman defeated.

"What would you like to say, Mrs. Lancaster? You inquire about my baptism, and now you bring me out to the woods for a stroll? Whatever you have to say to me, just say it."

"Very well. Nothing is an accident, Miss Fairbanks. I am not a believer in serendipity. I believe everything happens for a reason—that is why I was so willing to accept you when you arrived here. Although I am getting older, I am very much aware and in control of what happens in my own home. Do you believe me?"

"Yes," I answered sullenly. I did not enjoy the admission.

"My son, for all his beauty and affluence, has his gaps in character. You wouldn't think so to look at him, would you? Beautiful but not perfect. Much like his father. Like all the Lancaster men. No, the woman he marries must be strong and able to make tough choices, unmovable in the face of adversity. It is a talent to allow a man to believe he is control and yet keep the hint of scandal from his name."

What to make of this? I kept silent and still on the bench.

"I have been watching you these weeks, Mary Fairbanks. I believe you are strong and immovable and for whatever reason have set your cap for my son, although you could hope for a better life than what awaits you here. This is your chance to leave Marietta, Mary. If you do not leave now, I am afraid that you will find yourself like me. Empty."

Why I felt sympathy for this woman, I cannot say, but I did. It did not last long.

"I believe that somehow you have fallen in love with my son. Therefore, I will not object to this marriage even though it is built on dishonesty. Don't look at me like that, dear. The dishonesty has not been entirely on your side, of course."

"I have been honest with you, Mrs. Lancaster. I'm not hiding anything else."

She shook her head and pulled a tidy handkerchief out of her sleeve, then pressed it briefly to her nose as if she smelled something bad. It was probably me, although this place did have a musky sort of scent to it. Like rotting foliage. And other things.

"Did you think I was talking about you? Tell me, while we are on the subject, what happened to the real Mary Fairbanks? Will she arrive here one day to claim her prize? Will we become the scandal of Biloxi? I need to know these things so I can prepare."

I looked down at the path not just to discern the way forward but to avoid looking at her. How much should I tell her? How much was enough? I swallowed—my mouth felt dry, my throat even drier. "I assure you she will not. However, I fear that eventually someone will want answers."

"Why would they want answers? She was a woman of low character. Not someone the world cares about—much like you. There you are again with that sad look. Stop taking my words so personally. I think you and I will get along wonderfully if you trust me. There are many secrets here, secrets that one day will be yours to keep to yourself."

I wanted nothing more than to hear what she had to say, but I felt wretched. She didn't seem to notice that I was near to falling off the bench. What in the world was the matter with me? I focused on the far tree line, looking for something to fix my gaze on while this dizziness settled. It was a struggle, but I managed it.

"Do you know where you are, Mary?"

"How could I?" I popped back.

Mrs. Lancaster took my hand. Why did she insist on personal contact? I wasn't sure I could manage it with this sick feeling in the pit of my stomach. Somewhere, not too far away, I heard a woman crying, whimpering pitifully. The mistress of Marietta appeared not to notice a thing.

"This is the most sacred spot on all this property, all these acres, and it must be protected, Mary. You will probably think I am a bit mad, young lady, but you deserve to know the truth. My questions aren't to intimidate you but to determine if you can adequately do this job. Sacrifices must be made, sacrifices that will not be easy, but you must do it anyway. You must for your children. For John's children." She squeezed my hand and turned to me. We were only inches apart.

"The Lancaster name comes with great influence, wealth and respectability, but that comes at a cost, Mary. A horrible cost." I could hear footsteps not far away. I knew immediately it was the doe-eyed Portia. She was curious to see what we were doing. Mrs. Lancaster leaned forward still holding my hand. We were forehead to forehead now, as if we were truly mother and daughter. As if she were wishing me nothing but the best, yet this talk of sacrifice had truly unnerved me.

"Tell me what it is you have to tell me, ma'am. I will do my best to keep your secret and be a good daughter-in-law to you. All I want is to marry John and to love him forever. I swear to you." I closed my eyes and tried to keep my composure in this awkward position. Why the need for such familiarity? Shouldn't I leave? Shouldn't I run for my life?

"This is a hallowed spot, Mary. It is a boneyard. The bones of Marietta rest here, reminders of the many sacrifices all the women before you have made. He will expect a sacrifice and you must give it, or it will go badly for you. I cannot do it for you. If only I had a daughter."

She released my hand and rose from the bench. With her handkerchief she waved for me to join her. Were we going now? I wanted nothing to do with a boneyard. Did she mean graveyard? I saw no headstones, no crosses. Nothing to indicate that the dead were here except this queasy, uneasy feeling in the pit of my stomach. Oh, yes, now it was impossible to deny it. I knew that for sure.

I was sitting among the dead. The whispering grew louder, but still Mrs. Lancaster appeared not to notice a thing. It could not be only me hearing this strange murmuring. "Do you hear that? It sounds like many voices. Who else is here, Mrs. Lancaster? I think...I think your maid is following us."

"Yes, I hear them. I always hear them, Mary Fairbanks. Sometimes day and night, but they are not allowed to come in the house. They will try to lure you out, but never go, not at night. You must avoid this place unless you come to take care of his business. They know I am here, and soon they will know you too. I am the one who consigned many of them to darkness." She twisted slightly to glance at me before gathering her skirts and moving across the boneyard—if that is truly what this place was. I could see Portia out of the corner of my eye.

"You killed them? What are you saying? You expect me to kill too?" Was I in a nightmare? I glanced at the fern-covered ground, surprised to see some of the fronds shaking violently. Mrs. Lancaster stood amongst them, walking upon them with no regard.

"Every family has its secrets, Mary. Every family. This is ours. You will be entrusted with ours, so you must know. If you do not agree, if you refuse, he will take you or someone you love. That is why I asked you about your baptism. The unbaptized have no power over him. He will destroy you if you have no protection, but mind you, baptism protects only you. No one else. And it will not be enough to shield you if you refuse to bring him his due."

"Who? Who are you talking about?" I asked as terror arose within me. Portia was coming closer, but Mrs. Lancaster pretended not to notice her. What was happening? "I demand you tell me."

"You do not have to demand, Mary. I am telling you. I am telling you everything. It is only fair. It is how we do things here. You can choose to walk away if you like, but you will not walk very far. He will find you. He knows you now. He has smelled you, seen you. He has accepted you, and you must be his. You must protect John from him, and the Lancaster children."

"Who?" I demanded, my thighs shaking, my hands sweaty despite the unholy cold that arose from the ground beneath us.

"Death. He is Death, Mary. He is your master now."

I heard someone screaming. I thought it was Portia, but it was not. She was running away.

I was screaming. Screaming for all my worth.

Chapter Fourteen—Carrie Jo

Ashland and I huddled around the fireplace and cracked open a few bottles of water. It was thoughtful of Heather to leave us kindling and firewood, as well as a stocked pantry. If we hadn't been here to investigate a haunting, if we were just two sweethearts hoping for a romantic evening together, this would have been the perfect backdrop. But despite the mellow flames and the cheerful ambiance, Marietta had a real chill to it, especially after my most recent dream walk. I couldn't believe this. Could the family be cursed? We'd seen this kind of thing before. Idlewood came to mind, but at that location Death took the form of the Black Wolf.

What would it look like here?

"I don't think we can avoid that boneyard, Ashland. Horrible things happened here, but it all began out there. Before there was a Civil War graveyard, there were other bones, many of them." I shivered at the memory of my latest dream walk. It was too much to bear. "Poor girl."

"Don't pity her too much. We don't really know who the players are here. We have Mary Fairbanks, aka Vienna Fitzgerald, Mary Ellen Lancaster, aka Marietta, and many others. Why are they interacting now? Could the storm have awakened these souls? Do they want justice? Was Mrs. Lancaster a true believer in this so-called curse, or did she do horrible things because she was mad? If she did them at all. It's not out of the realm of possibility that she told Mary all that to deter her."

"I don't think so, Ash. We must go out there, but let's wait a few minutes. It needs to be darker, I think."

"Why do you say that?"

I shrugged as I took a deep drink of the water. Man, this baby loved her water. I patted my stomach without thinking but stopped when I caught Ashland's eye.

No need to worry him, Carrie Jo.

"Let's do a walk-through in here again. I promise not to dream walk; it's all you, babe."

He cocked a blonde eyebrow at me and grinned. "Or we could just stay here in front of the fire for a few minutes." Oh, great. He was feeling amorous. I totally misread that look on his face. I was thinking he was worried about me, and here he was wanting to take my clothes off. I thought I was the one who was supposed to feel amorous during pregnancy! He was really excited about being a father again, and apparently pretty dang excited about seeing my rounder figure.

"Really? Here?" I leaned in for a kiss when a loud hiss and a thud came from the other room. A scurry of footsteps followed, animal footsteps. Many feet and nails were scratching on the wooden floors. "What?" I leaped to my feet with Ash by my side. The lights flickered once, then twice, but then everything settled down. Nothing happened. We glanced at one another, Ashland put his finger to his lips, and I nodded in agreement.

Message received. I wasn't going to make a sound. Not a peep.

My hand was in his as we stepped into the other room. It did sound like an animal. I kept my eyes trained on the floor. It was certainly possible that a rat got inside during the renovations, or worse, a possum or raccoon. Those things could be nasty if crossed or threatened. The other option was that the creature came from the land of dark and spooky, maybe a paranormal entity that wanted to let us know we were not wanted here. Not in the least. If it weren't for Heather's situation, I would take that as a sign that we should leave, sooner rather than later. We surveyed the room, but there was a lot of furniture in here, lots of places for an animal or entity to hide if it had a mind to.

"Hello?" Ashland asked despite telling me to be quiet less than sixty seconds ago. I released his hand and wished I had a weapon to clutch, like a baseball bat.

Ghosts were one thing, raccoons another.

Ashland froze, his eyes fixed on the far door. It was a glass French door that led to one of the wide porches that flanked Marietta. I was looking in the opposite direction, through the open door to the other room. I swear I could see shadows move. A subtle sort of shifting. I stared and blinked; the fireplace offered a tiny bit of light. Was I really seeing what I thought I was?

Yes! A dark shadowy figure, long and lean, wrapped around the right side of the door frame. Its dark, hairless head stared at me. It had no eyes, but I had no doubt it was staring at me. The sickening feeling in my stomach, the creeping of my skin, those were all proof that I was in the presence of the paranormal. Then it crawled up and away. Oh, God! It was on the ceiling.

I was still staring in that direction when Ashland decided to join me. His body tensed, he took a step forward, and then all hell broke loose. The candleholder on the mantelpiece fell over, the love seat lurched, and unseen items rattled as the entity attempted to flee Ashland's all-seeing eye. "Be careful," I whispered needlessly as we bolted toward the open door. Luckily, Marietta was a one-story building, but there was a basement. From the rattling of the boards beneath our feet, I would say that was where the entity went.

And that would be where we'd go too. I clutched Ashland's hand and held the flashlight in the other. "Man or woman?" I asked him as we hurried down the hall to the closed door.

"I don't think it's either." His blue eyes narrowed as he surveyed me. "You want to stay up here?"

"It won't do any good. It knows I am here. It knows we are both here. Let's do this." I did not tell him I had that worrying dream walking feeling again. It was so weird; I experienced that quite often in this house. Marietta had many portals to the past, many doors back to the tragedies of yesterday.

Focus, Carrie Jo. Ashland needs you to stay close.

He tugged on the door, but it was locked. No, that couldn't be right. Heather and I had tried it earlier, and it opened just fine. Did she accidentally lock it? Maybe bumped the slide?

Ashland began feeling above the door for a key. I could hear banging on the other side. Pounding footsteps bounded down the steps, and another crash shocked me. Desperate and figuring we had nothing to lose, I reached for the door handle to give it a good shake. Could be a jam, right? I'd barely touched the door when it came open. I watched it swing open, and the blackness took my breath away.

"What the...really?" Ashland touched the doorknob and checked the lock. It was so weird, but it was working perfectly now. "Maybe it's stiff. Don't know, but we need to follow this thing. It's trying to run from us for a reason."

"Hey, don't do anything stupid, okay?" We crept down the steps together, me in front of Ashland this time. He would complain, but I didn't care. I had a feeling this thing wanted me, not him. It would be perfectly fine if it was just me here.

Just you...

I paused at the bottom of the stairs. "Did you say something?"

"No. What did you hear, Carrie Jo?"

"A few words, whispers. I can't be sure. It repeated back what I was just thinking. That is not a regular ghost, is it? Ghosts don't listen to your thoughts like that." It wasn't really a question, more like a statement. We had encountered quite a few ghosts together.

"What do you think? Try to protect your thoughts," Ashland said ruefully. "Hand me that flashlight, please. This one isn't cooperating at all. My batteries died."

"Here you go. Any ideas on how I do that? Protect my thoughts, I mean." My palms felt moist again, sweaty and itchy, so I wiped them on my blue jeans. I walked around in the front room; it appeared that the basement separated into two main rooms, not nine or ten like on the floor above. This should be easy enough, if I could keep my fear in check. I wasn't normally this afraid. Then as if it read my mind—again—something scratched me.

"Crap! Is that a nail?" I turned around, but I was nowhere near the stairs or anything else. "Ashland, look at my back, please. It hurts, and now it's on fire! It's so weird because it's burning from the inside out."

"Let me see." Ashland swung the light around, and I lifted the bottom of my shirt. He lifted it the rest of the way. I heard him hold his breath. "Scratches, three scratches, and they look deep! I think we should go tend to this."

My heart was pounding, and my eyes were trying to adjust to the darkness. We were not alone, not at all. This entity knew I was here at Marietta, chasing it, and it hated me. Totally and completely hated me. Why? I don't know, but that really ticked me off. Why pick on me?

I purposefully spoke to it. *We are here to help unless you have something to hide. Unless you have evil intent. Unless your goal is death and destruction. No sense in hiding from us.*

"Leave it, babe. We aren't going to run away because of a few scratches. Which way should we go?" I heard a growl in response.

Ashland heard it too. "There's our answer. This time, let me lead the way. If anyone is going to get scratched or hurt, let it be me."

I did not remind him that it hardly mattered who went through the door first. That if evil wanted to touch you, it would do just that. If it made him feel better to believe otherwise, I would not crush his hopeful thought. I was beginning to think we were in over our heads here at Marietta.

He spoke aloud to it now. "I know you are here; I can see you. You are not allowed to touch us. You are not allowed to scratch either of us. You crossed the line there. Now it's not going to go so easy for you."

It wasn't like Ashland to get aggressive with the spirit world. Not at all. But he darn sure was, getting all kinds of mouthy, and this wasn't a real ghost.

"Ashland? What are you doing?" I didn't like this new method of investigation. I reached for him to remind him that everything was going to be okay.

He pulled away from my touch. "Challenging him. He injured you, Carrie Jo! I'm not going to take this shit!" What in the world? Ashland did not swear, and he didn't lose his cool for no reason.

That's when I saw the black figure swaying in front of us. It had positioned itself in the doorway. It was leaning in toward us, like a 3D creature, emerging from one dimension to another.

"Your thoughts, Ash. Get them under control. Be positive."

He took a deep breath and closed his eyes. "Right. You're right."

I put my hand on his shoulder again. "It's okay. Right together, Ashland. Everything together. Every step of the way."

Step of the way…

Come, step this way, Mary.

I have been waiting for you.

Chapter Fifteen—Mary

"He is coming, Mary. He is as old as the ground. As old as the trees. He was here long before we were, long before the Others who lived here. I knew nothing about him, Mary. I knew nothing at all when I took Wade's hand and walked down the aisle to become his wife. At last you will see him. It is almost time. Stand close to me; he will not harm you."

I did as I was asked, my eyes flitting about trying to discern people in the darkness. But there was no one there, just trees and more trees...and the bones beneath my feet. *That is why I am shaky. That is why I feel sick.* My Irish roots never let me down. Never.

"You are not going to have long to wait. He is anxious to meet you."

The hair crept up on my arms. Even with these long sleeves on, I could feel the hair rising, reaching for the air around me.

Suddenly the leaves shifted beneath my feet. They blew up and around, twisting into a small tornado, a dust devil of dried leaves. Then it vanished and the collection of leaves and debris settled all around me. And then I felt a strange thing, the sound of snorting, like the kind one would hear if petting a horse or a cow. Whatever it was, it was so close to me. I could feel the breath on my skin. Mrs. Lancaster stood back and allowed it to surround me. She had a strange look on her face. As she observed me, her expressions were hard to read. Was she jealous? Relieved? Curious?

Hands touched my legs, caressed them and then tugged me down to the ground. I swirled my dress back to reveal what had a hold of me. It did me no good to struggle. Two dark hands held my ankles briefly before sliding into the ground. The dark had kind of crept up on me, and it was so dark out now that I couldn't see anything except what was right in front of me. I saw Mrs. Lancaster well enough, even though she seemed much farther away than before. Was she going to leave me here?

The hands returned, only this time, they slid up my legs. I screamed in surprise as the grasping limbs pinned me down, and yet Mrs. Lancaster did nothing. "Help me!"

"Let it happen, Mary. This is what you wanted, isn't it? He has to know you."

Before I could scream again, I twisted my body and felt a hand clamp over my mouth, muffling my voice completely. There was nothing I could do but suffer through the terror and humiliation of being groped by an invisible evil. Yes, it was certainly evil, wasn't it? A ghost? A dead person? I screamed against the disgusting hand that threatened to smother me. Death! I smelled death! I knew it well. A sickness had coursed through our village in County Cork when I was only six years old. It had taken so many that the bodies of the dead were piled up inside the church, yet my mother insisted we go and help tend to the dead. Strange that she was so scared of the dead once they were in the ground, terrified of ghosts, but dead bodies? No problem. But we had helped tidy them up, Mother and I and all my brothers except Cole. He had been sick and on the verge of death himself, so much so that the darkness never quite left him. It stayed with him for years until he left for military service. That had not lasted long. He had taken a rifle to himself and ended his melancholia in a bloody and succinct way.

"Please!" I gasped for air as the hand released me a fraction. But its fingers probed my body, probed me in inappropriate and painful fashion. And then as quickly as it had appeared, it released me. I lay on the soft grass and stared up at the black sky above me, weeping like a child. To my surprise, Mrs. Lancaster did not leave. She merely watched and waited.

"You passed the test, Mary Fairbanks. You have been accepted, it appears. That is a great honor. Who would have believed it? I was not sure that you would, but you have done it. Now comes the difficult part, giving him what he wants. Do you understand?"

As I sat up, there was a strange pain in my body, in an area not handled before. "You let it molest me. You stood there and allowed it to fondle me!" I walked back on my hands and clambered to my feet like an alley cat ready to scrap over a piece of rotten meat. "How dare you! How could you do that? What was that?"

"I did nothing at all. It is him. Death. He comes for us all, Mary. But now you have favor with him. He will take your offerings. Your children will be safe, for he has accepted you. I cannot explain why it is this way, but it is. Don't let the humiliation be for naught. When the time comes, you will give him what he wants, and you will protect this family—as I have always done. He likes the taste of you, Mary. He will not molest you again. Unless you fail to honor your promise."

I wiped tears from my eyes. "I promised nothing. Nothing! I hate you!" I could not believe this attack. It was terrible, and I wanted nothing to do with it. Eager to get out of her presence, I ran from the grove, through the patch of forest and back to Marietta. I had no plan other than to recover from the attack and then leave here forever.

But it was not to be.

Portia met me first. I was weeping when I came into the front room of the house. The servants were naturally nowhere to be found. It was as if they had known what would happen to me and wanted to avoid me at all costs. It was too much to take.

"Come with me, Miss Fairbanks. Come," her soft voice whispered in my ear. "Hurry, before she comes back. It will be all right. I know, I saw. I'm sorry I could not help you."

"It came for me. There's a horrible thing out there. Oh, no! I know what it was—I know."

"Shh...I know, but do not say its name. It will come inside if you do."

I cried even harder. "Please get John, Portia. Tell him I must see him. Please."

"She will return soon and will not allow you to tell him. It's part of the magic."

I took her hand as she hurried me down the hall to my room. She closed the door, locked it and led me to the bed. Portia hurriedly took a rag from the bowl beside my bed and rang it out. She returned and began dabbing my arms, face and hands clean.

"Fomoire. It is a demon, Portia. She trucks with demons. I cannot stay here. I cannot! It molested me! I am tainted forever!"

A banging at the door surprised me. I heard voices too, a male and a female. Was that John? After all this time, he would speak with me? How strange! It led me to believe that he knew exactly what was going to happen to me.

"Mary! Let me in! I hear you crying. Let me in, my love!"

Portia went stock still, unmoving and uncertain. The tapping continued. I wiped at my eyes with the back of my hand. Despite my misgivings, I wanted to run to the door and swing it wide open, to fall into his arms and tell him all that his mother had done. But that wouldn't be smart. How would he ever believe me? It seemed improbable, didn't it?

A demon erupted from the ground, John. It took my flower. It touched my soul. Save me! Your mother did this!

"Portia, open the door, please." I arranged my skirts and clutched my stomach. Oh, it hurt so bad. I suspected that I was bleeding. I would have to tend to that, but first, I must see John. He wanted to see me! I had been waiting for this moment. My fiancé had avoided me for so long, but now...

"No, Miss Fairbanks. You don't understand. Please listen to me." Portia fell on her knees before me and looked up into my face, tears in her eyes, her pretty lips quivering. "He is going to take my baby. That thing you saw, he will take the baby! Mine for yours! You have to believe me."

"Portia! Are you in there? What are you doing in there? Mary? Open the door!" John's voice sounded agitated. His response surprised me. Why would he be angry that Portia visited me? This was odd—this whole situation was so odd. I hadn't had so much as a decent conversation with him in the weeks I had been here. This was all too strange. I glanced from Portia to the door.

"What do you mean?" I whispered to her, my eyes never leaving the door.

"I am pregnant, Mary. John...he isn't what you think. He isn't innocent in all this. I also came here as his bride, but I was rejected. I fear what will happen to my baby. I fear it! Please, help me, Mary! Miss Fairbanks!"

Suddenly, the doorknob began to twist and shake. John's angry voice interrupted her desperate pleas. "Open the door, Mary! Portia, come out and leave her alone. My mother is looking for you. Come out now!"

"John, stop this!" I couldn't help but bark my warning at him. "Go away!" I put my hand on Portia's shoulder protectively, though I wasn't sure I believed her. Something was wrong, but what? If I had not had the dark experience in Marietta's boneyard, I wasn't sure that I would feel anything but annoyance. However, dark forces were at work here. Dark forces that may cause harm to Portia as they had done to me already.

I had to get to the bottom of all this. I needed answers!

Despite Portia's protests, I walked to the door and reached for the doorknob. I opened it, but John was not there. I saw nobody at all. Not a soul.

MARIETTA

I stepped out into the hallway and saw a tall, dark shadow slide down the hall. Portia walked up behind me, and her words chilled my soul.

"Oh, God! He is in the house. The Dark One is inside Marietta!"

She took off running, tears in her eyes, her whole body shaking. I called after her, but she was gone. She'd disappeared into her room, and no amount of knocking would convince her to come out. I wasn't sure what to do now.

Except leave. I needed to leave Marietta behind. Enough was enough. Finally, I knew what was here, and I wanted no part of it.

Fomoire! Heavens above! Lord, save me!

I began packing my clothes. I would leave now, even if no one would help me. I would walk if need be. Where I would go, I wasn't sure, but anywhere would be better than here.

Anywhere...

Chapter Sixteen—Carrie Jo

I wiped the tears from my eyes as I told Ashland my dream. It had been a horrible experience being Mary Fairbanks, feeling those hands crawling over my body, invading me, marking me for itself. I couldn't even imagine what happened to her. To know I would need to dream again, or dream walk...for some reason, I felt that was a dangerous idea. Yesterday's journey to the boneyard had not yielded much.

"That's not good at all. Reminds me of the Black Wolf. I hope it's not like that. Maybe it's just a grasping ghost, a negative human. I need to get a look at it, but for some reason it is avoiding me."

Ashland had seen a few ghosts meandering around the boneyard, but not the fomoire. They were the Civil War dead, patrolling the resting place of their fallen comrades. Not the thing that called itself Death. But my dream had been real. We had to go back and see it for ourselves. But first I needed to check in with Rachel.

"I'll call home. Will you make us some lunch? I can't believe we slept so late."

"Sure will. Send Lily my love. Are you going to call Detra Ann too?"

"Why don't you check on AJ? Then we can figure out what our game plan is, Ashland."

He smiled and walked out of the bedroom, leaving me alone.

Alone...yes. That's what I needed, to be alone.

Oh, dear. This dream wasn't over. Not by a long shot. I was still dreaming.

The door closed in front of me. I walked toward it to seek out Ashland, to let him know what was going on, but he was long gone. I wasn't in our time anymore. The familiar honey hue fused into my vision, and I was all alone.

And I was not myself or Mary Fairbanks. I was awash with sorrow. I began shaking as I became fully aware of what was happening.

Ashland...Wow, this experience is unexpected and powerful. I must go back. I must follow her. See what she saw, feel what she felt. She won't allow me to leave without knowing.

Portia!

She stood before me. This was strange. Usually, I dreamed as the other person, but Portia wanted to show me. The bedroom door opened with a long squeaking sound. Strange, I did not remember that door squeaking before. She had large brown eyes, dark circles beneath them, and her hair was unbound and hung heavily around her face. I could barely see her, but it was certainly her. She wore a yellowed white nightgown with long lacy sleeves and a dress with a dirty hem. I also saw that the frail-looking woman was significantly thinner than I remembered from my earlier dream. When I first saw Portia, through Mary's eyes, she had lovely skin with a natural glow. She looked nothing like that now. She raised her head to show me her gaunt face, and it was a terrible sight. Had she been starved? Was this an accurate portrayal of her condition? I said nothing, only watched and waited, trembling with dread.

Yes, her lovely appearance had changed dramatically. "What happened, Portia? What happened to you? Tell me," I said as she floated into the hallway backward, her eyes never leaving mine.

Ashland...I wish you were here.

I could not hear him; I was firmly planted in this current realm, in this time with the pitiful Portia. Even as I thought that, I heard another voice warning me.

Don't trust her!

But as Portia skidded away, I could do nothing but follow her. Nothing but scurry behind the floating apparition as she continued her backward journey down the hall to a closed door. Oh, but she was certainly pregnant. Her belly swollen, so swollen I wondered how much longer she could carry the baby. As she hovered before the door, moving up and down a few inches, she suddenly vanished as if she had been sucked through the door. Sucked into the past. As I stood outside the door, I felt the cold. The coldness of death permeated the air around me as I lifted my hand to open the door. Yes, I knew death quite well.

Before opening the door, I put my ear to it. What was on the other side? Who? Portia? I heard crying. A woman, a woman giving birth. I knew those words. I knew the screams and the pain and later the relief. I took a deep breath and opened the door. To my surprise, the room was full. There were too many people for decorum's sake, especially in Portia's time. Would men be allowed to wait for a baby to arrive? But there were dozens of men—and women and children. They were lined up against the walls, pale and gray, watching and waiting.

And it was not Portia who lay in the bed but Mary Fairbanks, the usurper, the Irishwoman who stole another's ticket. The woman who claimed John Lancaster as a husband, but was he such a prize? Was he a good man?

Portia was there, though. Her face was white and her body thin, but she was alive. At least then she had been alive. But now, her baby...she had clearly given birth. Where was Portia's baby? All I could do was watch and wait. I could not ask questions or do anything at all except stand amongst the crowd and witness Mary giving birth. She was sweating, and her damp hair stuck to her face and neck. No one held her hand, no one patted her face with a damp towel. No one comforted her with words of kindness and encouragement. A room full of witnesses stood around her, but there was no friend. I could feel that. The loneliness, the waiting for blood. The blood of the heir.

And that's when I saw the dark shadow sliding up the wall. It hovered over Mary's large bed, like a shadow canopy. It swelled and breathed excitedly in anticipation of the child's arrival. It wanted it, expected it. Mary's eyes opened wide, and she screamed. Because of the pain or because of the fomoire's presence, I could not say. It was most certainly waiting for blood and bone.

Blood and bone. Blood and bone! He comes for my blood and bone! One for another—one for another.

I could hear Portia's words echoing in my mind. She had tried to warn Mary, but she would not believe, and now it was too late. The baby would be born, and it would be far too late. Oh, the agony. I felt Portia's desperation, Mary's fear and pain. It was too much to bear. Too much to feel and experience.

Portia! Please let me help you!

My baby! My bones!

"Show me, Portia! Show me what happened!"

With a mighty sob, she flew backwards and vanished from the room.

"Show me, Portia! Let me go with you, Portia!" I cried.

Mary wailed one last time as her baby erupted from her womb, but I would not see the baby. Suddenly, I was in the boneyard with Portia.

Portia was running toward it. I was already there, waiting for her to arrive. I glanced down at my feet and watched the ground begin to shake. There was a disturbance in the soil. The dark figure, the one from the house, the one that had been watching over the birth of Mary's baby, had followed us here.

This was the thing Mary called a fomoire—a darkness straight from the bowels of the earth. And it was coming to collect its due. I heard a baby crying and Portia weeping. Someone was chasing her, perhaps a man. I heard him shouting, shouting her name.

Oh, but she was desperate. Desperate to leave! She had not meant to come here, but she got lost in the fog. The horrible fog. It had crept up from the ground during the birth. Crept up and over the ground. Crept up and threatened to bring me down.

I must leave. Take the baby! Please, take him.

She saw me, she saw me and ran with eyes wide open, clutching her crying baby.

The baby! Please! Help...

The ground began to open as the black shadow, the fomoire, raced toward her with its gaping mouth open. It found her quickly, and then she began to slide into the earth.

"No!" she screamed with all her might. "The baby!"

But it was too late. Far too late. The dark earth flew up. I could smell it, rich and musty. I screamed as I watched Portia's thin body falling into the earth. She would smother. Buried alive—I could not imagine.

I wanted to run to her, but the honey hue returned. The transition was happening, and I had to go back to the world of the living. Whatever powers ruled the land of dreams would not allow me to interfere with this situation.

"Please! The baby! Don't let him take the baby!"

I broke free and began to run toward her. Portia's face, full of terror and fear as she sank into the ground, faded. And then there was nothing. Nothing but the worn carpet of Marietta. Ashland called me from the kitchen, completely unaware of everything that was happening.

"Portia!" I screamed as I came alive fully to this realm.

I was still crying when Ashland found me.

Epilogue—Carrie Jo

Heather stepped away to talk with Mike Sellers, the owner of Rifle Dogs, an excellent cadaver dog recovery team. We had seen them work before. The dogs were alerting, which was to be expected because this was a cemetery. But even before that, this had been a boneyard. An ancient boneyard protected by an entity that demanded sacrifice. That entity took Portia right in front of me, and maybe her baby too. I had a sick feeling in the pit of my stomach. I wanted to know but also didn't want to know.

Ashland joined me as the dogs were led away. Luckily, or unluckily, they alerted just outside the cemetery, which meant we could dig. Heather wasted no time giving her permission to begin the bone recovery.

She joined us with a bleak look on her face. "I knew this was going to happen. I just didn't think it would happen so soon. What's really going on here, y'all?" She dabbed at her eyes with a tissue she pulled from her pocket. "I don't think I can watch this. Will you excuse me? I'm going to go inside. You guys want some iced tea?"

"Sure, Heather. I will join you. Ashland?"

He squeezed my hand comfortingly. "I'll stay here, just in case. I'll come inside if they find anything."

"Thanks," she said, and together we returned to Marietta. There was a news truck pulling in the driveway, and we both groaned at the sight. She said, "Great. That's great."

I interjected, "It was bound to happen, Heather. Anytime bones are found, the news media follows. I know that from experience. But the important thing is taking care of the people who've been reaching out to us. We can't quit, Heather, but you know what? We will go as far as you want. If it's too much, it's okay. I'll understand."

Heather and I ducked in the house and closed the door. I was happy to see Ashland hotfooting it to the van. We weren't officially representatives of Marietta, just trying to help. But Ashland knew the media, and he was the kind of guy that could get things done.

"No, I am going to see this through. I can't believe what you told me, what has happened in this house. Portia and Mary and God knows who else are out there. What does this mean? Is that demon awake again? Is that why people are seeing things here? Why are the bones turning up? It can't just be the storm. Does this entity want more sacrifices?" Heather's pretty face paled as we sat together on the overstuffed gingham sofa.

I had no answers, not yet. My work here was just beginning, but I would do my best to bring her the answers she needed before someone else got hurt. Eventually she stopped shaking, and we sipped our tea and waited for news.

We didn't have long to wait. Ashland came to tell us that two bodies were found, a woman and an infant, but the skeletons were missing their skulls. The coroner had come to remove the remains. It was a long day, but at the end of it, we left Biloxi knowing we'd done as Portia wanted.

Ashland and I found her body and her baby. We could not save the baby, not like she wanted, but at least the infant had been found. I wanted nothing more than to make sure Heather had peace, but there were too many questions left unanswered.

What really happened in the Lancaster family all those years ago? How could anyone make a pact with an evil entity? Why would Mrs. Lancaster recruit poor Mary to be a part of it? Why was Heather feeling as if something evil was working here?

Ashland and I drove from Biloxi in silence. We both decided to keep the Marietta project first and foremost on our list. In the meantime, though, something was up with Lily. Rachel told us the news about our niece's physical change, but there was more to it than that. Lily was the epitome of deep waters. She felt things on such a deep level, so intensely. The therapist said she was like this because of the trauma she had endured with her parents. Although I did not disagree with that, I believed Lily was such an emotionally deep person because she was my niece. Our bloodline flowed with gifted people.

"Bloodline...it is the bloodline. I don't know how, but it has to be the bloodline, Ashland."

"What? What do you mean? You mean at Marietta?"

"Yes, at Marietta. Something about Heather has to be triggering the activity. I don't think it was the storm. She took possession of the place right before the storm. Heather said she's always felt connected to the house, always loved it, even as a child. I think there's an attachment there. When we go back, we need to bring Detra Ann. I hate to say this, but I don't think Heather is being completely honest with us."

Ashland shook his head as we drove into Mobile County. "Why? Why would she hold back after contacting us?"

"She's afraid, I can feel that. But I don't know why she isn't telling us everything. Maybe she can't remember."

And then the road ahead of me disappeared. I was back at Marietta. I was holding onto the porch railing and could feel the cold wood beneath my hand. Dusk arrived, mosquitoes were lurking, and there were cicadas creaking in the trees surrounding the house. Mary and John were kissing. Mary was dressed in white; it must have been their wedding day.

White petals fell around them, and it was like a fairy tale. But then it turned into a Grimm's fairy tale because their perfect faces twisted, the skin melting away to show bones. Skeletal faces opened their mouths and screamed at me. I couldn't understand what they said, but it was clear to me they didn't want us to come back. Then the vision fluttered away with the sounds of birds' wings. It was a strange thing to see and hear. I yelped and clamped my hand over my mouth.

"It's true, Ashland. It's the bloodline. Something about the bloodline."

Ashland glanced at me. We were getting deep into traffic now. He could not hold my hand or comfort me as the tears streamed down my face, but he said gently, "If this is too much for you, please speak up. We don't have to do this. Remember that."

"No, we are doing it. I know which way to go. Let's go home and love our children. Next weekend we'll come back, and we will be ready for battle. All we need is a little time. A little time to prepare."

We didn't talk again until we pulled into the driveway. Lily and AJ were tumbling out the door to greet us like two balls of sunshine. I loved them so much. So very much. Thank God my bloodline wasn't cursed. Thank God everything had worked out okay for us. Seven Sisters was quiet, the ghosts were gone, and my family was safe. Time to live and love, at least for a few days before we stepped back into the paranormal world.

One more time.

FOOTSTEPS OF ANGELS

Marietta Series
Book Two
By M.L. Bullock

M.L. BULLOCK

A Cradle Song

Sleep, sleep, beauty bright,
Dreaming in the joys of night;
Sleep, sleep; in thy sleep
Little sorrows sit and weep.

Sweet babe, in thy face
Soft desires I can trace,
Secret joys and secret smiles,
Little pretty infant wiles.

As thy softest limbs I feel
Smiles as of the morning steal
O'er thy cheek, and o'er thy breast
Where thy little heart doth rest.

O the cunning wiles that creep
In thy little heart asleep!
When thy little heart doth wake,
Then the dreadful night shall break.

William Blake, 1789

Chapter One—Marietta

This was an inauspicious day—the heat was overbearing, and there was no late summer breeze. Another day with no rain. If this continued, it would be disastrous for the crops. Not only that, but the milk soured this morning, and many of the animals were sick from a mysterious malady, a crippling malaise that left some of the beasts without blood and bone. Not so mysterious to me. I knew the cause, but there wasn't anything I could do to stop it. I calmed the servants' fears and offered up any sensible lie or excuse I could imagine. They were a suspicious lot, as they should be. Suspicious of me, of my son.

Too much blood had spilled here at the place attached to my name.

My bloody wedding gift. A mansion as cursed and bleak as it was elegant and beautiful. If I had the chance to encounter my husband in the afterlife, I would most certainly kill him again.

How could he have done this to me? To our children and grandchildren?

Yes, my concerns were for the newest member of the family. Baby Lancaster wanted to enter the world. Unfortunately for us all, the fate of our family rested on my daughter-in-law's childlike shoulders. Mary had some sense of what existed here, but she refused to listen to me, to learn the full truth. It was not a topic of discussion she welcomed. She didn't trust me either.

Mary didn't know what I'd done for her. For my sons.

Portia's absence had separated me from John Lamar. He blamed me for her disappearance, and rightly so. I could not predict what the Beast would demand. I tried so many things over the years—even offering my own blood—but the Beast would not appear for me during these drunk offerings.

But ah, I was not a true Lancaster.

Dormancy was the best we could hope for. Seven years of peace. At least that had been true in the beginning, when I rid myself of Xavier's bastards. The Beast had accepted those and dutifully disappeared.

Where was John Lamar? Toying with a new girl, no doubt. Fool. My eldest son was always one to shirk responsibilities and satisfy his urges. So much like his father. Only John Lamar did not leave quite as wide a trail of children behind him, not like his father.

Mary moaned beside me, and I squeezed the girl's hand to remind her that she was not alone. She must accomplish this task. A live birth was necessary, the continuation of the legitimate bloodline. A future caretaker, someone to keep the peace between the Beast and the family. Hopefully she would have a boy. We needed a boy.

"You are doing fine, Mary. Just fine. Keep your eyes open and bear the pain. It will only last a little while," I whispered into her ear as I patted her forehead with a damp cloth. There wasn't much else I could do except encourage the tiny woman to bring forth my grandson.

The Beast had taken Portia and her child. It's not as if I'd known that would happen for a certainty. There was nothing to be done about that, but it bothered me that the full seven years had not been honored. It had been only a few months since the last sacrifice, and the sounds of war drums were heard often these days.

Ghostly war drums.

Things were not balanced between this world and the next. Not right at all. The slaves knew it too. They took their own protective measures against the angry spirits that dwelled in the shadows of this place. I did not forbid them. If they could fend it off, I would not object. How could I?

"Not my name," she murmured between grunts. "Not me. I don't belong here! Don't let it take my baby! Please, Marietta!"

"Hush, Mary. Don't talk nonsense, girl," I scolded her in low tones as she continued to clutch my hand. "All will be well. I promise you." My maid, Sally, and I exchanged a knowing look, but neither of us spoke. Mary continued to bear down, but progress remained slow. She was so small, so very tiny.

Perhaps the afterbirth would satisfy the cursed thing. The dead animals and the days without rain were cause for concern. I shivered and crossed my fingers against that very thing.

I must continue my work until Mary took my place, but I was tired. Oh, so tired. My sacrifices had carried the Lancaster family thus far. My poor Sophie.

After that, I'd managed to keep the creature at bay. But the Beast's unpredictable appearance wreaked havoc on my heart and mind. Poor Sophie. This was not the way things were supposed to be.

My late mother-in-law tried to prepare me, just as I tried to prepare Portia and now Mary. But the thing chose to kill Portia—and her baby.

What about Mary? She could no longer shirk her responsibilities.

Mary's child didn't want to enter this world, but it was time. He could not hide from his destiny any longer—whatever that may be. Mary wasn't trying hard enough. She'd been at this for hours, and there was barely any movement. Eventually, decisions needed to be made. I was glad that John Lamar was absent. I could see now that it had been wise of him to leave this bloody work in my hands.

None of these Lancaster men had the stomach to do what needed to be done.

"Look again, Sally!"

My servant obediently lifted the girl's bloody sheet and peered at her thighs. "She needs to push—I see the top of his head! He is crowning, ma'am!"

I breathed a sigh of relief. I was covered in sweat, and the room smelled like iron and blood. What now? Would I do the unthinkable? Would I sacrifice the woman for the child?

Of course I would.

John Lamar would not have stopped me even if he had been present. He was rarely here anymore, and when he was, he barely spoke to either Mary or me.

Portia had stolen his heart.

Did he care at all for Mary or her infant? Who could say?

I had worked so hard to bring them together. Mary was the one the bones selected. They spelled her name out more than once. The bones led me to Mary Fairbanks, but this woman...she wasn't who she claimed to be. I feared that whatever spirit drove the Beast knew this. Could this Mary trick the runes? Or the Beast?

I had been hopeful when John met Mary. He seemed interested, curious. A bit distracted from Portia, who held such power over him for so long. John Lamar had a heart attachment to Portia, and I assumed he fancied himself to be in love. He declared such to me a week after the elegant quadroon arrived. Portia had been John Lamar's chosen, but she wouldn't do. Her blood would not satisfy the Beast.

"This is on you, John Lamar." That had been my answer. To my mind, men were not capable of love or fidelity, but I had to admit John thought himself truly in love.

To his credit, John did put up a fuss when Portia disappeared. He suspected my hand in it but could not prove it, and in the end, he stopped asking about her.

So did Mary.

She seemed relieved that Portia was gone, too. She knew because she'd seen it happen. Mary knew what happened to Portia, and she said nothing.

As expected, John toyed with Mary for a few weeks and then moved on to someone else. Mary did not have the beauty and sophistication that Portia displayed. Poor Portia. She too believed herself in love with John Lamar, but luckily, I knew her secret. A dark secret that kept her quiet whilst I worked my plan. Silly woman. In the end, it had done her no good. The Beast took her.

Mary was not as strong as I'd hoped. Too small, with no hips to speak of, rather childlike, anatomically speaking. But how could I have known any of this from mere letters? I couldn't very well ask such a question, especially while impersonating my own son. What a bit of irony. I impersonated John Lamar while Mary, this Mary, impersonated the true Mary Fairbanks. Two tricksters we were.

Yes, what irony. *I, the great and haughty Marietta Lancaster, taken in by a common trickster.*

I gripped the young woman's hand and commanded her to push. "Mary! Mary? Wake up, girl!" The young woman roused. Her eyes flickered but then rolled back in her head, and she screamed with all her might.

"It's here! Can't you see it?" My daughter-in-law screamed a few more times and, with that declaration, passed out again. Once again, I placed the smelling salts under her nose and demanded that she wake up. She must do her part—I couldn't do it for her.

Yes, I had done all I could to appease the Beast that resided in the boneyard. But it was unpredictable, this terrible Lancaster curse. It manifested in horrible ways. Despite the heartache and the difficulty, I long ago stopped bemoaning my fate as caretaker here. I ceased begging heaven for help. I accepted what I must do for my children and grandchildren. I was a murderess. One of the damned.

I accepted that and willingly got blood on my hands. This had not been my fight. I hadn't caused it. This curse came with the land. The house before this one, the small one, had been cursed as well. Xavier Lancaster built Marietta for me, built it in my honor. But there had been no honor in it. All Xavier had done was bind me to this gruesome fate. He invested his fortune in seizing all the land around us. But the land came at a price.

An immeasurable, unspeakable price.

"Yes, my sweet Marietta. This is all for you." That's what he told me days after he married me, but it soon became clear to me that it was no honor. It was no honor at all.

It swallowed me up that day.

Xavier led me there. He told me nothing about the boneyard. Nothing about the Beast that lurked in the dirt of the clearing between the two small forests. Without concern, Xavier watched as I screamed, frozen to the spot. It came up from the ground, tearing up the dark soil with abandon and reaching for my ankles. As it gripped me mercilessly, I stared at the tall, thin being. A shadow, really, but a shadow with strength and teeth and claws. It climbed up my legs and lay on top of me, its black eyes boring into my soul. While I was still screaming, it scratched me with one long fingernail, clawed the side of my face and touched the bloody nail to its lipless mouth.

Sally's screams brought me back to this perilous moment.

"The head, it is emerging, mistress! Now is the time. She must wake up!" Sally declared, her eyes wide, her voice loud and booming. She always spoke too loudly, as she couldn't hear very well, but she was even louder under pressure.

"Mary!" I touched the pouch to the young woman's nose, but she would not stir. She was still alive, though, and her body still worked to push the baby out. Mary's back arched slightly, and she moaned incoherently. At least a part of her heard my voice.

"Thank goodness! Here it comes, mistress!"

I continued to coax Mary to wake up. It would be better for the baby if she did wake, but she only moaned and babbled, and I could not make out her words. I felt a stirring in the air. This place had always been a home for ghosts and otherworldly things.

A home for death.

The rocking chair in the corner of the room moved back and forth erratically, though there was no breeze, no moving of the air. Nary an open window. Sally's eyes widened at the sight, but I reminded her to stay focused on the task.

"The baby! Keep your eye on the baby! Don't let him go!"

"Yes, ma'am," Sally answered as she flipped the sheet back. The rocking chair continued to bang against the wall. Suddenly, the window slid open with a rough crashing sound, which caused me to gasp in surprised fright. The light-yellow curtains flapped in the wild breeze. A driving rain hit the house—a sign that supernatural forces were at play. I suspected that if I were to look out the window, I would see that it was raining on only the house, not the entire property. But there was nothing to do except continue to plead with Mary.

"Wake up, girl! Wake up, Mary!"

I clung to the girl's hand. These past months, I had worked so hard to bring this pregnancy about. Many times, I had to intervene in arguments between John and Mary. Finally, we would see the fruit of their union.

To my surprise, Mary and I had settled into a partnership. It was an uneasy one but a partnership, nonetheless. For whatever reason, Mary wanted John more than anything. And she believed—like many women do—that by delivering his child, by providing an heir for him and the Lancaster family, he would love her.

I encouraged this belief because it served my purpose, and I felt no guilt about it. It was better for everyone if Mary did believe that all would be well, if she believed that John loved her.

What happened to my son? John Lamar, my sweet boy, the one who once loved and trusted his mother. My heart hurt at the memory of our former closeness. But he had seen too much. He knew too much, and that had not been my fault. I had done everything within my power to prevent his ever finding out, but John Lamar was a curious child.

Curious enough to see with his own eyes what was hidden in the boneyard.

He would never understand, never appreciate all that I had given for him and for Oscar. Of course, Xavier was long dead. Happy to deliver all this misery into my lap. Despite his coldness, I loved John above all others. Even my Oscar. Yes, just like Mary, I loved John Lamar with all my being, but I would never gain his trust again.

At least I had Oscar, and he was far from here.

Yes, John Lamar was ruined. Completely and utterly ruined. He would never be a good man, as he had proven since Xavier's death. John Lamar would never be reliable, never committed to the continuation of his lineage, not like me, but I had hoped that would change. If not for him, for Oscar's sake. Yes, I loved John Lamar, but if he would not help me keep the Beast at bay, then I would have to turn to his brother. When death came for me, someone must take my place. Someone had to give the blood and bones to keep the wretched peace.

Maybe this was all for Oscar, after all.

If blood must be given, let it not be his or his children's. When I'd seen how things went with my older son, I didn't allow a day to pass. I had taken great pains to send Oscar away—to protect him from his brother's influence. A son was needed to continue the line, to protect us all. What would happen if there were no more children? Would the Beast demand their blood instead? I did not know what to expect. Truly, I did not.

Oscar was at school in Georgia, but he would be home soon, and I would have to find some way to keep John Lamar silent. Yes, I had done my best to make my expectations clear to him, but he refused to talk about it.

"I don't want to know anything else! I don't want to hear about it! This is superstitious nonsense, Mother!" He had never spoken to me so disrespectfully, but I did not push him on the matter. "Where is Portia? Tell me you didn't have a hand in her disappearance! What are you doing in that boneyard? Why all this talk of evil and death? I would have been happy with Portia! Did you kill her? Did you harm her? I swear, Mother! If you touched a hair on her head…"

I refused to answer him, but neither did I deny his accusations. Let him think what he wanted. I hadn't expected his resistance. Initially, I planned on lying to him, telling him what he wanted to hear—or didn't want to hear—but when it came down to it, I could not. He'd seen for himself what lay in the boneyard.

What waited for us all.

But I wanted him to know what I had done for him. I wanted him to know about the curse his father left in my care. I derived a strange satisfaction from seeing his face break, seeing the awareness break his spirit. Yes, he knew the truth, and there was no turning back.

Poor Mary. Poor John Lamar.

John's son would not be taken, despite their separation! The baby would need to be protected! When the time came, I would be ready. At least I'd bought them some time—seven years. That was the length of the curse. Seven years. But it had only been five!

Surely, Portia's unexpected sacrifice would suffice.

It would be enough. It had to be.

I had made mistakes before. The Beast did not always play by the rules, rules I had to figure out largely on my own. Oh, I couldn't bear to think about it. Not now. Not when my grandson was about to arrive.

That had been so long ago, I barely remembered my daughter's sweet face. No, I didn't want to remember those brown curls and trusting hazel eyes. Only seven. Just seven. Her brother John Lamar away with his father on his first ever hunt.

One would be taken, one would remain.

Yet I remembered the sounds of my own screaming as Sophie was pulled down, down, down, into the dirt. The horror of being buried alive terrified me. I'd dug like a madman, but it had been no use. The Beast had taken her, and she would not return. If I were any kind of mother, I would have ended it then. But would sacrificing myself be enough?

What about burning the place to the ground? I could not be sure. How was I to know such things?

Mary finally awoke with yet another scream. The rocking chair tipped over, and a blast of bloody odor filled the room. Sally whispered a prayer as the baby emerged into the world. He had a loud, lusty voice. Always a good sign.

I knew it was a boy. I had known all along. I knew a great many things. The bones told me, and I always believed the bones.

They had not let me down so far.

Chapter Two—Rachel

The drive to Biloxi wouldn't take long, and the view along Beach Boulevard was breathtaking. Strange that I loved the ocean so much but rarely went to the water anymore. But there would be no time for taking strolls. Besides, I was anxious to share all the information I gathered about Marietta with the Stuarts. I was honored that they would invite me along. It had been a while since I'd been involved in a full-blown Carrie Jo and Ashland investigation.

Because of my involvement with the Brotherhood, I suspected that Ashland and Carrie Jo kept me at arm's length just a little bit. I know they loved me, like an oddball sister. But there was that little bit of distrust because of all that had gone down with our group.

As far as I could tell from my own experience, the Brotherhood was merely a group of scholars who wanted to get to the bottom of local hauntings. They were open to all sorts of phenomena, including ESP, psychometry, and yes, mediumship. On occasion, they asked me about the Stuarts, but I never told them anything of importance. Eventually, they stopped asking. I wasn't down with backstabbing my friends. Despite what CJ and Ashland might suspect.

Seven Sisters continued to be a place of interest for anyone fascinated with ghosts, dream catching and the rarely talked about phenomenon of time travel. So much so that CJ decided to close the house for tours. I didn't blame her for that. There were a lot of shady characters out there who had no qualms about coming into your home and doing things they shouldn't.

It was the unfortunate truth—the dark side of this paranormal world. There were a lot of bad actors out there. People that didn't mind stirring up a hornets' nest and then leaving you to deal with the angry spirits. Bad human beings that treated ghosts and the spirit world in general with a singular lack of respect. This was all entertainment to most of them.

Sure, occasionally, a tour guest would regale us with an interesting story. Everyone has a "ghost" story of one kind or another, but even true-blue witnesses have a hard time believing what they've seen themselves.

Back when Seven Sisters was open to the public, I led more than my share of tours. We were so proud of our work, so proud of Seven Sisters coming to life again. But inevitably we'd discover weird fetishes left behind under cushions and behind doors. Or the odd scrawling of graffiti, a half-burned candle, and even more disturbing things. No matter how hard we tried to corral guests and keep them out of the residence, it was nearly impossible to keep an eye out all the time.

Eventually, Carrie Jo put her size-seven foot down, and the tours came to an end. It was a smart move.

And now Heather, the owner of Marietta, wanted to open her historic home to the public. I hoped she knew what she was in for and had adequate staffing. Even though Marietta wasn't as large as Seven Sisters, it had a significant boneyard and other historic locations nearby.

Lots of bad things could happen if allowed.

I was sitting in the back seat. Ashland was driving, of course, and Carrie Jo had just finished a phone call with Detra Ann. Her other bestie decided against coming to Marietta even though CJ asked her to repeatedly. I got the feeling that Detra Ann wanted to step away from all things supernatural, but that wasn't going to be easily achieved.

No one who owned an antiques store would ever be completely free of the paranormal.

The three of us were only going to stay the weekend—at least this go-around. AJ was with Detra Ann, since he loved her daughter, Chloe, and Lily had gone to tennis camp. I was so proud of Lily. She was like the little sister I never had. It was amazing how intertwined all our families were. It was perfect except for me and Angus.

"What do you have for us, Rachel? I can tell you are champing at the bit to tell us what you know. Thanks for coming, by the way. It's like old times, isn't it?" Carrie Jo's pretty smile reminded me of the first time I met her. She was always so excited about life. CJ loved history as much as I did. Ashland did too. Maybe that's what made our friendship so tight. We were history and research nerds of the highest order.

"Yes! Hopefully not quite as terrifying, but I am excited about working with y'all. I did a recon last weekend—I was careful not to be detected. I managed to investigate the property without being noticed. I didn't go inside, though. I didn't want to spook Heather. From what I observed, there's a problem on the grounds. The energy is uniquely..." I struggled to find the right word. I didn't want to doom us with words like "evil" or "cursed," but that's how it felt. "It was not a welcoming energy; I'll put it that way."

Carrie Jo glanced at me in her visor mirror. "I agree." She wasn't smiling at all. "I saw something—in Mary's vision. Or dream. Gobsmacked, that's how it left me. So, the thing that molested Mary, what happened to Portia, it is not just symbolic. There is something on that property under the ground. Is that what you're saying?"

"Yes, that's what I believe. But why? And what?"

"In my latest dream, I was looking through Marietta's eyes. It was horrible, Rachel. She knew there was something here, and she contributed to its strength. She referred to it as the Beast. It was here on the property when her husband built the house. And even before that, or so Marietta believed. I can't even express how terrifying it was to witness how it appeared firsthand. Sometimes being a dream catcher really sucks." She shivered as she slowly recalled the details.

When she was done, it was my turn to shiver. "I can honestly say, I no longer want your gift. I don't know how you do it, Carrie Jo. I sense things, but I don't have flat-out visions, nor do I see ghosts like you do, Ashland. Well, not on the regular." I dug the folder out of my backpack. "Here it is. I dug up some interesting stuff that could fit with Marietta's experiences. Have either one of you ever heard of a grim?"

"You mean like the Grim Reaper? The guy with the sickle?" Ashland asked with a slight grin on his face.

I frowned at him as if to scold him for not taking this information seriously. "This particular grim is nothing like that. It's not a cartoon or a figment of someone's imagination. According to legend, this thing is deadly and dangerous. I can't understand why it would be terrorizing the living, though. According to my research, grims are found mostly in English and Scandinavian graveyards. When a new cemetery was established, the church or landowner would assign a protector. Usually a dog. A black dog—that's a grim. These black dogs were supposed to protect the dead from grave robbers, witches, warlocks, even the devil. A grim had great power. Here's the terrible part: the tradition was that the dog had to be buried alive under either the cornerstone of the church or the corner of the cemetery property. Unfortunately, settlers from those areas continued the practice when they moved to America. Even down here."

Carrie Jo half spun around in her seat as much as her seatbelt would allow her. "Are you kidding, Rachel? That's horrible. An actual living animal buried in the graveyard alive. I can't think of anything more heartbreaking. Wait. Are you saying that there is a grim on the Marietta property?"

"According to the records I found, yes. A grim was sanctioned by the church when Marietta was built. There was a small church on the property, but it is long gone, burned to the ground. You know that there were several houses on that land before Marietta was built. People had already been buried on the property before the Lancaster family moved in. And the Lancasters all met with foul ends. Even the Native Americans considered the land tainted."

The couple exchanged glances, and we rode in silence for a minute. Okay, it was a lot to take in. I gave them time to process it all. They didn't ask any questions, so I picked up my narrative.

"Anyway, more about the grim. The English settlers believed that when a new churchyard was opened, the first person buried there had to guard it against the devil. Sounds like a horrible assignment, huh? Since no human soul wanted to do the job or should be expected to spend eternity fighting evil, it was the grim's job. The Irish believed a little differently. They believed that the spirit of the person most recently buried in a churchyard had to protect the dead from evil until the next funeral. Then the newly buried would become the new guardian. They called this the Graveyard Watch. I don't know why I am telling you this—obviously, the Lancasters weren't Irish—but it is an interesting bit of history. Look at this church record. It's a rare find. It's from the chapel that used to be on the Marietta property. Luckily, the smaller churches had to send records of deaths and births to the basilica in Mobile. That's where I found this."

Carrie Jo studied the paper and handed it back to me. "Rachel, you've outdone yourself with this research. How on earth did you uncover all this?" she asked as she sipped her iced coffee. I didn't want to tell her, but I wasn't going to keep it to myself. No secrets between us. Honesty was the best policy.

"Okay. Full disclosure. The Brotherhood archives. They've got a library like you've never seen, but I had to request records. Or rather, the Brotherhood asked, and the basilica delivered. I could show you sometime if you're interested," I offered with a smile.

Carrie Jo smiled back at me in the mirror. "Maybe."

Ashland broke the silence that followed. "You know, I think I have heard of this practice. Grims aren't just dogs, right? I have heard of pigs and other livestock being buried but never dogs."

"That's right, Ashland. In Scandinavia, they often buried black pigs as protectors. But here in the south, it was most often a black dog. They have more than one in Mobile. You've probably seen them at Magnolia Cemetery. There's one in the old section, in a back corner. That black dog statue."

"Interesting and heartbreaking. I can't believe it. That's so sad." Carrie Jo slid her eyeglasses over her face. The sun was so bright now. At least the clouds had parted. It was nice to see the sun. It had been raining for days. "Here's a question: If it is a grim I saw, if that's what we're dealing with, why would it turn on the owners? Why would a guardian demand a sacrifice? And another thing, the image I saw in Marietta's mind didn't look like a dog. It was tall and had a humanoid shape to it."

I twisted my lips as I considered her question. "Um, well, there is more than enough evidence to suggest that before it was a church cemetery, it was a Native American burial ground. People have been burying people on that land for hundreds of years. I just wonder if that might be part of the conflict? Native American beliefs about the afterlife vary greatly from tribe to tribe, but many of the southern Native American tribes also believed in protectors for the dead. They could appear in different ways too."

"Really?" Ashland asked curiously. "I never thought of that."

"The Pascagoula and Biloxi tribes believed that after the souls of the dead passed into the spirit world, they could occasionally still communicate with the living through dreams or the intercession of medicine people. There is an interesting account written by a French officer about the Biloxi from the year 1730. Want to hear it?"

Carrie Jo turned again. "Ooh, read it."

"'The Pascagoula and the Biloxi tribes have curious thoughts about death and dying. They do not immediately inter their chief when he is dead. They dry his body in fire and smoke to make it like a mummified body or skeleton. After having reduced it to this condition, they bury the chief in the place occupied by his predecessor. As such, he is assigned the role of Protector of the Dead, also known as a Watcher. He will perform this role until the next chief takes his place. It is then that he can move on to enjoy peace with his fathers. Once his job is complete, they move the mummified chief and place him with the bodies of other chiefs in a sacred location, where they are arranged in succession on their feet like statues. There is no specific information about where the sacred location is, but it might be above ground or below it.'"

"Geesh. We might literally be talking about a spiritual conflict between this grim and a Native American protector. I can't even imagine what the atmosphere will be like at Marietta."

"I'm not through," I murmured as I flipped the page and continued reading. "It gets worse. 'Regarding the Watcher, he is buried with a long pole painted red. This is his medicine stick. In his other hand, he holds a war club or an ax, which he can use to defend the other buried chiefs, their wives, and their children, if required. The living or the dead. It is said he can use these magical items to attack any who dare attempt to pillage the sacred land.'"

Traffic forced us to creep along Beach Boulevard. I took a moment to enjoy the beach scenery.

"Whatever happened to the Biloxi tribe? I admit I don't know much about the local Native American tribes, but I am very interested," Ashland said as he adjusted his rearview mirror.

"A smallpox epidemic nearly took the Biloxi tribe out. They left the land and went to join their brethren to the north, the Tunica. But they have many burial mounds in the south Mississippi and south Alabama regions."

"I guess this adds to the mystery, right?" Ashland declared as he eased the car into the right lane. We'd arrive at the house soon. I was glad we'd be staying there. It was nice of Heather to open the place back up to the Stuarts and me. Really nice.

"Is it the grim? A Biloxi chief? Something else? I don't know. I can find no records of a grim going rogue, or one demanding blood, but there's a first time for everything, I suppose. There are no headstones, no markers in that graveyard. No evidence of a grim statue. I wonder if it is in the wooded section. Maybe we should check that out?"

Carrie Jo shook her head. "It is so strange. Heather referred to that area as a boneyard, not a graveyard. So did Marietta. There's no crypt that I know of. No mausoleum, no headstones. Nothing to mark any resting places. It's just a wide-open clearing with trees surrounding it. It was the same back in Mary's time. Crazy, huh?"

"Maybe it's underground?" I suggested as I flipped through the folder again.

"This close to the coast?" Ashland commented with clear disbelief. "The water table wouldn't allow that kind of construction. Would it?" He glanced at Carrie Jo, who peered at him over her sunglasses.

"Anything is possible, babe. As if you needed to be reminded of that."

He grinned back at her. They were so cute together. They were always so happy, even when they weren't quite getting along. Talk about soulmates. I didn't want to feel jealous, but I sure wished for that very thing myself. What must that feel like, to be yourself with someone and not scare the hell out of them? I wouldn't want to spend my life being a pretend version of myself—and let's face it, I am into the weirdest stuff. Not many men want to talk about death rituals or crystal skulls. I almost had that once with Angus. For a short time. In the end, none of it was real.

Nope, I wasn't going to think of Angus. Backstabbing cheater. At least Chip had moved on and wasn't ringing my doorbell anymore. Nope. Not today. That would totally ruin my good mood. *Goodbye, losers!*

I shrugged my shoulders. "It was just a guess. I'm sure we'll find something this weekend. Ooh, there it is. It's such a lovely place. Why are such beautiful houses always so haunted? Why do we love them so much?"

"Well, when you inherit one, you do what you have to. I can't speak for you, though," Ashland joked as his blinker began tapping. He turned off the boulevard, and we headed toward the house.

"Okay, you got me." I couldn't help but laugh.

It was true that Ashland's family home, Seven Sisters, had been extremely haunted. That house had a long and twisted history. What would we find at Marietta? Secret rooms and hidden staircases? Although I had a map of the interior of the home, I was eager to check the place out in person. Maybe take some readings and some measurements. Historic homes as old as Marietta often had hidden rooms. And underground ones. Despite Ashland's reticence to believe there could be an underground room, I wasn't ruling the possibility out yet.

A woman waved at us from the porch; that must be Heather. As soon as we parked the car, lightning popped over us. "Geez Louise! Where did that come from?" Carrie Jo exclaimed as she waved back at Heather.

Ashland parked the car. "I guess we better run for it. I see storm clouds rolling in off the ocean. Looks like it might settle in for a while. You guys go ahead. I'll grab the luggage."

"Thanks, Ashland." I grabbed my backpack and hurried out of the car. A blanket of humid, clammy air met me. Yeah, the air was shifting. Storm fronts were colliding, and not just meteorologically. I sensed the spiritual world swelling up around us. I smelled the electricity in the air. That was kind of my secret power.

I could smell blood long after it had been spilled. I could smell spirits. I know, that's weird, but it was true. Good ones, bad ones. Indifferent ones.

MARIETTA

Yep, I could smell danger, and I smelled it here at Marietta despite Heather's smiling face and the beautiful surroundings. Oh, yeah. I could smell death and a strangeness that I couldn't identify. And it was coming for us.

Chapter Three—Mary

My baby cried for me. A pitiful sound, one that spoke to the depths of my heart. I slipped in and out of consciousness during the birth. Each time I woke, the pain was more intense. The agony of childbirth overwhelmed me. Where was John Lamar? The baby was supposed to bring us together. Yes, even now, as I hung between life and death, I knew that if John Lamar wanted another child, I would not refuse him. Despite his recent chilliness toward me.

Where was my husband? He'd been gone for far too long. Didn't he realize that our baby was coming? Where could he be?

I needed to see my child, see the baby's face, but there was no one in the room. My heart sank, and I couldn't help but think the worst. The worst possible scenarios played out in my mind. My abdomen swollen, my thighs bloody, I struggled to sit up.

"Mrs. Lancaster...the baby. Where's my baby?" My eyes fluttered as they tried to focus. My bedroom was dank and dark; it smelled like sweat and blood. The rocking chair was turned upside down, the dresser turned at a weird angle, the door wide open.

I shouted again, "Please, Mrs. Lancaster!"

Somewhere in the house, I could hear my baby crying. It had to be my baby. I could hear Mrs. Lancaster singing; I knew her voice. She often hummed and sang as she sewed her embroidery pieces or when we strolled in the garden. Yes, I knew her voice. The sounds of the baby and Mrs. Lancaster began to fade, as if they were leaving the house.

Leaving Marietta! My own sweet child! What was she going to do to him? Give him to the fomoire?

Yes, it had to be a boy, my baby boy! I'd dreamed about him long before he arrived. The crying grew more faint, as if he were going further away. Mrs. Lancaster was taking him away from the house, away from me. What could she be doing?

Oh, God! No!

My damp nightgown clung to me, but I was determined to see. From my window I would be able to see the boneyard, to see the horrible place I'd worked so hard to avoid these past many months. The evil spirit was out there, and it waited for me, for my son. It had claimed Portia and her baby. It had claimed many others, I knew, but it wasn't going to claim my son!

"No! Marietta! He's your grandson! You cannot do it!" I shouted toward the open window; the curtains hung torn and twisted. What had happened in here? I couldn't understand any of this. The baby continued to cry. I slid out of my bed and landed on the floor with a thump, the sheets twisted around my legs. I was a bloody mess, and my legs shook from the blood loss, but I had to gain my strength. No way could I make it down the stairs, but I could crawl to the window. I could certainly do that for my son.

"Marietta! No! Please don't! Mrs. Lancaster!" I begged as I sobbed. My sweet child didn't deserve to be born into such an evil family. I long planned to leave this place. John Lamar would understand. He wanted to leave, too. I knew it in my heart!

My tears fell, and my heart broke in my chest. All the struggle, all the prayers. Had it all been for naught? I'd done everything she wanted, everything Marietta instructed. I loved John Lamar with all my heart, with all my body. But in the end, he had let me down and our child too.

I smelled rain in the air, and the floor under the window was wet. Had it rained? I couldn't remember. My pale hands slapped the wet floor as I pulled myself to the wall. My legs were not cooperating, and with every move, I felt another surge of warm blood. Despite my fear, a strange strength rose within me.

I must see. I must see for myself where she was going.

"Marietta! Don't take my baby to him! He is innocent!"

I heard the door swing open. "Mary! What are you doing on the floor?" Marietta's voice came from behind me. I twisted around, my back against the wall, the window above me. This didn't make sense. I heard the baby crying outside, with Marietta crooning over him. But that wasn't right, because Marietta was standing over me now.

She squatted down beside me, an expression of concern on her face. What was happening? Had I passed into a world of insanity? Could childbirth drive a woman crazy? I was so weak and Marietta so strong that she easily lifted me from the floor and placed me back in my bed. She wadded up the bloody sheets and threw them in the corner of the room as she called for someone to fetch them. Marietta reached for a freshly folded blanket, which she must've brought in with her. It smelled clean and fresh, like sunshine and green grass.

"Where's the baby? Listen! I can hear my baby crying now. Can't you hear the baby crying? Don't keep him from me!" Even as I begged, the crying did indeed get louder. Horrible, pitiful weeping. The poor child needed his mother. He needed me! "Please, Marietta! Have mercy. Bring me my child. Don't let it get him!"

Marietta kept her face a mask, an unmoving and unemotional mask. "What are you talking about? Your baby is asleep, Mary. I will bring him to you after we clean you up. You are a mess. What were you thinking crawling across the floor?"

Despite her peaceful words, I continued to hear a baby crying pitifully. How could she say she did not hear the terrible crying? Marietta Lancaster's calm expression did not bring me peace. It was a skill she had, one that I admired at times. One never knew what her thoughts were when she took on this look, this emotionless, blank expression.

Mary Fairbanks, the real Mary Fairbanks, once said the same about me. "You don't fool me, Vienna. I see the deep waters in you. Those eyes betray you." No doubt Marietta was far more intelligent than I would ever be. In an unpleasant way. I too committed crimes, things I would forever regret, but I never trucked with evil. Not like Marietta Lancaster. Not in such a direct way, and what was hidden here at Marietta was pure evil. I still did not understand it.

"Bring me my son! I have to see him!"

"There, there, Mary. What are you squalling about? Sally will bring the baby to you in just a moment. She's cleaning him up. We must protect him, you know. I prepared oils for him. For his skin, to keep away any evil. You would do well to tend to your own self. Look at you—you are a mess, daughter-in-law. The doctor will be here soon. I suppose the unpredictable weather has kept him away. If you don't stay in bed, this bleeding will not stop. Women do bleed to death, Mary. Then who will take care of the baby? It's easy enough to find a wet nurse, but a child needs his mother. Stay abed and let us care for you."

I did not have the heart or the energy to fight with her, but the tears flowed easily down my cheeks. All I could think about was my baby, Jason. My brothers were far away and my dear mother dead all these years. But the brother I loved most, Jason, he would be honored by this gesture if he knew. I would never find my way home again, never see Ireland, but at least in this, I would feel comfort. Jason would be my family, not these strangers. Not these strange Lancasters. If my husband refused to leave, I would do it myself, for Jason's sake and for mine.

In the distance, I heard a baby shrieking, an inconsolable pleading for his mother. It had to be my child. Was there another infant here at Marietta? As I clenched my fists and prepared to fight with my mother-in-law, Sally appeared with a carefully wrapped bundle in her arms. Could it be true? Was this my child, safe and sound?

"Jason?"

"Ah, what a good name. It sounds strong, Mary. I like it." Marietta sat on the side of the bed as I tucked back the blankets to view my son's face. He was perfect with soft blond hair, like a baby duck. I kissed his head and couldn't fight back the tears. Only these were tears of joy.

Outside my window, toward that horrible place where *it* waited, the thing that had molested me all those months ago, the cries echoed. An infant's cry was unlike any other. Not a child, not an adult, and certainly no animal.

This was a baby in distress. If not mine, then whose?

Don't let this be a trick. Don't let this be anything but my child.

Sally left us alone after packing towels between my legs. Settling against the pillow, I looked down at my sleeping son and breathed a sigh of relief. Yes, he was ours. He was so like his father. Slightly upturned nose, the noble bridge between his eyebrows, tufts of white-blond hair. He was like a luminous angel, a cherub sent from on high.

Yet the cries of the other infant outside stirred my soul. I couldn't bring myself to ask Marietta the truth. Did I want to know?

Holding my sleeping child, I could do nothing but stare down at his perfect pink lips, examine every inch of his lovely face. Despite my joy, the yells of the infant continued. My mother-in-law offered no explanation and continued to wear her blank expression, which revealed nothing. Whatever was happening outside, I would never know. Did I want to?

"Marietta..." I whispered the beginning of my question, but the screams suddenly stopped. Whatever happened, whatever had occurred, it was over.

Whatever evil had happened, whatever exchange had been made, it was done. Marietta walked soberly to the window and closed it and the curtains. She carefully repositioned the chair and shoved the dresser back against the wall. It was all over now.

All of it.

I could not cry. I could not feel anything. Without a word, Marietta left the room and closed the door behind her.

It was then that I decided, come what may, we would certainly leave this horrible place. With or without John, we would flee Marietta, both the house and the woman, and her wretched curse.

I whispered this promise to my sleeping child as I held him. Such a peaceful moment, such a wonderful time, to finally be a mother. Except this bloody stain. To think my son would be the cause of such an evil act. This child was all I ever wanted. No home, no matter how fine, was worth all this. Now, because of my child, I had to make tough decisions. The evil here would not be stopped—it would not relent. But I would not allow it to take my child. Not my own little Jason.

Jason Owen Lancaster.

That would be his true name, but when we fled, I would have to think of another. We would have to hide our identities, for Marietta Lancaster would not easily let us go. Even though it could mean death for her own grandson. Hadn't Portia's baby also been her grandson? She couldn't or wouldn't protect him.

I knew the truth of it. I knew that my husband and Portia had been lovers, continued to be lovers until her disappearance. Until her murder. No, Marietta would not easily let me go, but John Lamar must be made to understand. I would tell him everything, and he would see that we needed to go. We must leave to protect the baby. Our future was not here.

Sometime in the night, before the moon was full, I heard the loud wailing again. Not a child this time but a woman. I couldn't make out much more. Yes, it was an argument between a man and a woman. I heard a man's voice! As she wept for all her worth—it had to be Marietta—a man's footsteps came up the steps.

Sturdy and steady, he walked up all thirteen steps and then came to the door of my room, where he paused.

As I clutched the baby, perhaps a little too tightly, Jason began to fuss. My room had no light, not a lamp, not a hint of moonlight. Nothing but blackness. As the door creaked open, I discerned a figure, a man's shape. He was holding a lamp and carrying a bag.

"John Lamar?"

He hesitated as I stared at the black silhouette. Who was this? Could this be the fomoire taking on a human shape? He stepped into the room, and I got a better look at him. This was no Celtic demon, no being from the Underworld. Dr. Morris! He had visited me a few times during my pregnancy. Marietta continued to cry downstairs; I could hear Sally crying too. Something was terribly wrong, terribly amiss.

"I have bad news, Mrs. Lancaster. Very bad news, ma'am. It is the reason why I could not be present for the birth of your son. I am happy that you are safely delivered." He put the lamp on the table by the door but did not come closer. He cleared his throat as he clutched his bag.

"What is it, doctor?" I licked my dry lips. I was powerfully thirsty suddenly, extremely thirsty. My mouth felt full of sand, my tongue thick. "May I have some water?" He obliged me by pouring a glass of water from the pitcher. I sipped the water but couldn't avoid looking at his sad, defeated face.

"Your husband has died, Mrs. Lancaster. I found him dead on the road just a few hours ago. I am sorry, ma'am. I tried to revive him, but he was dead. I am sorry to report this sad news on what should be a joyous occasion."

I shook my head in disbelief. "I don't believe you. My husband is a healthy man. I would know if he were sick. I would know that. He is not dead, doctor. I think you are mistaken."

He patted my hand kindly as he sat on the bed next to me. "I am not mistaken, ma'am. I have known John Lamar all his life. I helped deliver him, you see. Unfortunately, death is not predictable. A man can be perfectly healthy, then be struck down with no warning. My condolences to you, Mrs. Lancaster. At least you have your son. Perhaps that will bring you comfort."

At least I have my son.

Those words caught in my mind, in my throat. My mind collapsed in on me. How to process this? Could I believe this was accurate? *No. It's not true.* I whispered it again and again, but my mother-in-law's weeping testified to the horrible truth. The nursemaid came to feed Jason, and the doctor left me alone after prescribing a tonic to soothe my grief.

At least I have my son. My poor son. He would never know his father. He would never see him or be held by him. *At least I have my son...*

Suddenly, a strange fury I hadn't expected rose within me. Yes, I had my son, and I would keep him alive and safe, no matter what I had to do. The sorrow of losing John Lamar was real, visceral, but my maternal instincts overrode my grief. If I didn't leave here, Jason would die too. Marietta may well be willing to sacrifice her children to the fomoire, but I was not. Not mine or anyone else's.

I had not made any deals with the devil. I would not lose a single child to appease the thing that lived in the boneyard.

Never.

At least I have my son.

Eventually, I fell asleep. When I woke from time to time, I heard Marietta crying. At least she had remorse for John Lamar's death. I couldn't help but believe that this was entirely her fault—the woman who trucked with devils, who offered up innocent sacrifices to the evil one. Her machinations led me here, led me to love and lose John Lamar. Led me—and my son—into danger of a sort I could not yet fully perceive.

I was determined to get stronger. Day by day. I would be strong and smart for Jason.

We would leave this evil place behind quickly. Perhaps we would go back to Ireland after all. These past months, I managed to squirrel away a sum of money. Enough to take us far away and live without worry for at least a year. Maybe not Ireland. Maybe somewhere else here in America. I had enough to take us far, far away.

I woke in the late morning, my heart breaking again as I recalled the loss of my husband. He had never genuinely loved me, not like I hoped and desired, but I had loved him with all my being. With all my soul. Despite this sad truth, I could not bring myself to cry for him. As I struggled to cope with the horrible reality, I caught sight of a strange silvery shimmer in the corner of the room. The outline of a man, or possibly a woman. Only an outline, though.

Was I still dreaming?

No. That couldn't be right. I pinched myself and knew that I was wide awake. Who was my unwanted visitor? I blinked again and again; I even covered my face with a blanket like a child, but when I pulled the quilt away, the shimmery figure remained.

Fear like I had never felt before crawled up my body, from my feet to my arms and finally to my neck.

"Hello?" I managed to ask through my dry lips. "I see you. Who are you?"

For a moment, the shimmery outline took on color, a clearer shape. This was a woman in strange clothing, with a face I did not recognize. Many of her features were impossible to see, but she had a head full of brown curls, loose and unbound, like a young girl's. And then she was gone, as quickly as she had appeared.

As she vanished, she took all the warmth in the room with her. Had I just seen a ghost? Perhaps the mother of the child who left the world so mercilessly just last night?

What was happening here at Marietta?

"Jason," I cried in the dark. "Jason!" I called even louder until Sally came to check on me. I did not have a maid of my own, even though Marietta suggested I take on one. It did not feel appropriate to do so. Who was I to have a servant or a slave? No one. Just a poor immigrant from Ireland.

"Please, bring me the baby."

She paused and did not immediately go to do my bidding. She would never hesitate for Marietta. "He is sleeping, ma'am. Shirley laid him down only a few minutes ago. He is a hungry baby."

"Bring me my son, Sally, or I swear I will crawl out of this room to find him."

With a bob of her head and a disapproving look, she left me alone and soon returned with my sleeping child. I held him and kept my eyes on the corner of the room until I too finally fell asleep.

Thankfully, I did not dream.

Chapter Four—Carrie Jo

My first night at Marietta, this go-around, was quite revealing. I woke up awash with Mary's feelings. Her fear, her sadness, and more than anything, her pain. To make matters even weirder, for the first time ever, I think she saw me.

And I felt my own baby move!

I wasn't that far along, only four months, but I'd been pregnant before. I knew what a baby bounce felt like. Was my child seeing visions? Was that the reason for this early movement? Surely babies didn't comprehend this sort of thing. I hoped not. Things here at Marietta were far too scary for a baby. Yeah, just thinking about it gave me the shivers.

Maybe this wasn't the best idea after all. Way to go, Carrie Jo.

"Ashland?" I whispered as my hand went to my stomach. I couldn't wait to tell him the news, but he wasn't in the room. Marietta was only one floor, but it was a large, rambling house. Many bedrooms, lots of nooks and crannies. I quickly got dressed and found Rachel and Ashland on the side porch, the one closest to the boneyard. Rachel was scribbling in her leather-bound journal while Ashland strolled the porch with his phone to his ear. From what I could hear, he was talking to Lily. Even though he didn't have her on speakerphone, she was so excited that I could hear her without technology's help. That made my heart happy. Just a year ago, I would never have imagined Lily leaving the house for a sleepover, much less tennis camp.

"Is Aunt CJ around?"

Ashland glanced up and spotted me, a big grin on his face. Man, how was it that I was still so in love with him?

Ashland Stuart. His beautiful soul and handsome face still made my heart skip a beat.

Pinch me. Is my life real?

"Yes, she's right here. Good morning, babe. It's Lily."

He kissed me, and I took a seat beside Rachel on the wicker couch. The cushions were wonderfully comfortable. Ooh, was that orange juice? The thirstiness that Mary experienced after childbirth stayed with me. As if he read my mind, Ash poured me a glass, and I drank half of it without much effort.

"Hey, Lily! How is tennis camp? Is your cabinmate nice?"

"Yes, she is, and I like camp," she answered with an excitement that I hadn't expected. It was touch and go before she left. Lily went back and forth at first. Should she go? Should she stay? Eventually, she decided this was what she wanted, and I was so proud of her for stepping outside of her comfort zone.

"It's a lot of work, but I've got this. My backhand is smooth, or so Coach Rice tells me. She is a powerhouse. If I can get to be as good as her, I'll be happy."

I smiled at hearing her enthusiasm. "I'm glad you're getting to rub shoulders with her. Coach Rice is a legend, or at least that's what Uncle Ashland says. He knows everyone in the sports world. What else is new? Making lots of friends, Lil?"

"Here's the thing. Um. Yes, I met a friend, Aunt Carrie Jo." Her giant pause at the end of that declaration hinted that there was more to this story. Lots more. Did I want to know? Of course I did. Someone needed to look out for her. If not her uncle and me, then who?

"Met? A guy friend?" I asked, trying to keep my game face in place. It wouldn't pay to sound too enthusiastic. Teenagers hated that. Or at least ours did. Lily was now fourteen going on thirty. She was always calm, cool and collected, at least in most situations. "Tell me about him." I slapped Rachel's arm with my eyes and mouth open. Luckily, she'd stopped scribbling in her book.

"Ouch," she whispered, but she was clearly interested in what we were talking about. I mouthed the word "boyfriend" to her, but she had no idea what I was saying. Ashland wasn't paying attention, thankfully. He was on his laptop, presumably checking out more historical records about this place.

Lily whispered into the phone, "Yeah, he's a guy. I have a guy friend."

"That's wonderful, Lily. Is he your boyfriend? Is that what you're saying?" Ashland glanced up. Okay, he too was clearly interested in this tidbit of information.

"Not really. Um, but he's different."

"Different? Different how? Is he older?" I had a sinking feeling in the pit of my stomach. The hairs on the back of my neck were standing up, too. I'd managed to pull my hair up in a sloppy ponytail this morning, but that's about all at this point.

"Are you alone? I don't want Uncle Ashland to hear this," she asked in a whisper as I clamped my lips shut. I couldn't lie to her.

"Um, no. Should I be? What's going on, Lily?" I left the glass on the table and waved Ashland away. He clearly didn't mind eavesdropping on our conversation, but I couldn't allow that. "Okay, I am alone now. No one can hear us. What do you need to tell me?" Chills rushed up my arms.

Lily cleared her throat; it was a nervous tic, a sure tell that she was uncertain or unhappy about something.

"Lily, whatever it is, you can tell me. What do you mean, he's different? Let's start with that," I said, trying to sound cheerful and patient. "Is he an exchange student?" That was a dumb question, but I couldn't think of what would qualify as "different" in a boyfriend for my niece.

She sighed and cleared her throat again. "He's not really a boyfriend. Just a friend, but I like him. I don't want you to freak out. Okay?"

I paused inside the front room and stood in front of one of the mirrors. Strange that they would put two mirrors across from one another. Really strange. They were huge, massive mirrors too.

"I'm here, not freaking out." I slapped a big smile on my face. It was true, people can hear smiles. I really wanted her to trust me.

"Okay, good. Well, I first met him in the Moonlight Garden. It was right before I left. His name is Mitchell. But he is here at camp too. I thought I wouldn't see him again, but he's here."

Lily stopped talking for a moment. I didn't know what to do, press her harder or wait for her confession.

"He was a visitor at Seven Sisters? We haven't had tours in months. Was he trespassing?" Lily cleared her throat and gave me a frustrated sigh. Then the silence was deafening. "What is it about Mitchell, Lily? Is there something I should know? You said he was different."

Lily sounded flat-out exasperated at my questions now. "Nothing. I just wanted to tell you about him."

I didn't "speak teenager," not like Ashland, who was a natural at it, but even I knew she was lying to me. She changed her mind about what she was going to tell me. Dang! I was no good at being an aunt.

"Um, okay." *Be cool. Don't make a big deal out of the fact some kid was hanging around our house and Lily never mentioned it to you.* "Well, that's good, I guess. He's at tennis camp too, huh? What a coincidence. Will we get to meet him?"

"Maybe. I'm not sure. I just wanted to tell you about him. Uh-oh, I've got to go. Coach Rice is calling me. I'll call later. Probably tomorrow. Bye, Aunt CJ."

"Bye, Lily." She hung up the phone, and I moseyed back to the porch shaking my head. The odd, creepy feeling stayed with me.

"What was that about?" Rachel asked curiously. "Does Lily want to come home? I hope not. She's talented, a natural athlete. I'd hate to see her quit before she really gave it a shot."

I shook my head. "No. She's not quitting. In fact, she sounds like she's having fun."

Ashland crossed his arms as he studied my face. "And? What about this boyfriend?"

"You heard that, huh? His name is Mitchell, and she says he's a friend. Not a boyfriend. What's the game plan for today, guys?" I didn't know why, but I didn't tell Ashland that she'd met Mitchell at Seven Sisters before she left. There needed to be a level of trust between us two girls. Aunt and niece. Some things her uncle didn't need to know. Not yet.

Ashland held my hand sweetly. "You aren't going to tell me what's happening with Lily?" my husband asked with genuine suspicion and disappointment.

"Girl stuff. I am sworn to secrecy," I lied calmly. "Actually, she clammed up on me. Whatever she was going to tell me, she didn't." I didn't like telling bald-faced lies, but I knew Lily wouldn't approve since she asked me to step out of the room. That part I wasn't making up—she asked for privacy, and I was obliged to give it to her. Maybe I'd tell him later once I figured out what the deal was with Mitchell.

Should I peek into her dreams? No, I didn't dare. What if by doing so I opened a door for her to walk into mine? That would not be good since I was here at Marietta. How could I protect her from the ghosts of Marietta, the fomoire or whatever lurked in the boneyard? I wasn't sure what was out there yet, but it was nothing good. Not at all.

Rachel closed her journal and finished her coffee. "Fine. Be mysterious. Teenagers. Any dreams, Carrie Jo? Have you seen anything?"

"Actually, yes." I sat down at the table again as Rachel broke out her pen and notebook. "Mary presented herself to me. I got to experience the childbirth—she had a son, you know. That was not enjoyable at all. It made my own baby jump." Ashland flashed a concerned glance in my direction. "We're both fine. But what I saw, it was terrifying."

For the next half hour, I shared everything I witnessed. From the information I gathered about the Beast in the boneyard to the end, when I suspected Mary may have seen me, I shared it all. Could I have been the silvery silhouette she saw? If so, that could present a problem. It was bad luck to involve myself in past events. I'd done it before with terrible results.

I did my best to answer their questions, but I didn't see as much as I would have liked. Mary's knowledge, at this point in the timeline, was much more limited than Marietta's. I hoped to connect with the older woman again. She knew more than anyone else. Knew about the Beast, knew about the family history. I needed to see through her eyes, but so far, I had not been successful at peeking into her past. Maybe I'd try again later.

Ashland tapped the table thoughtfully. "It's my turn, Carrie Jo. I'm dying to get into that boneyard. I've only seen residual spirits in the house, but they could be hiding from me. For some reason, they are collecting outside the house. It's like they're afraid to come inside."

"Afraid of us?" Rachel asked as she tucked her dark hair behind her ear. "Why would they be afraid of us?"

Ashland narrowed his eyes as he considered her question. "I don't think it's so much that they are afraid of us as they are being collected. Literally collected. Pulled toward the boneyard. Maybe the fomoire—or, as Carrie Jo put it, the Beast—needs energy, so he's using the spirits here. I've heard of this before. You remember the maelstrom of the Leaf Academy. Midas and his group encountered one. A strong spirit that captures and harnesses the power of those it ensnares. Maybe it's like that."

I shivered at the reminder. Ashland didn't mention that the maelstrom spirit killed a woman, and that the horrible death shook up Midas Demopolis so badly that he quit paranormal investigation altogether.

Then he shook his head. "Don't get alarmed, guys. Not yet. I'm not certain, just guessing. I need to walk outside and see who is willing to talk with me."

Rachel got up and cracked her fingers as if she were itching for a fight. "Great. Let me grab my camera and I'll be ready. Let's make use of the daylight. I'll set up IR cameras around the house and property tonight and see what we capture."

I raised an eyebrow at her but didn't object. When did we become a paranormal investigation team? I never thought my feet would carry me down this path when I graduated from college.

We'd been doing this a while, only without equipment. Previously, we'd only used my dreams, my dream walks and Ashland's ghost sightings.

Well, I guess it was time for an upgrade if we were going to do this thing right. This was what I wanted, right?

"I need my shoes. Be right back, Ashland."

Despite what I'd seen in my dreams, I was truly excited. Besides being a mother and a wife, a historian and researcher and dream catcher, I was now a paranormal investigator.

This was my true calling. And I was going to see it through.

Chapter Five—Ashland

Unlike my wife, it wasn't easy for me to connect with the dead. It took willpower and, at times, blind luck. I'd spent half my life denying my gift. At times, it remained awkward when I embraced it. Chances are, if I hadn't met Carrie Jo, I'd still be pretending that I didn't see dead people. Embracing my ability cost me a few friends, made me the target of a few jokes, but it was worth it.

It was worth my sanity. I did feel more grounded nowadays. Happier. More fulfilled as a person. As a wise man once said, "Being yourself is the best person to be." Who said that? I couldn't remember, but those words comforted me.

Out of respect for the dead I hoped to encounter, I stepped quietly as the three of us walked out to the boneyard. Strange to call it that. Why not a cemetery or a graveyard? Why were there no headstones or tombstones out here? Imagine burying someone without leaving a marker? How had that started? We needed to find out why and how.

Glancing back at the house, I thought again that Marietta had lovely bones. A beautiful house with the view of a lifetime, the Gulf of Mexico. To think that this house remained standing throughout hurricanes, tropical storms, and the like. Sure, part of it had to be rebuilt after Katrina, but even that monster hurricane couldn't take out the grand old home. Besides being a residence for the Lancaster family and the family before that—their name slipped my mind now—it had also been used as a military barracks during the Civil War, and another portion of the property had been the location of a military hospital.

No wonder so many soldiers walked the grounds. I sensed their presence now. Their thoughts were redundant.

Reporting for duty.

Must clean my gun.

I miss my wife.

We paused outside the boneyard, Rachel with her equipment, Carrie Jo with her eyes glistening, seeing the other world in another time. For some reason, I couldn't shake the feeling that someone was watching us from the house. I glanced back at Marietta once more and thought I saw a curtain move. Was someone inside, hoping we would stay away? Maybe it was a trick of the eyes. An air-conditioning vent could move a curtain.

No, it was not merely a feeling. A strange uneasiness hit me like a semitruck, so much so that I made an "oof" sound. Carrie Jo followed my gaze but like me stood quietly, saying nothing for a few minutes. Finally, she asked, "What is it, babe?"

"Energy. An uneasy feeling. Very strong. I can't see anyone yet, but I hear the voices of soldiers. Let's get started, Carrie Jo. Good Lord." I nearly bent double as she touched my shoulder. "It's like electricity—this is a powerful place. Really powerful. How far away from the house would you say this was? Two acres?"

"At least that. It's a bit away. You lead the way, Ashland. We will follow your lead. Rachel is going to take pictures. I'm going to walk with you. I'll be right here if you need me."

I squeezed her hand and released it. My skin tingled; my eyes burned slightly. This always happened when there were multiple spirits around. I didn't detect anything ominous. No rogue grim, hellhound or elemental.

But suddenly I saw plenty of ghosts. The further I walked into the boneyard, the more I could see.

The wandering dead hadn't noticed me yet as they floated, stomped and scurried back and forth. Most were coming from the wooded lot behind the cemetery. I had to close my eyes for a few seconds to adjust to the strangeness of it all. The dead were from different time periods. I opened my eyes and took slow, even breaths to steady myself.

I saw a man in tan pants, a dirty white shirt, suspenders, and a simple black hat. If I had to guess, I would say he was from the pioneer era. As if he heard me appraising him, he slowed his walk and raised a lantern as if he were peering at me through the darkness. It wasn't dark yet, more like twilight, but this place already had loads of activity.

Activity like I have never seen.

A young girl followed the lantern man. I couldn't see her face, only a worn cotton dress and an oversized bonnet. They disappeared back into the foliage while two Native American women emerged with baskets full of food in their hands. They saw me too but immediately vanished before my eyes. They were startled, clearly unhappy that I could see them, but I had no chance to speak with them. Would they have even understood me? I wasn't sure they would understand my language.

Rachel's camera snapped photo after photo. It was a bit distracting, so I walked the other way, more to the west while she went east. Carrie Jo hung out in the middle and gave me some space. I needed it so I could focus on my ghostly surroundings. I needed answers for what was going on here, and who better to ask than the ghosts themselves? They'd seen everything for so long.

They were witnesses to the good and the evil here at Marietta.

A soldier dressed in Confederate garb stared at me, apparently surprised that I saw him. He stepped toward me, and despite wanting to run as fast as I could in the other direction, I held my ground. Yeah, my fight-or-flight sense warred against my intention. The soldier's worn boots, torn pants and ragged jacket were proof that he'd been in battle. Or something. Was he buried here too, hidden away in an unmarked grave?

"Hello. My name is Ashland. What's your name?"

He opened his mouth, but instead of answering me, only an empty scream emerged. His eyes turned black, and his mouth opened wide. Too wide! It became a yawning cave of anger, and a scream blasted from his dead lungs as he launched himself at me. Yeah, I could hear it now. The soldier blew through me as quickly as any stormy wind. As he surged through my body, the end of his life played in my mind.

Private Hollis Murphy.

Drowned in his foxhole.

Shot and bleeding, left behind by his own brothers in arms. He couldn't even be sure who shot him. A Yankee invader or one of his own? The battle had not been a good one. Mass confusion with blasts firing all around them until one struck him like an angry hornet.

In the forehead, but it did not kill him immediately.

No. He drowned in muddy water, abandoned and lost.

Why he had presented himself in such a hostile way, I couldn't say, but I finally managed to speak to him. "You are dead, Private Murphy. I'm sorry about what happened to you. It is time to move on, soldier. Your time here has ended."

The dead soldier didn't reappear, and I felt him nowhere around me.

Like many lost souls, all he needed was to relay his story to someone who would listen. After the restless dead shared what they needed to share, they usually left and presumably found their way to wherever it was they needed to go. Why was it like this? Why were some dead restless? Why didn't they all move into the afterlife smoothly? I couldn't say. Nor did I have any good theories on the subject. Not everyone who dies needs counseling. Not everyone who passes needs to tell their story, but I had met many who did.

Private Murphy had been one of those.

Carrie Jo was right beside me. We were both kneeling on the damp ground. I was trying to catch my breath, but CJ kept still and silent, obviously sensing that we were not alone.

Over the past few years, I mastered the art of opening myself up to the dead. Not to use my body—hell no to that—but I did open myself to hearing and seeing and experiencing. It's strange how we protect ourselves without thinking about it. Or at least I had before. Not listening, ignoring the sounds of crying, the whispers. Wrapping myself mentally with a shroud of steel that nothing could penetrate unless the ghost caught me off guard.

Now I did the opposite. I still visualized the protection, only now I pictured myself lowering those shields.

Here I am, in a graveyard, lowering my shields. Welcoming the dead to come to me.

And they saw me. They were all around me. Beneath me. What had I gotten myself into?

This was simply too much—there were too many of them.

As if she read my mind, my wife was there, her hand in mine, her soft voice in my ear. "I'm right here, Ashland. Let's do this one together."

How she got to me so quickly, how she knew I needed her, I didn't know, but I was so glad to feel her beside me. She stepped close, and the dead shifted in appearance. They were no longer angry, horrible things but people. People like me. Alive and walking normally. And then, as if someone switched off a light switch, they didn't appear to notice us at all.

Ah, so that's the difference between Carrie Jo and me. She sees the dead in her own way, but the dead don't see her. They aren't angry at her. They did not consider her an intruder into their realm. Not usually, anyway. Things got a bit screwed up when she attempted to interact with a dead young woman at Seven Sisters once, but that was all in the past.

Here we were, the two of us. Rachel was gone, probably left behind in the present while Carrie Jo and I walked into the past.

Yes, we were dream walking! That's why things had changed. I quietly breathed a sigh of relief as my wife took over the task of navigating the spirit world.

This indeed was a long time ago, before there was even a house or any structure at all. I saw the pioneer man again, the one in the black hat, the white shirt, and suspenders. But where was the little girl? I saw a wagon, and a lantern with a dull yellow light hung from the back. It was dark. This darkness was unlike any other I ever experienced. I could see no other lights, nothing to push back the darkness on the landscape. There were hardly any trees, no electrical lights or residences.

Just a man, his wife and their daughter in the wilderness.

He was working on a busted wagon wheel, softly swearing under his breath while his wife tried to comfort the whiny child. The image was beginning to fade, but I wanted to see more.

No, I needed to see more.

Carrie Jo must have been reading my mind. "Let me help you, Ashland. May I?"

"Yes, Carrie Jo. Of course. I'll follow your lead."

She squeezed my fingers and took a step ahead of me but did not let me go. We were fully stepping into the dream world, and there was no turning back.

No turning back at all.

Chapter Six—Adam Crossley

"Adam, we can't stay here. You heard the man at the fort. This place is evil; we shouldn't be here at all. You never listen to me, husband, and look at what's happened! What are we going to do?"

The man spat on the ground, which served to silence his fearful wife. "Not talk of evil, Jemima. I will not have that kind of talk around my daughter. We will stay here for the night and that's that. We can't abandon the wagon. What do you suggest? That we walk on foot back to the fort?"

The woman hurried to him and spoke in a low whisper. "No! But it's not safe here. Look around us. There is no protection, nothing but bones, Adam. The man at the fort warned us not to come this way! This place is..." She bit her lip, but Adam knew what she wanted to say. Evil. Everything was evil in Jemima's world. There was a devil around every corner. There was no more terrified woman in this wild country. Of that, he was sure.

Adam rose from the ground, the knees of his pants wet with mud. "I know what the man said, Jemima, but here we are with a busted wheel. Why do you have to be so damn superstitious?" He threw down his hammer as he towered over her. He would never hurt her but often used intimidation tactics to keep her in line. Jemima was one to believe that crows were a sign of death and that spilled salt meant certain catastrophe. The truth was, Adam did not intend to come this way, not at first. But after reviewing the worn map, and according to his figuring, passing through this desolate place would cut half a day off their travels.

"Don't you swear at me, Adam Crossley! I will not be spoken to like that!" Jemima sniffed and wiped at her nose with the back of her hand. Her bottom lip trembled and her voice broke. He suddenly felt softness for her. Despite her superstitious ways and all her fears, he loved his wife. Loved her so much that he wanted to build her a better life. A life away from all those that would hate them because they were black. A life that would let them love and live safely.

He touched her arm briefly to comfort her. He wasn't one for public displays of affection. Adam didn't know how to soothe her worries. No one had ever soothed his. He hadn't grown up in a loving home. His mother had no warmth in her, none for Adam. Only for his sister. After Audrey died, their mother had left him. Moved away and left him in the shack by himself. Until he married Jemima, he had nary a bit of softness in his life. He liked her softness but not the hysteria.

"Go back to the wagon and stay with Kitty. I'll have to find some way to repair this wheel in the morning when the light is better. I need a chuck; there's no getting around it. I may have to walk back to the fort." He sighed at the thought of walking all that way. No way could his family walk that far in any reasonable amount of time, and he didn't dare leave their wagon full of belongings unattended. Adam decided not to mention that tonight, though. That would only add fuel to the proverbial fire.

"Sleeping in a graveyard? Have you gone mad, husband?" Her eyes were wide as she took in the stick arrangements. Trace scents of decomposition hit him occasionally. He knew this place wasn't for the living, but he could not tell her that.

"Stop it, Jemima. We have no choice in the matter."

Strips of fabric fluttered in the late evening breeze. Pieces of cloaks and tunics and furs. Strands of leather and feathers. No doubt this land had long ago been claimed by the natives. He hadn't meant to linger here; he hadn't meant it at all. Still, he shivered as he argued with her.

I refuse to allow fear to prevent me from continuing this journey.

Adam sighed as he ignored his own fear and trepidation. His wife's fear was large enough for the both of them. Putting hers down made him feel braver.

"They are dead. Dead Indians, Jemima. What do you think they'll do to you?"

She set her mouth, her already thin lips disappearing. Her dark skin and luminous brown eyes shone despite the lack of light. "I am not sleeping in a graveyard, Adam Crossley. No matter what you say. Neither will our daughter. We need to leave this place."

"Where will we go, Jemima? The town is at least eight miles back." She didn't answer his question but began to cry. "There's nothing to worry about, Jemima. I will make the hike back as soon as the sun comes up. I'll hire a wagon to carry me back. With any luck, we will be back on the road before noon. Please, wife. It's just for the night. Just for one night. If it makes you any happier, we can camp away from the wagon. Over there, in the clearing."

Jemima's shoulders slumped. "We were supposed to be in Harmony Springs tonight. My cousin will be worried over us." She pouted as she crossed her arms and poked at the grass with the toe of her boot. A sure sign that she agreed with her husband's suggestions. She didn't like it, but it made sense to her. She wouldn't argue with him anymore. He quietly breathed a sigh of relief.

"Yes, and when we see Oda tomorrow, she will be glad to see us. I know this is not what we planned. None of it, Jemima, but this is our best option. Please, dear. Don't be fearful. You and Kitty find sticks for a fire. We will set up camp in that direction." Despite his uncomfortableness he hugged her, and she appeared to be appreciative of the comfort.

Adam kissed her forehead. "Listen closely; you can hear the ocean. I imagine it is just beyond that row of trees there." He was doing his best to remain calm and supportive, but he was worried as well. Not about the dead so much but about the living. Biloxi wasn't really a town, more like a collection of scattered houses and a sparse main street. A gambling town. Nothing more than a stopover between New Orleans and Mobile. At least they had food and drink, but sleeping outdoors with no defense? That was risky.

It would be better to stay with the wagon—in the wagon—but Jemima would not agree to that. He knew his wife well enough to know that. Kitty and Jemima set about gathering sticks before it got too dark. They would sleep just beyond the burial ground, off the property completely.

To be honest, Adam hadn't intended to lead the wagon through this strange property. But he'd closed his weary eyes for a minute, as he often did on long days in the wagon. The horses knew to move forward, to keep walking. They were good horses. Reliable animals.

Until tonight.

Brutus and Napoleon stomped and snorted, unhappy that they were presumably left behind. Yes, they were probably right. He shouldn't leave them here. Adam would remove their harnesses and stake them near the camp.

"Hush now, Napoleon. We aren't going to leave you behind." He patted the dappled gray and began unhooking the harness. As he struggled with the worn leather, he got an uneasy feeling as if he were being watched, and closely at that. Adam paused and glanced around him from beneath the lowered brim of his hat. He saw no one, and there was nowhere to hide.

Except that row of trees, a small swatch of forest between the burial ground and the ocean. Just beyond the clearing where they would be spending the night. About a hundred feet away, there was another tree line, but it was a cluster of young trees. Pines, mostly.

How could anyone be watching them? They hadn't seen anyone on the way, and there were no houses or shelters out in the wilderness. According to the man at the fort, there were no more natives living in this area. They all fled to the north, away from the whites who'd brought them smallpox.

As he worked with his horses, he occasionally peered into the growing darkness, but he saw no one. He continued his work and led the horses out of the sacred ground solemnly. Yes, this had been a terrible mistake, shutting his eyes, not paying attention to the horses' track. And then to make things worse, he had a busted wheel. How it busted, he couldn't say. He didn't see a thing, not a rock or any kind of obstruction that might have caused a break. The wagon had little wear; the wheels were new. It was unexplainable.

As he led the horses away, he glanced down again. No, there was nothing at all. Not even a bump in the road.

Well, you probably struck something a ways back. It just took a while to break the wheel. Yeah, that had to be it.

Goodness! He was getting as jumpy as Jemima.

His wife and daughter had gathered a conservative stick pile, but they'd need more before bed. Let them eat a meal and get settled first. Once they slept, he would scuttle around for more fuel. Adam planned on keeping his eyes open for as long as possible.

It didn't take long to get the fire going. Jemima and Kitty set about cooking a simple meal, and the smell of bacon had his stomach rumbling. That and some fry bread and he'd sleep like a baby.

Adam's own mother had been Cherokee, his father black. He had a great respect for the native races here in America, but he did not know much about them. Only a few songs, a few prayers. Nothing much. Why should he feel so on edge?

About the time the pots had been cleaned and the pallets made, with the stars twinkling above them, he heard a flute. Only four or five notes of a wooden flute. His grandfather used to play a similar instrument. It was the only music he knew. The sound so soft and gentle that he wondered if he heard it.

Until he saw his wife's face. No, when he witnessed Jemima's fearful expression, he knew he had indeed heard music.

"What was that, Daddy?" Kitty had already piled up on her blanket, her eyes closed, but she wasn't quite asleep yet. She whimpered to her father, but Jemima quickly settled her fears.

"It's alright, Kitty. The woods make strange sounds. Go to sleep now. Your papa is watching over us. Lay down and count the stars, darling. Count until you're sleepy." Jemima tucked the smaller quilt up around Kitty's neck and patted her softly.

"Yes, ma'am."

Adam reached under his pallet and pulled out his rifle. Kitty snuggled down as Jemima threw the last of the wood on the fire. It wasn't freezing tonight, but there was a chill in the air. Yes, he would have to get more wood to protect them from the cold and any wild animals. The couple did not speak, but Jemima refused to sleep without him.

For hours he sat next to his wife until finally she settled down with her head in his lap. His rifle rested beside him. Kitty snored softly on her pallet. He would have to get up in a minute and gather that wood. Maybe then he would be able to sleep too.

Adam yawned, despite his need to protect his family. Well, he was only a man, after all. A mortal man who needed to eat, sleep, and do other things. How long had it been since they'd made love? He missed those moments, which had become too infrequent in recent months.

Adam rubbed his eyes and for a moment thought he caught movement. No, he was sleepy. That's all. Staring into the darkness and imagining shadows moving would only serve to make tomorrow an incredibly tiring day. He needed his rest. At least a few hours.

The flute music, that had been the power of his own imagination.

What had that been? Reeds? They were close to the ocean. *Come to think of it, reeds didn't grow by the ocean, did they?* Who knew, but he had seen or heard nothing disturbing since those few notes.

"Jem, lay on the blanket. I have to get more wood," he whispered softly, and she did as he asked without arguing. Whippoorwills began to sing, not far away either. His mother never liked the sound of the whippoorwill. Mother believed the birds brought bad luck to women, especially unmarried women. He never understood her native ways, and she'd not been eager to explain them to him. He wished now he'd insisted on learning more about his mother's culture.

Shivering against the sudden chill, he tucked his jacket up around his neck. He left the rifle on the blanket and walked toward the far tree line. He wouldn't go far, just far enough to get what they needed. Strange that this clearing had been so neatly preserved, as if by an invisible force that claimed it. That kept it.

Where would he find wood? Oddly enough, there wasn't much on the ground. No branches or limbs. Jemima and Kitty picked the place clean earlier, apparently. But there should be something here, something they could burn. He could not let the fire go out in this vast blackness. Too many ne'er-do-wells out this way. That's what they said at the fort.

Biloxi was a gambling town, not that he saw much in the way of a town, but gamblers...he knew their kind. Mostly, gamblers were losers. They'd sell their mothers' souls for the next card game. What would they do to him and his family if they believed he had something valuable? He didn't want to imagine that, but people like that had no moral compass. Not at all. And the fact that he was half black, it didn't always help in these situations. He didn't mind being black—he was a proud black man—but there were a lot of bigots roaming the hills.

It was a fact of life.

"This isn't right," he mumbled to himself as he stalked around, hoping to find wood. Why was it so sparse when there were two large swathes of woods? He didn't go too deep into the forest, since he wanted to keep an eye on his family, but he desperately wanted to find fuel. Being here in the dark, the idea of getting lost in these strange woods, made him sick to his stomach.

Adam would never tell his wife this, but the longer they were here, the more anxious he became. It was not a good feeling. It was as if the ground had been picked clean and swept by others.

Other ill-fated travelers.

Ill-fated? What was wrong with him? He didn't usually behave like this. He was not one to be nervous about the darkness or the woods, but he was practically in tears and feeling desperate.

Desperate times called for desperate measures. He'd read that before, in an old book by some philosopher whose name he'd forgotten. That was something, at least. He knew how to read, thanks to his grandfather. Wonder what his Papa would think about this situation?

Adam glanced over his shoulder, as if someone would see him do the unthinkable. "Go away," he whispered to whoever might be watching him, for indeed, they were being watched. Every move, every step. Watched. "I'm not here to hurt you."

The man stood still in the fragrant woods, but the feeling began to dissipate. He no longer felt as if he were being threatened or watched. He breathed a sigh of relief. In the moonlight he could see fairly well despite the trees, but there was no ground clutter. No broken branches or limbs.

Desperate measures...

He had to do this. "Forgive me," he said quietly as he grabbed the shaft of a pole and easily removed it from the ground. The ancient structure fell apart, and he collected all the wood. There were no visible remains—obviously, they had been collected long ago—but this had been someone's burial spot. Some brave warrior, a beloved family member, a chief, perhaps. But he needed the wood. He gathered it all up, ignoring the musty smell of the cloth strips that remained stuck to the dry wood.

Immediately upon collecting the bundle of odd sticks and fabric, his teeth began chattering. Adam scurried out of the woods like his pants were on fire.

Jemima did not stir, and he was thankful. He tossed the wood onto the fire, praying that his wife would not wake up and drill him with questions.

He warmed his hands by the fire, but even hanging out by the flames didn't stop the chattering. He carefully added the remainder of the items to the fire.

In fact, he got colder. Much colder. His teeth chattered loudly, so loudly he thought he would wake his wife and daughter. He eyed Jemima again, but she didn't move. Now he wished she would. He wanted her to be by his side. He was supposed to protect her, but he was not feeling confident. Could he protect his family?

Should he wake her up? Should he try to lie down himself? No, that was impossible now. Footsteps. He heard footsteps all around him. Light steps, like moccasins, not boots.

Before he could call Jemima, the ground began to shake.

Chapter Seven—Carrie Jo

"That was intense, Ashland. Really intense." My body shook, a residue of the profound dream walk. My body responded like that when the dream was intense—or evil. Perhaps with the added fuel from Ashland's abilities, we'd stepped too deeply into the paranormal realm. I sometimes forgot how strong my husband's abilities were. He liked playing them down and was always content to let me shine. But honestly, I was beginning to wonder if he hadn't passed me up in a paranormal sense. Still, he didn't enjoy dream walking. He'd rather talk to the dead than step back in time.

"Ash, baby, are you okay?" He was sitting on the ground with a stunned expression on his handsome face. His blue eyes were red, as if he'd been crying. Maybe it was the heat. It had gotten quite warm out here this afternoon.

He ran his hands through his damp hair. "Yeah, I am fine. Why would he take down that burial structure? It wasn't that cold. It wasn't like they really needed that fire. They had enough to cook a meal and stay warm. He had to know he was only inviting trouble."

Rachel squatted down between us with the camera pointed in our direction. I hoped she didn't film us on our dream walk when I asked her not to. "Who? What did y'all see? Someone disrespected the boneyard? Desecrated a burial structure? Did you see the grim? What? Don't leave me hanging, guys."

Gathering my composure, I asked her to put the camera down. She begrudgingly complied, and I explained to her what we witnessed: a young pioneer family traveling through Biloxi to parts unknown. I told her how desperation drove Adam to make that poor decision, and fear. It had to be fear, but how that ended, we couldn't say. The dream ended before we had the chance to see what else would happen.

Yes, he disrespected the burial grounds by dismantling the structure. The ground shaking that occurred before the dream door closed reminded me of what Mary experienced when she visited the boneyard. Rachel believed a grim could be stalking this place, but what we saw led me to believe that it could be a Native American protector lashing out. We talked amongst ourselves, despite the biting flies and darkening skies. Finally, we were breaking through and getting some answers, but I wasn't satisfied with the little bit we'd seen.

I felt electric.

I didn't want to complain, and I sure wouldn't tell Ashland, but he'd been the one to break the walk. The dream door was still open—wide open, and it was waiting for me. I had to walk again.

But this time I wanted to walk alone.

"I need to go back, guys. Just for a few minutes. Adam wants to show us what he did, Ashland. He wants help. You know he does. You saw him first. If he's still here—and I believe he is—he might be willing to show us the rest of his encounter."

Ashland glanced around the boneyard as if he were hoping to see a reason why he should refuse to agree with me. But we were beyond that. Past the point of no return.

To his credit, he was as curious as I was, and Heather needed us to figure all this out. As things currently stood, it wasn't completely safe here, or at least not comfortable. Not in the boneyard, not inside Marietta. Ugh. This spirit was biding its time. It would make a move soon. Nothing and no one would be able to keep it out. Eventually, nothing would stop it from breaching the house. Not spells or incantations, salt or sage. This thing was near ancient. But which thing? The Native American or the grim? Or something else?

Suddenly, my ears began to ring. I was not one to suffer from tinnitus, but the ringing persisted. The ringing became so loud it almost took my breath away. Then the whispering started. The voices of dozens of people were talking, threatening, spewing out hateful things. It made me feel sick.

"This is so weird. Voices, Ashland. Guys! Can't you hear them?" I asked as my heart began to race.

Both Rachel and Ashland shook their heads. These voices, they were coming from the dream world. They were calling to me. I could hear them say my name over and over again.

Carrie Jo, please. Come, Carrie Jo.

"I need to dream walk again. I don't know what's happening. They were provoked, Ashland. The grim and the protector. They were both provoked. It's not just a grim here. Not just a protector. They really had nothing to do with one another. It is something else. Something we are missing. I need to confirm that."

Ashland shook his head in disbelief. "Are you saying that there is another spirit here in the boneyard? Are you prepared to deal with that? Let me go with you. I can do it. Just give me a second, okay?"

"I think I need to do this walk solo, babe. I'm going to be fine. This is what I do, remember?"

He kissed my cheek but didn't say he agreed with me.

"Imagine how the Native Americans feel? They were here long before the settlers. Having the grim here would tick them off. One would think, right? And now we're talking about another instigator?" Rachel took another picture, this time of the boneyard.

Ashland nodded, but his eyes were blinking erratically. It was kind of a tic of his, proof that his psychic wheels were turning. And that potentially, the effects of his old illness had returned. "Yeah, possibly, but we need to be sure how this all works. The ghosts have vanished with the dream. I can't see anything now. I guess you're right. I don't think I could do a dream walk again."

Dusting the leaves off my bottom, I stood on my feet and wiped my hands together. "There's no shame in your game, Ashland Stuart. I can do this. Let me walk while the veil is still thin."

"I hate seeing you disappear right before my eyes. It freaks me out, and I always worry," Ashland confessed as he took my hand. I squeezed his hand to reassure him and then released it.

"I'd expect no less from you. But I am not a newbie, Ash. I've done this about a hundred times. I'll walk back to Adam, and I promise I won't stay long."

"I agree with her," Rachel added. "We need to strike while the iron is hot. I mean, I wish I could go with you, but I'd be less than useless. Hey, can I film you?"

I frowned at her. "Seriously, Rachel? You want to film me dream walking?"

"Please? I won't share it with anyone. It would just be for me. For my own studies. I could compare it to other evidence I have. Wouldn't you like to know if there were other dream walkers out there? People you could network and work with?"

She made it sound reasonable, but how could she ask me that? I didn't want to think negatively about my friend, but her involvement with the Brotherhood bothered me. And now she wanted to film me? David warned us about the mystical group, but Rachel continued to engage with them. They were a strange, secretive organization that studied the supernatural, but they were too sneaky for my taste.

"No, Rachel. I don't agree with that. Please respect my privacy. I don't want to see myself on YouTube."

Her crestfallen expression spoke volumes. "I would never do that. If you say no, it's a no." Rachel put the camera down and stood with us. "How can I help you?"

"I am going to take a walk. That's it." I hugged Rachel to let her know I had no hard feelings, but I made a mental note to talk with her later. We needed to put this Brotherhood thing to rest. I squeezed Ashland's hand and kissed his cheek. "I'll be right over there." I tilted my head toward the back side of the boneyard. "That's where they were, Adam, Jemima and Kitty. I should be able to reconnect with them quite easily."

"Sounds good, CJ. We'll be here, but don't take risks. You know the rules. Don't interact with them. Don't make contact. I know you know all this, but I worry," Ashland confessed with his hand on my shoulder. He had every right to be worried. The last time I interacted with the past, it nearly cost him his life.

The rules for dream walking were simple:

Change the past, you change the present. And sometimes the future. My job was to witness and observe. Not prevent tragedy or change the course of history. Time didn't like to be tinkered with. No matter how tragic the event, how heartbreaking the scenario, the Universe didn't appreciate my hands working in its magic.

"Ashland, you better believe that I am not taking chances. I haven't forgotten what happened. And I haven't forgotten I am not alone." I casually and briefly rubbed my tiny belly. The baby wasn't moving around at the moment. She had been much more active in recent days. I pushed fear out of my mind, fear that I was putting our baby in danger.

Why? Dream walking didn't involve anything dangerous, no drugs. No hallucinogens. Just a little faith in my abilities.

"Go, take your walk. I'll be here waiting."

"Okay, guys," I smiled at them confidently and headed to the tree line. The ringing in my ears stopped, and so did the threats. Everything got quiet. So strange. My eyes scanned the tree line. I fixed my vision on one tree. Just one. And then one branch, and then one leaf. I kept my gaze fixed, just like I'd been taught.

Yes, I heard the spirits before I saw them. A soft mumbling. Chanting. I discerned that it wasn't evil. It wasn't threatening me, but unfortunately, this was not Adam Crossley. Not his wife and child. I almost turned back.

No, Carrie Jo. Keep your eyes on the leaf. See how pretty and green it is? The sunlight was shining through it, making it even brighter.

"Adam? Jemima?" I whispered hopefully. It did no good. This wasn't what I had planned, not what I intended. I continued to focus, and then time began to slip away. It changed. The honey-hued dream world swallowed me up. I saw things through the familiar sepia filter for the first few minutes.

The air smelled sweeter. Purer. The grass was soft beneath my bare feet. Where did my shoes go?

Flute music filled the air. It sounded hypnotic. Sweet, melodic. There was also the soft tapping of drums. The sound welcomed me. This wasn't war music; this was a protective spell. Someone was doing their best to protect this holy ground.

Yes, it was both holy and sacred.

Thump, thump, thump.

And just like that, the air shifted. The dull honey hue blurred my vision. I reminded myself that this was normal. The first few minutes of a dream walk made me feel uncomfortable, but it always faded.

No, I wasn't alone. There was a man with me. He was watching me, his sparkling black eyes curious and assessing. He was bare-chested and strong despite his age. The man had a regality about him. Yes, that was the word. He shone with otherworldly beauty, but he was as old as anyone I'd ever met. Probably older than I could guess. It did not diminish him at all. He was a force to be reckoned with. It would be important to let him know right from the beginning that I came in peace. I had no desire to go to war with this man. Unlike other ghosts, he knew I was here. He knew without me doing or saying a word. He knew many things except why I'd come.

The sepia lens lifted, and the air brightened. Then it darkened. It was night here. The stars sparkled above us, and I saw familiar alignments like the Big Dipper and the Little Dipper. I smelled wood burning, the fragrance of charred meat, and a plethora of herbs. Some herbs I recognized, some I did not.

Why are you here?

Oh, boy. Don't interact, don't interact. That's the rule, right? But this was different. What would Ashland do? He'd do the same thing, I was certain. The old man was in tune with the dream world, and I felt an odd kinship with him even though I had no idea who he might be, except one of the dead who rested here. Maybe a chief? Could he be the protector? Well, he'd addressed me, and I had to answer him. What else could I do except run back to my own time? How would that look?

"The lady in the house asked me to come. Her name is Heather. She is afraid because of what is happening here. I am a dream walker."

Go your way, dream walker. This does not involve you. Go in peace.

"But my friend is afraid. She asked me to come speak to you."

He said nothing but stared at me, his intelligent eyes blinking slowly as he assessed me. Through squinted eyes, he studied me as he pulled on his long pipe.

I felt compelled to continue making my case. "There is something dwelling here in the boneyard. It has been here a long time, and it is getting stronger. You must know that. It has stolen the peace of this place. Has Heather done something to disturb those that rest here?"

Go, dream walker. The ancient dead must rest in peace, or they will rise. Yes, evil things were done here, wanderer. Many things. Leave while you can.

"What is your name? My name is Carrie Jo." I thumped on my chest; my hands moved through the air in slow motion. So strange. Yes, it was so strange here in this time between times.

Yes, we are between times. I have no name. None that you would understand.

His mouth did not move as he puffed on his long pipe, but I heard his voice in my mind. Perfectly. Without fear. I experienced no fear in his presence. But that didn't mean I wasn't in danger. I smelled the delicious scent of tobacco. No, he was not going to tell me his name. He was not obligated to do so. I had no idea how to compel him.

"Nobody wants to harm you. Nobody here or in the house wants to hurt you. Whatever happened before, it has nothing to do with my friend. If you are at war with another spirit, I can help. I have helped others before."

Harm has been done. We have not forgotten. I am the Watcher. I have been awakened, and I will not rest until all have been punished.

Drums began tapping slightly. The soft, honey-hued air around me shifted. The man's dark eyes peered into mine as he stepped closer. Was he forcing me to leave? Yes, he wanted me to go. The drums made him stronger.

"My friend has done no harm! Please, listen to me!"

Her blood testifies against her.

I staggered back a half-step but pushed against the invisible wall he was building against me. I didn't sense hostility, but there would be no reasoning with him. He had one purpose and just the one.

Go from here!

He shook his staff before pounding the feathered-covered stick on the ground, leaving me breathless.

Everything changed, and I returned to my own time, to my husband and friend. I landed on the ground on my backside. Ashland and Rachel were standing over me. All I could do was lie on the grass and shudder under the man's power.

"Carrie Jo? CJ! Can you see us? What happened to you?" Ashland knelt beside me. He held my hand and patted it repeatedly until I managed to answer him. He relentlessly questioned me until I could sit up. I put my arms around his neck and held him tight. I was glad to be back. Glad to be with him. I don't know why, but I cried.

A strange feeling of helplessness crept over me. I hadn't broken through to the Watcher. I hadn't convinced him to help us. The only thing he'd done was acknowledge that there were indeed other spirits here, spirits that were not friendly. And the Watcher was on assignment against them, but not only them. Heather too!

Now I knew the truth. I'd seen the Watcher face to face. Fierce and determined, the Watcher would do what was necessary to protect his people. Even if that meant declaring war on Marietta.

I continued to cry. Ashland picked me up and carried me inside. Rachel walked silently behind us. I knew one thing for certain—if we were going to resolve this situation, this wasn't going to be easy.

And the cost would be high.

Chapter Eight—Rachel

"How about a glass of water?" I suggested to my friends. They were both clearly shaken up. So was I. As we headed inside, the negative energy didn't let up. And the house was entirely too quiet. Why did I get the sensation that someone would be listening to our conversation? I went to the kitchen and grabbed three bottles of water. Carrie Jo had gotten started without me. She was telling Ashland about the man she encountered during her dream walk, apparently not Adam the pioneer but a Native American man who identified himself as a Watcher.

"You met a Watcher? I knew they existed, but I've never read of anyone interacting with one." I cracked open the bottle of water and took a big sip before flipping through a book. I listened as Carrie Jo recounted what occurred during her dream walk. "What did he look like, CJ?" After skimming through the table of contents, I traded the book for another. This wasn't what I was looking for. I'd read a passage before about the Watchers in the Native American community. I remembered that they had to be either a chief or a shaman. The candidates for the task of Watcher had to be brave, had to be strong and faithful to the tribe.

I brought three books for this investigation, each containing information about local Native American burial practices. Sadly enough, there weren't a lot of details about the Biloxi tribe, which I assumed would be at this location. The secrets of the Biloxi—specifically, their oral history—remained lost, but they would probably be very much like their kin the Tunica.

"What did he look like?" Ashland asked as he leaned back on the couch. Carrie Jo was still shaking.

"Long, shaggy, dark hair. Old, like a hundred years old. But not crippled up like an old person might be. He was very strong, guys. Strong with his energy. He didn't try to hurt me, but he forced me back. Um, let's see. He had dark eyes, painted markings on his chest. He had a staff, with feathers on it. The Watcher tapped the ground once and closed the dream door, which forced me out. He didn't want to talk to me. The only thing he really said was, 'They must rest in peace, or they will rise up.'" She snapped her fingers. "Oh, and he said that harm had been done and that Heather's blood testifies against her."

For some reason, the atmosphere thickened as she recounted the experience. I even glanced down the hallway a couple of times before I continued searching my reference material for answers. Ugh. I didn't like this. It was as if what we experienced in the boneyard had followed us inside.

"This has been going on for centuries. There's a battle between this dark spirit and the Watcher, but how and why, I don't know. Why is it coming to a head now?" Carrie Jo asked as she leaned back. I noticed that my friend's eyes were watching the hallway too. We glanced at one another, but neither of us said anything. I thumbed through the book and finally found the page I was looking for. "Hey, did he look anything like this?" I held up the book, and Carrie Jo accepted it. She touched the page and nodded her head.

"Yes. The Watcher was older, though. I mean, really old. The markings on his arms were similar. He wasn't wearing a vest; he was bare-chested but wore deerskin trousers. The man was covered in dirt, like he just rolled out of the grave. Is that an illustration of a shaman? Who is that?"

"Yes, but from the Tunica tribe. The Tunica were closely related to the Biloxi. According to this book, it was a great honor and responsibility to be chosen as a Watcher. Whoever the tribe selected, usually one man per generation, he had to be very devout, strong physically, mentally and spiritually. And one more thing."

Ashland leaned forward and set his empty bottle on the coffee table. "What's that? I'm almost afraid to ask."

"He had to be willing to relinquish his soul for his tribe. At least temporarily. The Watcher had to allow his soul to be in limbo until the next protector took his place. He could move on to his rest only when his job was finished."

Carrie Jo gasped in shock. "What happens if there is no other Watcher? If his entire tribe is dead, or they moved, what happens to him? He's never allowed to move on?"

Her very troubling question hung in the air. I had no answer for her and no idea what it would mean. But it did make me feel sorry for him. The Watcher was no elemental, no spiritual protector. He had once been a living human with a life and probably a family.

Ashland appeared as tense as I'd ever seen him. He too was now glancing toward the hallway. I had to ask, "Do you see someone, Ashland?"

"No, but I sure as heck feel a presence."

The three of us waited, but nothing manifested. I quickly scrambled through my bags and found the REM pod and EMF detector. I put the REM pod on the other side of the living room and the EMF detector on the coffee table. I was no pro at using them, but practice makes perfect, as they say.

"This man, after he died, they would have allowed his bones to be picked clean by nature, and then he would be interred. In some areas, they would place the bones of the dead in a cave, but there are no caves around here. Not that I am aware of, at any rate. What about you? Any hints about a cave or cave system?"

Carrie Jo handed the book back as she shook her curls. "I don't know, Rachel. I've not heard of a cave system. And I don't suggest we go looking for him. Messing with his resting place is really going to tick the Watcher off. He was warning me about that. They already want vengeance for a wrong that we don't understand. Let's hold off on looking for his resting place until we get a handle on what the Lancasters were doing here. I get the feeling that the Native

Americans didn't appreciate them feeding the Beast, as Marietta called it. They were offended by it. Enough to feel as if they need to protect this space a hundred and fifty years after the last Lancaster left."

I bit my lip, wondering if now would be the time to tell them the rest. I had a hunch, a theory about the reason for the continued haunting. I didn't think this was just about the bones and the hurricane. This was about Heather. Yeah, I needed to fess up. I had to if I was going to keep everyone safe.

Genealogy didn't lie, but I didn't have her permission to investigate her lineage. Carrie Jo wouldn't be happy about my delving into a client's background without the proper permission. Better to get forgiveness than permission. Some would say I had a lack of integrity, but that's just not true. I had integrity, but I also had a strong drive to find the truth, no matter what it cost. And this personality trait of mine had cost me a lot.

"Um, guys. I need to tell you something. I did a bit of research. Heather is a true-blue Lancaster. She's a direct descendant of Ezra Lancaster, who was a grandson of Xavier and Marietta Lancaster. The only thing is, Heather was adopted. She doesn't know she's a Lancaster." I felt my phone vibrating in my pocket, but I chose to ignore it. Time to face the music. I hoped they wouldn't be too upset about my prying into the client's background. "The only reason I did it was because of what Heather said. She had a strange pull to this place, remember? She couldn't understand why, but it was as if she were compelled to come back here, to buy it. Make it her own."

"She's really a Lancaster?" Carrie Jo asked, and I breathed a quiet sigh of relief.

I nodded my head. "Yes, she is a Lancaster. A hundred percent. Only, I don't think she knows it. Did you?"

Ashland answered, "No, I don't think so. But what about the pioneer family? Did they have anything to do with the war going on here? If they were just passing through, why are they still hanging around? That's concerning to me." He asked his wife, "Did they die on this property? And if so, how?"

As if in response to his question, the REM pod across the room sounded off, followed by the grandfather clock in the front room. It was six o'clock already, and we'd barely gotten started with our investigation. Had we lost time in the boneyard? There was no other explanation for it. That was quite curious. I made a mental note of that. This would not be the first time I'd experienced a time slip in a case.

Case. That was a good word for it.

Carrie Jo's green eyes widened slightly. According to everyone's body language, we all experienced the shift in the atmosphere. A strange silence fell over Marietta. The air conditioning ceased to blow, which created even more of a vacuum of silence. We heard the soft tapping of shoes across the floor above us.

Only there was no floor above us.

Could those footsteps have come from another part of the house? Maybe the roof? Without saying a word, the three of us went to the front door to verify that no one had come inside after us.

We found nothing at all.

The strange stillness hung in the air until the air conditioner kicked back on.

I reached for Carrie Jo's hand. "Hey, it's okay. Let's all grab a bite to eat. I think we need some normalcy for a bit, don't y'all?"

"I couldn't agree more," CJ answered as she hugged me. "You're right. I'm starving. I can't get over the fact that Heather is a Lancaster. How do we present her with this information? Rach, you know how I feel about this sort of thing. I don't think it's our place to tell her. Not unless she asks. Agreed?"

I did not agree with her, but as she was the boss, I was not going to argue about it. Seriously, I respected Carrie Jo all the way. After changing clothes and washing up, the three of us met in the kitchen and devoured sandwiches and sodas. Not the best meal choice, but as we were working on a case, we didn't have time to cook a healthier one.

I noticed that Carrie Jo's eyes had dark circles beneath them, as if she hadn't slept in a month of Sundays. I didn't want to say anything, but that concerned me. CJ had a baby to think about—not just this haunted house and land. I glanced at Ashland, but he didn't appear to notice anything odd. He had mayo on the side of his mouth. I handed him a napkin as a courtesy. He took the hint and wiped the condiment away. Was the Marietta case weighing on CJ? My poor friend had been through enough these past few years.

"Carrie Jo, are you feeling okay?" I asked politely. I didn't want to make a big deal about it, but her appearance was truly concerning. I'd been around her all day, and she didn't look like this earlier. Not before that dream walk. My question appeared to fuel Ashland's curiosity, too.

"Hey, stop staring at me. I'm okay, y'all. I will admit I am tired, but that's it. If I remember correctly, I was tired the first trimester with AJ, too. At least I don't have morning sickness this time. Not often, anyway." She sighed as she dusted breadcrumbs off her hands. "Would you guys mind if I took a nap? Normally I'd amp up on coffee, but that's not good for the baby. If I don't take at least a quick nap, I don't think I'll make it through tonight's investigation. I assume we're going back out to the boneyard. That seems like the logical thing to do."

Ashland rubbed her shoulders and kissed the top of her head. "Yes, of course. Get some rest, babe. But try not to dream, okay?"

"How do I prevent that?" She laughed playfully. "Tell you what I'll do. I'll set my alarm for an hour. I won't sleep longer than that, okay, Ash?"

"Okay, honey. Better yet, I'll stay with you and wake you in an hour." He snapped his fingers. "Rachel, would you mind if I stayed with Carrie Jo? After the boneyard, I could use a nap myself. You won't feel like I'm abandoning you, will you?"

"Heck, no. I'll go ahead and check the batteries in the infrared cameras and then set them up. I'm not tired. Go ahead, guys. I'll be perfectly fine." Ashland left the room with Carrie Jo in tow. They were walking hand in hand. I was happy to see them acting like teenagers.

One day I'd be a part of a dynamic duo too. It was going to happen. I just needed to have a little faith. And a whole lot of luck.

I had plenty of that, but I was also a woman of science. Speaking of which, I needed to call Nate. I promised to give him an update on my Marietta findings. Not on the Stuarts but on this house and land. I hadn't mentioned it to Carrie Jo and Ashland yet, but there were quite a few houses along this section of Beach Boulevard that had reported hauntings. It might have something to do with the spiritual war happening here, or it might not. Who knows?

That was one reason why I was here.

That and I wanted to work with my friends. Sometimes it was hard balancing the two. But I could handle it.

I had a never-ending thirst for learning. As my Gran liked to remind me, I was a lifetime student. Unlike my college roomies, I liked going to class. I liked taking notes, proving theories right. Or at times wrong. I liked challenging the status quo in all things.

I set up two cameras in the boneyard, along with a few sensors, and then sat in the shade while finishing my now-tepid water. Fishing my phone out of my pocket, I tapped on Nate's contact number.

"Hey there, Rachel. How is it going at Marietta?"

"It's complicated; that much I can say. I am still looking for the grim. Even though the record shows there is one on the property, it's not at all easy to find. There are no statues. No gravestones. Nothing at all to lead me in the right direction."

"Have you tried dowsing rods?" Nate asked with a touch of simple naivety. That was Nate's gift. He had a way of suggesting the most simplistic ideas. Often, they were the right ideas. I couldn't help but chuckle.

"You know, I don't think I packed a pair of dowsing rods. I've got a night-vision camera, some SLS cameras and laser panels, but no dowsing rods."

He laughed at my answer. "Ah, you are such an overthinker. Trust your instincts, Rachel. You are as much a sensitive as your friends. Just in a different way. Trust that sense of smell. Remember what I always tell you: your body is the best detection device. Body chills, unusual odors, hairs responding to electricity. Walk by yourself. Without depending on others. I promise you'll find what you're looking for."

"Okay. I'll give it a shot. But you know me, I trust technology more than I trust myself."

He chuckled again, and I couldn't help but smile. I liked Nate. Not in a girlfriend/boyfriend kind of way. He was more like an older brother, but a good one. One you liked to keep around. I'd never had any siblings, so it was a welcome relationship.

"How is the dream catcher and her psychic husband?"

"Great. Both of them. Carrie Jo is taking a nap now. She looks tired, and I'm worried about her. Hey, did you hear anything yet? You know, about the Gaar House?"

Nate didn't laugh this time. Instead, a long moment of silence passed between us. I didn't like this response. Where his excitement? "Rachel, I don't think that the Gaar House would be a good case for you. In fact, I'm taking it off the board. It's too risky for most people. The Brotherhood is going to pass on this one, so that should tell you something."

"What? What do you mean, going to pass? This is what we do. It's the Gaar House. I worked hard to get us in that place. We can't quit now—this is my reputation on the line. They've asked us for help, Nate. It's got it all. Poltergeist activity, full apparitions, sounds, smells. And you know I need this investigation to make my final report. I need this for my certification. I thought I had your backing."

"You do have my backing, Rachel, but I don't have the final say in this. The Brotherhood made this decision, not me. They want to protect you, not suppress you. Listen, focus on your current case. I have it on good authority that the Brotherhood will be happy to accept Marietta as the subject of your report."

I couldn't believe my ears.

I needed something sensational for my final report. I'd been working so hard these past years with the Brotherhood. I'd done everything they asked of me, and I was this close to receiving my final certification—to becoming one of them. After that, I would travel all over the world conducting research on their behalf. It was a dream job, the offer of a lifetime. Now, Nate wanted to pull the plug on my dreams.

I could think of nothing to say. No way was Marietta a big enough case to be considered worthy of a final report. What was going on here? "Marietta? How does Marietta compare to the Gaar House? In what way, shape or form?" I sneered at his suggestions. I didn't mean to sound snotty, but this wasn't what I planned.

"I'm not talking about investigating Marietta alone. To make this report really stand out, you should observe and report on your fellow investigators, Rachel. It's not spying. It is reporting."

I sprang to my feet. My face flushed red; my heart was broken. "I told you I wasn't going to do that. I told you all along. Why are you doing this, Nate? These are my friends, and they trust me. All this time...is this what you wanted all this time? All my studies, all my reports. They meant nothing?"

"No, Rachel. That's not true. Let's talk about it when you get back. Clearly, you are missing the point. It's not how you make it seem, Rachel. I'm not asking you to spy on your friends. That's not true at all."

I paced the boneyard. The humidity stifled my breathing, and mosquitoes hung around my face and ears. What a joke! All this time, I had been so blind. Oh, God. Did this mean I needed to walk away? I had to tell Carrie Jo. No, I better not do that. What a fool I'd been!

"I have to go, Nate. I have a grim to find. Talk to you later." I did not give him a chance to object or to ask me anything else.

I hung up the phone and kicked a few rocks. This was not how I expected things to go. Not at all. Carrie Jo tried to warn me, but I didn't want to believe her. Maybe I was making too much of this. Maybe I misunderstood Nate completely. Had I overreacted?

God, please let that be true. I didn't want to lose all this time I'd invested in the Brotherhood, but if they were truly asking me to snitch on my friends, to tell secrets, I'd be gone—and without regret.

After a few minutes of feeling sorry for myself, I got a handle on my fury and got down to business.

Nate had one thing right.

I had abilities. Even without the backing of the Brotherhood, I could do this.

I would do this. I just needed a minute to sort this out.

I needed to think.

No. I needed Gran. I hoped she picked up the phone. She was the only one who would understand. She'd know what to do. Gran always saw the bigger picture. I continue to be blindsided by the people I trust.

And I was pretty sure I'd made a horrible mistake.

Chapter Nine—Ashland

Carrie Jo slept quietly beside me. She woke up once—just long enough to insist that I let her sleep alone. "I can't sleep with you staring at me, Ashland. You worry too much, babe. I'm fine. I'm so exhausted, I don't think I could dream if I wanted to."

"Fine." I smiled down at her sleepy face and kissed her softly. "I don't necessarily believe that, but I'll get lost. Sleep, Carrie Jo." I slid out of the bed and covered her up. She smiled once and closed her eyes. Her dark brown curls were scattered around the pillow like a wild halo. I loved her curly hair. Her glistening green eyes. Her easy way of loving me and everyone she cared about. I was one lucky guy, and I knew it.

How was it that I felt as if I'd known her forever? Like we'd never been apart. Always friends. Always in love. Before Carrie Jo, I never thought much about soulmates and the like, but if such things existed, she was mine. I couldn't imagine life without her. Yes, Carrie Jo was my soulmate. There was no other explanation for the connection and love I had with her.

Closing the creaking door as quietly as I could, I slipped out into the hallway and knew immediately what I would do. I had to go back and seek out Adam Crossley, the dead pioneer. Without Carrie Jo's gift in operation—hers was certainly stronger than mine—I could operate without fear of drawing her in. Hopefully.

I didn't see Rachel, not at first. She was on her cell phone walking around the front yard, and she looked frustrated, judging by the way she stomped her feet and waved her free hand. I didn't want to get involved in her personal life, but it was concerning. She still had connections to the Brotherhood, and I would never trust them. Not in a hundred years. Couldn't say why, exactly. It's not like I'd been best friends with any of the previous Brotherhood members. I didn't know anything truly nefarious, but all the secrecy...I didn't care for that too much. And they had too much of an interest in my wife and me. They wanted to study us, like we were two bugs in a jar. I would never go for that. I peeked out the window again. Rachel was sitting on a bench now, not paying attention to the house at all.

I took that as a sign. She mentioned earlier that she'd be setting up cameras out here, so I decided to get a move on. I wouldn't have long to be by myself, and that's exactly what I needed. Funny how that worked. CJ used to insist on dream walking solo, and that always worried me. Now, I was just as bad. I craved silence and solitude when working with ghosts. Many times, when we were home at Seven Sisters, I would go outside at night, after everyone was asleep, and walk the gardens. I didn't always see ghosts out there, but they appeared on occasion. Most of the time, they needed someone to talk to so they could move on. Other spirits wouldn't speak to me at all. They weren't ready for living human intervention.

One night at Seven Sisters, I encountered the ghosts of several black men. Sad, broken, and understandably so. These men were longing for their families. It took some work, but I assured them that their families were not lost but waiting for them. Their loved ones were on the other side of the light door. That was the night I realized I had to do this. I had to work with the dead and help them find comfort. Those men, those haggard looking, hopeless dead slaves, deserved peace. It was the least I could do, especially as a descendant of the Beaumont family.

I made the trek to the boneyard. With some luck, I would encounter Adam Crossley again. The dead pioneer triggered activity, unhappy activity, here. He had done the unthinkable, although to him, it had just been a case of survival.

I remember how Adam Crossley appeared when I first met him, a menacing expression on his face, his body tense, angry and protective of his family. He had not been open to talking then, until Carrie Jo stood with me. Her strength gave me strength. But I couldn't rely on that forever. I needed to hone my abilities without putting my wife in harm's way.

Yes, it was solitude that I needed.

I wanted to work my own mojo without anyone's help. Stand on my own two feet. It was important to me that I get a handle on this ability of mine. But what were the chances that I would encounter the pioneer again? There had to be countless untold bodies buried in the boneyard. There had to be. But I was going to give it a shot, regardless. Adam presented himself at least once already. He might reappear if I spoke my intentions to him. I needed him to know that I wasn't judging him. I needed his help. I needed to know what was happening here.

For Heather's sake and the sake of anyone who stepped onto this property.

Excitement and apprehension crept over me. This was not a feeling I was used to. I was rarely apprehensive when approaching the dead, but this place, this strange and confusing location, did not put me at ease.

I could see the boneyard. I passed the tree line and was closing in on the clearing. Before crossing into the space, I stood still for a moment and settled my mind and spirit. I grounded myself with a few deep breaths, remembering to focus not only with my natural eyes but with my spirit. It was difficult to describe to others how I was able to see the dead, but this was the best explanation I could come up with.

You had to look with both sets of eyes. How you activated that second set of eyes, how you tuned in to your spiritual eyes, I had no idea. I was born like this. I was born to do this.

I stepped into the clearing, and the thick grass made no sound as I stepped carefully and as respectfully as possible. I slowly surveyed my surroundings. It was completely quiet, and I felt a distinct sense of loneliness. Not fearfully so, but certainly alone. I heard no birdsong, no leaves falling. I heard nothing at all. Not even insects, which was very unusual for this time of year.

It was also a telling sign that I was not alone. Yeah, someone was watching me. I slowly tilted my head to get a good view of the woods around me. Then I looked back toward the trail that led from Marietta, but there was no sign of Rachel. Where had she gone?

Good. She should be here soon enough, so I could not delay.

Calmly and in a somewhat quiet voice, I spoke aloud. "I'm looking for the man I saw earlier. Adam Crossley. My name is Ashland. Are you still here? I saw what happened. I know what you did, Adam. I'm not here to condemn you, sir. I only want to help. Please, let me help you."

The wind did not stir, the trees did not move, but the humidity sweltered up from the ground. How odd. Didn't the humidity usually come from the atmosphere?

I don't know. Maybe. Maybe not. How very strange.

I closed my eyes briefly, reminding myself to breathe. And when I opened them, I saw the dead man I'd come to see. Adam Crossley watched me. His eyes fixed on me, burned into me, and there was no love or understanding there. It was as if he hated me. Hated me for knowing what I'd witnessed. How was I going to make him understand that I did not blame him for the evil that had been released here? Adam was about twenty feet away from me. He was wearing the same clothes as before. Nothing about him had changed, but at least he did not present himself as some terrible, gruesome corpse this time. He was a man, like me. The only difference between us was a few hundred years.

Go away! Leave us alone!

I had to keep trying. "Adam. My name is Ashland. I can help you, Adam. I know you didn't mean any harm, but harm has been done. Let me help you make it right." I spoke with true sincerity and even extended my hand to him as a gesture of goodwill.

What happened next was completely unexpected and unwanted.

Like the soldier I'd seen earlier, Adam Crossley took off at full speed and ran toward me. Only he didn't blow through me. He stayed with me as I fell to the ground flat on my back. His body felt physical, like a living man. His dark eyes bore into mine, and a low growl grumbled from his chest. Crossley's hands were on mine, his legs on mine. I pushed against him, trying my best to push him away. Then his physical body vanished, but the weight of the man lingered for a moment.

And then nothing.

Wait. No, that's not right. Adam Crossley remained with me. I couldn't see him, but I felt him. He hung on to my soul, and I screamed at the shock of it.

You want to see? You want to know? I'll show you...

*****

I poked at the fire to stoke it up a little higher. Fire kept away both man and beasts. Usually. The old rotten fabric I'd stolen from the burial ground burned quickly, but the dry poles made excellent fuel. Excellent, but they wouldn't last all night. I'd have to get more. Then what would I do?

As I stirred the flames with a green branch I found earlier, I heard a man's voice, a low whisper barely discernible to my ears. I was so tired, plain worn out to the bone, so it was no wonder I didn't hear correctly. And it was completely possible that I was merely hearing things. My grandpappy used to say, "Go to bed, son, and quit sniffing for ghosts." I never really knew what that meant, except maybe quit looking for trouble. A tired mind is a man's worst enemy. Yeah, that had to be it. I could sleep for a whole day, if given the chance. I rubbed at my eyes with the back of my dirty hand, and the smoke made my vision blurry for a few seconds.

But then I heard the voice again.

This was the worst scenario possible, stuck out here alone with no sign of civilization nearby. The kind of men we'd meet in these parts would most likely be criminals of one kind or another. Still squatting before the fire, I paused my prodding. I cocked my ear by turning my head to the left and then to the right, but I heard nothing else.

What in the world had I heard? A thought occurred to me, a dark and disturbing thought.

What if the voices I heard were Indians? Angry natives who saw what I'd done. I hadn't meant any great disrespect; I only wanted to keep me and mine safe through the night. That couldn't be it. There were no more natives along this stretch of the Mississippi. How could it be possible, since they'd all but died out? The man at the fort said the natives had cleared out long ago, the ones that survived the plague. Decades ago, as far as he knew. Maybe longer, but then again, it was impossible to know.

Under normal circumstances, I would never desecrate anyone's resting place. But if it was between life and death, my family's life and death, then I would do what I had to do.

My stomach felt as if I'd swallowed a rock. A sharp one. It hurt, either from hunger or from fear. I couldn't be sure. Sitting as still as possible, I whispered into the dark, "Hello?" I didn't want to wake my family. Not until I could be sure that I wasn't merely hearing things.

My surveillance offered up nothing, so I turned back to my task. I yawned—the warmth of the fire and the waiting pallet were tempting me. I again heard the voice. It happened again, as if the whisperer watched and waited for me to turn away to become vulnerable. I didn't like this at all.

For a moment or two, I felt a splash of water hit my face. Could it be rain? I prayed against that possibility. I didn't want to deal with rain on top of everything else.

The only other place to find shelter would be inside or beneath the broken-down wagon. There was no way would I ask Jemima and Kitty to do that. Not if it rested in that musty graveyard. My stomach growled, for the sparse meal had not satisfied me, but I would not complain.

This had been my idea. My dream.

We needed a new start. All of my mistakes, all my past sins had returned to me, and it was time to move. I had hidden nothing from my wife; she knew everything about me, yet I felt compelled to make this move. For all our sakes.

Jemima would forgive me, but I was quite certain I would never forgive myself. Never.

Subduing the man who intended to harvest my life. Seeing the life slip away in his eyes. Seeing that I lived, and he died. Killing a man, whether on purpose or by accident, was something I would've never imagined these hands doing. Yes, I was capable of murder and now knew that a murderous beast lived inside of me, and that it could happen again. In fact, one kill had not been enough. I killed and killed again. All men. All deserving of death. Cruel men, they were. But each time I killed, the beast within me grew stronger. Jemima didn't know what I had done, but the law did. And they would catch up with this black man eventually. She did not know my horrible secrets, and I never wanted her to find out.

What if Jemima knew how it made me feel? How the killing, although done in the name of self-protection, at least the first time, excited me. It made me feel things I'd never felt before. Strong, invincible, powerful. I hated myself for those feelings. That would count for something, surely. A kind of repentance.

And then again, I heard the whispering. The strange whispering. Unintelligible words spoken with an urgency that forced me to address it. Leaning over, I tucked the cover up around my wife's and daughter's shoulders. Jemima stirred briefly but did not waken, thankfully.

That's when I heard the first of the footsteps. Yes, one set, then another. There were two interlopers out here. I lifted a flaming stick and waved it in front of me, hoping to get a clear view of the intruders as their feet pounded the ground. Oh, yes. That sound I knew. The clear sound of moccasins.

I knew that sound. I was familiar with the sound of moccasins running on dry ground and in wet grass. It was vastly different from the sound of boots or sandals. The footsteps raced back and forth just beyond the edge of their impromptu camp. Yes, those footsteps echoed from the burial ground. Yes! There must be someone else out here.

I broke the stick over my knee in a threatening manner. That dangerous angry beast within me threatened to rise as I stomped toward the sound. I'd just been in the burial ground moments ago and heard nothing. Saw no one. The darkness offered no clues as to who was watching me. Who was stalking me?

I could not be sure, but in a threatening voice—not one so loud that it would wake my wife—I whispered fiercely, "Show yourself! I hear you, you bastard. I know you're there! I've got a gun!"

Yes, I did have a gun, but for some reason, it was not in my hands. My fury, my protective nature, caused me to leave it behind. It was not like me to be vulnerable. Whoever ran in the darkness certainly did not mean well. Again, I heard words, words of an unknown language that troubled me, but this time the words were not distant. Rather, the voices rang in my ears.

Yaz zan si otse! I see you, Beast. Go from here!

I stepped across the boundary line and waved the fading flame before me. My hand flew to my ear to wave away the unwanted voice. What in the world was going on? How could the stranger get so close to me without being detected? How could he know my secret?

I did not understand that. A flurry of footsteps ran toward me again, the sound of many men. Only this time, they were coming from behind. As I spun about to finally meet the strangers, I gasped as an invisible hand with sharp fingernails scratched my face. Swear words came unbidden to my mouth. I stabbed at the air around me with my stick, but there was nothing and no one. Only the faint sounds of footsteps.

Yaz zan si otse, cof yaz!

More words this time. More words that were surely meant as a threat. A warning. I should leave, but how could I? Running through the darkness with my wife and young daughter would be dangerous. My hand went to the place where I had been scratched. Sticky and wet, had to be blood. Yes, I could see that much from the dwindling flame.

What was the meaning of all this?

Not far away, I heard the tapping of a single drum. A small one, like the kind my grandfather would use when he summoned his ancestors. And then came the yipping. Not the yipping of coyotes or wolves, but the distinctive sounds of men bent on war.

Or revenge. Could my own ancient blood be the reason for the beast within me?

"Damn you!"

A creaking sound to the left of me caught my attention. The sound of poles clattering to the ground, the tearing of cloth, footsteps thumping on the ground. It was as if the place had come alive.

No, not alive. It was full of the dead. I swung the glowing stick around in fast circles. It did not provide much in the way of light. In fact, my dim torch grew dimmer by the second. Soon, it would be completely extinguished, and I would be here in this horrible place with God knows what. I raced toward my crooked wagon, hoping to find some sort of weapon. Instead, I fell to the ground, and a tremendous slap caused blood to fill my mouth. I couldn't speak, couldn't move. I could do nothing but wait for the nightmare to end.

You are the nightmare! Go from here!

That's when the ground beneath me began to move. As if something buried would emerge. More of the dead? More of the angry natives who sought revenge for my earlier desecration? My mind stung with the shock of it all. This couldn't be happening. This must be a nightmare. I should wake up!

Yes, wake up, Crossley!

But before I put two thoughts together, the ground shook again. Only it wasn't a corpse climbing out of a grave, but rather an animal. A big black animal with paws as big as my head. It rose from the black dirt and shook the soil off its back with a mighty roar. The dead scampered away, but their whispers continued. No, not whispers. They were chanting. Chanting for my death.

What of Jemima and Kitty? What of my family?

Glowing red eyes stared at me, and the creature—a dog, a cat, some hellish combination of the two—snarled at me. My voice found my tongue, and I began to scream.

I screamed because hell was coming for me and I deserved it.

I deserved this ending, and so did the Beast inside me.

Chapter Ten—Carrie Jo

Even though I was dead tired, I managed to dream. I hadn't expected that. I really hadn't. Those first few minutes, the honey-hued color stuck with me; it was so thick it wouldn't allow me to see clearly. But then a magnificent ocean breeze blew in off the coast, the sepia cloud vanished, and I realized I was not alone.

Ashland lay on the ground, his face staring up at the heavens, wide-eyed and unmoving. Luckily, I could see that he was breathing. Yes, breathing normally but mesmerized by whatever it was he saw from his vantage point. I glanced up at the night sky, but there wasn't a hint of anything remotely strange or unusual. Just glittering southern skies.

But the boneyard had become a lively place, a place of deathly celebration. Men and women wailed, their grief-stricken faces covered in paint and mud. The ground rumbled beneath my feet as if it too were grieving for the dead. These people were not just here to bury their dead. They too were suffering and sickly. Even in this strange light, I could see that their skin was marked with boils and bleeding ulcers. Yes, they were a sickly lot who would have no one to bury them. They honored those they could, but who would honor them?

Oh, yes, smallpox. That's right. This was part of the history. The Biloxi were nearly wiped out by this horrid plague. Thanks to the white man. What cruel gifts we brought these people. What a horrible sight!

None of the dead spoke a word, but they shared the language of grief. One by one, they fell—women holding babies, men carrying children, old men leaning on the younger ones. All were skinny, so thin that they must have been starving.

This had been their place.

Their burial ground.

A place they would always honor and expect to be honored. Until the first desecration and then the one to come. Oh, God! I heard their voices in my ear, and it was too much. Too many voices speaking all at once, crying, begging. I could not decipher the language, but it pulled sorrow out of me. Deep, horrible sorrow and something else. Fear! They were afraid, but of what? Us? The Crossley family?

No, that wasn't right. My skin crawled as I began to understand exactly what it was they were afraid of. They were afraid of the creature, the one that took Portia and stalked the Lancaster family. No, these unfortunate dead had nothing to do with that. Nothing at all. They were trapped here, not resting in peace but restless in fear.

Oh, God! Ashland! We must get out of this dream!

Racing toward my husband, I fell beside him, reached for his hands, and immediately began shaking him. His hands were as cold as ice, as if he too were dead, but he was not dead, merely dreaming. He'd planned to find ghosts, obviously, but the power of this place drew him into the dream world. Maybe it was because I slept. I had pulled him into mine. I couldn't be sure, but at least he was alive. Just seeing. Only looking at and observing what others could not. Except me.

Ashland, I'm here! I'm right here! We have to go! Please, wake up!

He wasn't moving at all. What was happening here? Why couldn't he shake this dream? If I couldn't wake him, at least I would protect him. I lifted his head and placed it in my lap. I would protect him with my last breath, in this realm or the one we came from.

My heart raced as time sped up around us. Bodies were pitched high on poles, wrapped in sacred garments. The blasting sea breeze, the screeching of the predators who did their job without mercy. Birds, coyotes and all sorts of animals cleaned the bones and left them behind.

The screams grew louder, the absolute exultation of agony reached a fever pitch, and then the air grew stagnant. The dead, the many, many dead, had left.

Except Adam Crossley. The color of the sky shifted again; it became a dark purple, and a glittering of stars shone down on us. Instead of structures laden with the precious dead, the poles were in heaps on the ground. Time had passed, much time. This place had been left for many years, or so was the sense I got.

"Ashland, we need to go. Ashland? Babe?" I decided to try again. Ashland and I needed to get out of here. The worst was about to happen. The absolute worst. I could feel it in my bones. The ground rumbled again. There was a wagon not far away—the Crossleys' wagon. The broken wheel was evidence of the accident. I glanced around as I waited for my husband to respond. He was breathing normally, and his eyes were blinking. How had this happened? It was as if he too were dream walking. Or something like it. I would have to figure it out...after we got out of here.

There he was—Adam Crossley! On his back, not far from the wagon. His face was bleeding, his eyes wide with fear. His dark skin glistened with sweat, the kind of sweat caused by fear. Deep and abiding fear.

And I saw the creature. Black, so black it was almost blue. It was the largest dog I'd ever seen, like something from a previous ice age. Its menacing growl pulled a scream from Adam as he began to try and crawl away. He was on his stomach, crawling away from the hole left by the Beast. This must be the Lancaster Beast! The one that fed on children and women, the one that demanded sacrifice! I watched in horror as Adam's attempt to escape quickly ended. His struggle did not last long.

Ashland begged to get up. I wanted to help him, but my eyes were transfixed on the horrible scene that played out before me. Was the Beast going to kill Adam? Is that what happened to the pioneer? What about his family?

Just as I thought that, I watched the Beast place his massive paw on the back of the black man. He didn't kill him; I could hear him scream, but others were screaming too now. Not just the ghosts of the natives who'd been trying to warn him. They began to fade; they knew it was too late. I watched in horror as Adam and the Beast became one horrible being.

But even as Adam screamed and roared, other screams rose. The screams of Adam's wife and daughter. They had seen Adam pinned to the ground, seen him struggle to get away.

"Adam! Adam!" Jemima cried fearfully. "Adam, no!"

"Run, Jemima! Take Kitty and run! Please!" Adam pleaded as he struggled to breathe. His transformation was almost complete. I could see the tears streaming down his cheek. He could do nothing but watch and wait. What a terrible sight! A terrible situation! "Run, Jemima! Don't come here! Stay off the land!"

But Jemima had a gun, a long, black gun. And although she was screaming and crying, with Kitty tugging on the back of her skirt, she was brave. So brave that she clearly had every intention of killing the Beast.

Ashland sat beside me, his eyes damp, his face flushed. "She has to stay off the property, Carrie Jo. It cannot get her if she stays out of the boneyard. We must warn her. We have to stop this." He was dead serious even though he himself knew exactly what could happen if we were to interfere with history. Bad things happened when you interfered with past lives. Bad things.

"No, Ash. You know we can't." I whispered to him as together we rose to our feet. "We can only observe. Not interact. That's rule number one."

"But," he began to argue with me in a broken voice.

"I know," I answered him as we watched in horror the slaughter of Jemima and Kitty.

The animal taunted Jemima by circling the edge of the boneyard. She fired the gun but did not strike the Beast, only the wagon. "Adam? Where are you?" To get a better shot, she would have to get closer. That was her reasoning. I didn't need to hear it; I knew it. I would have done the same thing. Jemima had no idea that the boundary she was about to cross was going to doom her.

Jemima shot the gun again, but to no avail. She sank to her knees and began to scream, scream like her soul was on fire. Kitty staggered behind her. The child was confused, and in that moment, as quick as a lightning strike, she was dead. The Beast landed on her and ripped her to pieces. An eruption of blood and bones fell on Jemima, who continued to run to the wagon. "Adam!"

Her face was the epitome of regret, horror and grief. She did not make it to his side but fell on the ground. The Beast was on top of her, and I could watch no more. I even said, "NO MORE!" as loudly as I could to break the spell, break the dream.

Together, Ashland and I were standing in the boneyard, both crying, looking around for fear that the Beast would somehow return and finish its bloody work. It wasn't done, that was for sure, although it did not have the power it once did. It did not have the power to rise yet, but it wanted to. Oh, yes, I could feel the evil permeating from the ground.

It needed a new sacrifice. It needed a Lancaster. The Beast wanted Heather.

"Do you see him?" Ashland whispered as he pointed to the center of the boneyard. I had to confess I did not.

"Adam is the Beast!"

"Stay here, CJ. Please, stay right here."

I didn't argue with him, but the horrible memories sickened me. I could easily throw up thinking about the slaughter. The death of that child; she had to be only slightly younger than our Lily. Her death would forever be burned into my memory.

"Ashland," I whispered as he continued to walk to where the wagon would have been those hundreds of years ago. As I stared into the darkness, I began to discern a figure. The Watcher! The old man who we'd seen before. Ashland stood before the bare-chested native, but as far as I could tell, no words were exchanged.

The old man gave Ashland a painted stick. Worn feathers fluttered from the end; it was wrapped in painted rope and embellished with symbols. The man turned and walked away, disappearing from the clearing.

It was then that I understood. What we'd seen, what we'd witnessed. The Biloxi were abandoning this holy land forever. The weeping, the burials we'd seen, they would be no more. Those that were buried here were gone forever. Moved on to the light or wherever it is that they were destined to go. Where do we go when we die? Our destiny isn't to be ghosts, that much I was sure of, yet some of us remained behind.

Some of us rested in our burial grounds.

Some of us did not.

Ashland returned to me, the stick in his hand, a gift from a man older than any we'd ever met. I couldn't wrap my mind around all that this meant. Especially for Ashland. Why did he carry the stick? To the Biloxi, it had been a cherished and sacred item, a symbol of authority in death and life.

"What did he say? What are we supposed to do?" I asked fearfully. I had another question to ask but decided against it. *Would the Beast come back again?* Did I really need to ask that?

"He said it was time to go to war. That this was not his battle anymore. It is ours."

"Ours?" I asked as I stared at the stick and touched it gingerly. As soon as my finger touched the pole I felt a shock, like static electricity. No doubt this item had a bit of magic to it, but what did we know about banishing a hellhound, or whatever this thing might be?

"Yes, ours. It's not a coincidence we're here. We have to help these people rest, Carrie Jo. They deserve to have their land back. They can't rest here; he won't allow that. The Beast wants to kill the vulnerable, especially children."

Instinctively, my hand flew to my tiny baby bump. Ashland didn't notice as he was surveying the boneyard, stick in hand. "Let's go, Ash. We need to talk to Rachel and tell her what we've seen. We need a plan, don't you think?"

"Yes, you're right. Let's go, Carrie Jo. Stay close, okay?"

"Don't worry. I'm sticking to you like glue. I don't like this place. Not at all. I hate this place, Ashland. I hate it."

We walked back to Marietta in silence, hand in hand.

Chapter Eleven—Rachel

I should have already set the cameras, since it was dark already, but I couldn't shake my disappointment. My time with the Brotherhood was coming to an end because this was a line I wasn't going to cross. Imagine asking me to spy on my friends. Nate didn't really want a report on Marietta. I didn't believe that for a second. What they wanted was more info on Ashland and Carrie Jo Stuart. And of course, by extension, Lily and AJ. Give me a break. Like I'd do that. I told them from the beginning I would never spy on my friends, and they pretended to be okay with it.

Now what was I going to do with my life? All that work, and for what?

I walked back outside carrying my backpack and two tripods. I darn near walked into the Stuarts, who were emerging from the woods that led to the Boneyard. "Sorry I'm late getting these set up. Hey, what do you have there? Did you find it in the burial ground?"

Ashland and CJ exchanged a worried glance and nodded. "Yes, but that's not all we found." Mosquitoes circled us, but they didn't seem to mind. I swatted away as they told me what they'd seen. Strange how Ashland's ghost walk and Carrie Jo's dream walk combined like that. I wondered what that meant—were their powers growing, fueled by one another's gifts? We'd seen that before. I mean, the Brotherhood had seen that before. I read about it; it was a topic of much discussion in our study groups. And here I had evidence of just that. When gifted people work together, their gifts become stronger, or in some cases, one or both will wane. Definitely not the latter for Carrie Jo and Ashland.

The old stab of jealousy struck me, but I reminded myself it was wrong to feel jealous of the people I loved. Sure, I wanted the same thing, someone to love me in all my weirdness, but that did not justify being jealous of two people who'd only been good to me.

"Good Lord, you mean the Beast is Adam Crossley? Ugh, why didn't I have these cameras up? Man, I'm sorry about that."

"It's fine. I don't think you would have captured much anyway. What we saw was in another realm, for the most part. Do you have any idea how long we were gone? What time is it?" Carrie Jo asked me as I shuffled my equipment to glance at my watch.

"Only about an hour. But wow, it got dark kind of early. I still can't believe that Adam and the Beast are one and the same. And that medicine stick, the Watcher actually handed it to you?" I put all my equipment down except my camera and immediately began snapping photos. I was no expert on Native American artifacts, but it had interesting markings and colorful paint.

"Touch the stick, Rachel. Tell me what you sense." After taking a few more photos, I reached out to touch the wooden stick. So old, such craftsmanship. There was no telling how many hands had held this magical item before Ashland received it from the hands of a Watcher, the ghost that abandoned this place. My fingers rubbed across the wood, but I did not sense or experience anything. Only sadness, but that was probably because of the story they told me. It sounded incredible, from the Beast to the ghosts of the Biloxi, but this was the world the three of us lived in. The paranormal world.

"Nothing, but you can't go by me. Any gifts I have come and go. They aren't like yours. I'm the weirdo that smells things. I better get these cameras set up."

Ashland shook his head. "Change of plans. We don't need footage. We know what's here and what we're up against. We don't need the gear. We need salt, and lots of it. We may not stop this Beast, but let's make sure it can't leave the boneyard."

"Why would it leave the boneyard?" I asked, surprised at the fear I heard in my voice. I didn't mean for that question to come out like that. "It hasn't left it before."

Ashland's answer made my skin crawl. "The Beast has no opposition now. There's no Watcher to keep it in check. The Beast had grown stronger and the Watcher weaker. He's abdicated his responsibility, maybe because he knows he no longer has the strength. I don't know. But we need a barrier so that when we banish this thing, it doesn't escape the land."

Carrie Jo bit her lip. "Wow, I haven't thought that far ahead, but I'd say you're right. This stick isn't going to be enough, Ash. You don't have the authority to use it. Not really. I need to go back to Marietta Lancaster's time. I need to see how it ends for Mary and maybe figure out why Marietta fed this thing to begin with."

"I don't know, Carrie Jo. Is it safe to dream walk again so soon after a dream?" I asked with genuine concern.

"The sooner we get this over with, the better. Let me help you tote the gear back. Ashland, I doubt seriously that Heather has all the salt you need. You're going to have to go find some." The three of us walked back to the house, and Ashland put the stick inside the door near the coat rack and then headed out.

"I'll be right back, guys. Please, stay in the house. I mean, CJ, don't even think about it."

His wife gave him the stink-eye, and he vanished out the door.

We dumped the gear on the couch, and I felt kind of helpless. What was I bringing to the table here? Nothing much. I couldn't believe this was happening. "Let's eat something. You need to feed that little guy. Or girl."

"I thought you were in the girl camp." Carrie Jo smiled prettily. She was truly a beautiful woman. So tiny, though. Petite and perfect.

"Oh, I am, but boy or girl, this child will be awesome. You don't know how lucky you are, Carrie Jo. Really, really lucky." I didn't mean to sound resentful; it just came out like that.

"One day you'll have your own family too, Rachel. If that's what you want. I believe that completely. You haven't given up on love, have you?"

I took the bread out of the breadbox and went in search of lunchmeat and mayonnaise. How to answer that? I wasn't sure. Had I given up on love? I think so. Maybe it was time to let that dream go.

"Life throws curve balls sometimes," was all I could think to say. "Who knows what the future holds for me? Or for any of us, for that matter."

Carrie Jo's expression, a mixture of sadness and something else, caused me to turn my eyes away from her. I was the worst friend on the planet. Why would I say something like that at a time like this? "Hey, don't listen to me. I'm not lucky in love, just friends. Let's eat. Ham and cheese okay with you?"

Her smile returned, and we slathered mayo on bread and assembled sandwiches. I expected Ashland to be right back, but an hour went by and there was no sign of him. Carrie Jo called his cell phone, but we heard it ringing in the living room. I guess he'd been so flustered he'd forgotten it.

"He'll be back any minute, Carrie Jo. Let's see what's in the pantry. I know there's at least one container of salt. We could start with that," I said hopefully.

"You heard Ashland. It's not safe, Rachel. You didn't see what we saw. So many dead. So many Native Americans dying of smallpox. Then the Crossley family got murdered. The Beast was nothing like anything I've ever seen. I swear it resembled a large panther and a rottweiler. It is indescribable, really. I don't think it's a grim, Rach. I mean, it didn't look like an ordinary dog. Then this thing came up out of the ground and merged with Adam."

I tapped my pen on my notebook. I needed to write all this down. I began talking out loud. "So not a grim, but we know there is a creature and then the Watcher. But the Watcher gave Ashland his medicine stick. That means he has abdicated his role as the Watcher. I didn't think they could do that, but then again, a human spirit still has free will. Could the grim have morphed with Adam? Become something else?"

"I guess it's possible, but how?" Carrie Jo sat beside me and began cracking her fingers, a thing she did when she was nervous about something. "The sacrifices! The sacrifices that the Lancaster family made! The grim was supposed to keep the devil away, but they—"

"They drew him in! They made a deal with him. I bet that's what happened. That's a hellhound, Carrie Jo. A freaking hellhound, a servant of the devil. Oh, my God! Who would do something so evil?"

Carrie Jo got up and began pacing back and forth. Her face was pale as she took in this turn of events. "Wait until Ashland hears this. It wasn't Mary. She came to Marietta after this had been going on. Marietta claims it was happening when she got here, too. Now it's awake again because another Lancaster is here. Heather! Oh, no! It wants Heather to bring it an offering! It must have started with Adam in the early 1800s or late 1700s."

"No, it wants to serve Heather, but it needs a sacrifice, preferably a child. Or a woman. Or a..." I couldn't finish the sentence. It didn't matter. Carrie Jo knew the truth now. The total and complete truth.

The Beast wanted her, and her baby. As if she read my mind, Carrie Jo whispered, "I have to go back. Before Ashland gets back. Once he figures this out, he'll never let me go. I need to see Mary, Rachel. I have to dream walk."

"But you've been doing it all day, CJ. You have to rest and then..."

She shook her head. "Nope. I tell you what, though, I'll let you record me. I'm willing to make a deal here, Rachel. I have to go. I won't have much time."

"Carrie Jo, you don't mean that. I am not going to do that. The Brotherhood doesn't need to see this. They don't deserve to see it. I'm done with them, CJ! All this time, it's you they wanted, but I didn't know. I swear, I didn't know. I thought they cared about me. I thought they wanted to improve my gifts, that I was important to them, but I was wrong. So very wrong. I am sorry. You must know I would never betray you. Never ever."

Carrie Jo suddenly hugged me up. "Of course. I know that. I know you would never do that. Never ever. I have always trusted you, Rachel. What's going on?"

I couldn't help but cry, not because I was guilty but because this felt as if it were the end of something.

But the end of what?

"What am I going to say if Ashland comes back and you're dream walking? He'll have a cow, not to mention chew me out."

To my surprise, CJ took my hand. "Then come with me, Rachel. Come with me, but keep quiet. All we can do is watch and observe. Don't touch anything and stay with me. You have to stay with me. Okay? Deal?"

Her offer surprised me, but I couldn't say no. I wanted to dream walk with Carrie Jo! This was the chance of a lifetime. I may never have another opportunity like this.

"I'll leave Ashland a note. I don't want him to worry about us."

"Good idea," I agreed as I provided her with a pen and a piece of paper.

She quickly scribbled a note and then took my hand. "What do I do? Tell me how this works."

"You focus on a small item. Like that butterfly box over there. See the butterfly? See the wings? Just look at it and tell me about it and don't let go of my hand. You have to stay with me, okay?"

"Okay, Carrie Jo. I trust you. I'm looking at the butterfly. I am watching the butterfly..."

Then the room began to spin, and the density of the air shifted, as if it thickened slightly. For a moment, I panicked. Was I going to smother? As if she read my mind, Carrie Jo squeezed my hand. "Keep your eye on the butterfly, Rachel. Stay focused and breathe. The sensation will pass in a few seconds."

I saw the light shift. I breathed a sigh of relief. We were inside Marietta.

I could hear a woman screaming. I immediately began running behind Carrie Jo.

Chapter Twelve—Marietta

I watched with some amusement as my petite daughter-in-law haphazardly stuffed a few mismatched items in a traveling bag. She wasn't thinking clearly; she didn't understand what would happen if she tried to leave, but I did.

I, Marietta Lancaster, knew firsthand what would happen if Mary stepped off this property, especially with that child in her arms. She would be torn to shreds before her feet made it to the end of the driveway. Portia tried that too, but the Beast stalked her until she relented and returned. In her case, her attempt angered the Beast. He took her anyway. Her and her child. I couldn't think about it too much. I didn't dare to mourn over them.

The Beast would know; he always knew when one of his own planned to escape. The Beast could smell the Lancaster blood. Or so Xavier told me. Could it truly have once been his grandfather, the ill-fated Percival Lancaster, who'd made his own deal with the devil? Or something altogether different?

How to explain it all to her? Maybe I should have done that to start with. Maybe I should have told her all this in the beginning, but I had been afraid. Too afraid to bring anyone here that would make a fuss. Finding John Lamar's wife had been challenging for me. I couldn't marry him off to a local girl, although for a time, when he was fifteen, he had been smitten with the heavenly-minded Miss Amy Prentiss. After a few words with me in private, her father decided that the Lancasters were not a suitable match. We were not a religious family.

The devil roamed the grounds here at Marietta. No, I couldn't allow poor Amy to endure such a test. She was so sweet and pious, it would have driven her mad. She wasn't strong enough to endure the tests that would surely come her way. The loss of children, the death of other children. Madness took many Lancasters, at least the ones who knew the truth. Not my Oscar, though. I kept him far away from this place. As far as possible. So far, he'd seen nothing and experienced nothing, although he had not yet married. The real test would come then. How far did this creature's arm reach? Being part spirit, it may be far indeed.

But I'd chosen Mary Fairbanks, and I was not disappointed by her thus far. She had given birth to a son, which meant the Beast would be satisfied for yet another generation. Why had it killed my son? Why? I couldn't say, but I was eager to preserve my grandson, and even Mary Fairbanks. It appeared that all my hard work would end this evening. And I'd worked so extremely hard to bring her here. The letters, the trips to that godforsaken town to see her for myself. It had been the other one I'd selected, the real Miss Mary Fairbanks, but this one had been a better replacement. Our Mary, although an imposter, had a good heart and earnestly loved John Lamar, traits that I am sure would have been missing in the real Mary Fairbanks. She'd been a calculating prostitute. The woman before me made quite an improvement. She had her own mysterious past, but she was faithful to my son and, until now, obedient to me.

"You'll never make me stay here, Marietta Lancaster. My husband is dead, and there's nothing left for me. I know what you are and what you have done, mother-in-law. I know everything. If I stay here, it will come for Jason. It will take him, won't it?"

I sat in the straight-back chair and made no move to stop her. I'd already made plans to appease the Beast, already had my eye on another offering. Didn't Mary understand what I was doing? Why would I make her stay? Why would I need to make her stay? If she wanted to die, how could I stop her? All that it meant was my poor Oscar would have to return home, for the Beast would not be happy with any blood other than Lancaster blood.

"Seven years, Mary. Only every seven years. That is what I had been told. I didn't believe it; Eugenie Lancaster had always been a dramatic woman, an actress before she came to America and married Xavier's father. But what she told me terrified me. Of course, I ran to Xavier and told him everything, but he said he knew nothing. He lied to me, Mary. He knew it all. At least John Lamar knew very little. He did not lie to you."

Mary wiped her nose on a handkerchief she pulled from her oversized skirt pocket. "But you stayed. Even when you knew, Mrs. Lancaster. You let the children die."

Her words stung, but I continued to speak. I wasn't going to address her accusation.

"Nobody knew, but I was already pregnant. It's not something that's done, you know. Ladies don't do that sort of thing, give themselves before they marry. That's not how it happened. It was not my Xavier; he was a total gentleman. He never so much as kissed me until after we were married."

"Who was it, then, Mrs. Lancaster? Who was the father?" she asked, her voice echoing through the room. It reminded me that we were probably not alone. We were never alone here. Especially now that the Beast could enter the house. Did Mary know that yet? Did she know that the boundary had been breached? Probably not. She did not want to know anything, did she? I ignored her question.

My poor Sophie...

"I didn't know a thing, Mary. I married Xavier because I loved him. He knew everything and didn't tell me a thing. He knew about the curse and brought me here to feed the Beast. I wasn't even his first wife. I was his third. Did you know that?"

Mary shook her head; her wide-eyed expression did not surprise me. I would scarcely believe any of this if I hadn't lived it myself.

"Oh, don't worry, dear. John Lamar didn't know, Mary. Not in the beginning. He suspected something was amiss, but he did not know for certain. Don't blame him for bringing you to our home. He didn't know very much."

She didn't appear to believe me.

"John Lamar was not what you would call a gentleman. I know he cared for you, even loved you, perhaps. But like his father, and his father before him, John Lamar was cursed. The Lancaster name is in all ways afflicted."

"Cursed? Afflicted? I would say this is more than a curse, Marietta. We, the wives of these men, are the cursed ones. If I stay here and one day you are gone, I'll be the one leading women here and offering up the innocent. I can't do that—you can't ask me to do that. Never! You may as well kill me now if that is your true intention. Kill me, Marietta, for I'll not stay another day!"

"You shall and you will! You must do it for your son. If not, it will take him. It will take him like it took my Sophie. Like the others. Give it what it wants, and Jason will live. Is that what you want? Do you want him to die?"

"Do you? Do you want me to die?"

I didn't take the bait. I decided to keep going. She had to know everything before she made her decision. I felt tired. I couldn't be responsible for another death. Unless I had to. No, Mary needed to give this next offering. Yes, that's how it should be. I'd made my mind up about that.

"Something happened, Mary. Eugenie died without leaving me much instruction. What she told me all those years ago sounded crazy, so I ignored her rantings. I should have listened. Maybe I did something wrong and angered it. Maybe this is all my fault, Mary Fairbanks, but it did not start with me. I am trying to keep my family safe. That is all I wanted to do. Now it is your turn. I will not live forever. Then what will you do?"

Mary began to cry as she sank on the bed. "He's dead, Marietta. John Lamar is gone, and now there's only my son. Do I stay and continue to anger God with these unholy acts? I cannot do that. And I cannot bring another innocent woman into this situation. We need to leave, mother-in-law. We can leave together if you'll just listen to me. Please, say you will come with me."

Mary's pleading didn't stir my heart. I already knew what would happen if we attempted to do so.

"Do you think I haven't tried? Do you think I haven't crossed the boundary with my own child? It took my Sophie, Mary Fairbanks. My firstborn. It was only supposed to be every seven years. She was the bastard child, and it came for her." Mary gasped at my tired confession. "I didn't have the heart to tell Portia, and she and my son were in love, or so they believed. But it took her. You saw it yourself, didn't you?"

A tear streamed down Mary's small, heart-shaped face. "What happens if I cross the boundary, Marietta? What will happen to me? What about Jason?"

"It will come. The Beast will rip you to pieces. Or it will pull you beneath the ground and you will be buried alive." I smiled at her not because I found joy in the telling but because I had thought the same thing once upon a time.

"Do you think you are the first to try? It knows what you plan to do. It will find you. If it becomes angry enough, it will come in the house, Mary Fairbanks. And nothing will stop it. Nothing and no one."

She suddenly sprang to her feet. "I don't believe you! Nothing has that kind of power! Nothing! I have to go; I have to take Jason!" She lurched the bag off the bed, the contents half spilling on the ground. She didn't care. Mary had every intention of leaving, regardless of my warning. My honest and truthful warning.

"It's too late, Mary. The baby is gone. Jason is gone. He's safe, I promise you that, but he won't be if we don't do what we must. If we don't give the Beast what he wants. Please, Mary. Do not fight me on this. Do not make me do something I will regret."

Mary shrieked as she opened the door and ran to the nursery. As I predicted, the baby was nowhere to be found. Of course, I would never harm the child. He was my grandson, after all. But she had to do the deed. It had to be Mary; she was, after all, Jason's mother. Yes, it must be her.

"I want my son! Give me my son, Marietta! How can you do this? How?" Mary cried desperately and even shook my arms. But I would not be moved. I was doing this for her own good. So that she would not know the pain of loss. She would thank me later. However, Mary could not run from this any longer. It was her turn to satisfy the Beast. It was time for fresh blood, so to speak.

I rose from my seat and fluffed my skirt. I may as well tell her the truth. "Sally has taken Jason, on my order. You must give an offering. I will accompany you, but it is your turn, Mary. You are the child's mother. Just as I inherited this curse, so will you. Everything has been prepared for you. The offering is waiting for us."

Mary smothered a scream with her hands. "An offering? You mean a child! You want me to murder a child! I will never do that. Never! Give me my son, Marietta! We will not stay in this evil place! You will burn, Marietta Lancaster. Have you no fear of God?" Mary's Irish accent conveyed her deep feelings. Her Irish brogue always gave her away when she felt anxious or, in this case, horrified.

"You will go, or you will not see him again." It was not my wish to do this, but she had no choice. Just as I had no choice. I folded my hands peacefully and took a step toward her. She would do this. It was my turn to leave. I'd been waiting for her; the bones declared her the inheritor, the proper wife for John Lamar. She would have to do all that was required of her. I had appeased her, coddled her long enough.

Mary would kill for her son, or she would die. I would keep the boy myself and continue to do what I had to do for the sake of my family.

MARIETTA

Mary, Mary. What will you do?

Chapter Thirteen—Carrie Jo

My body shook. No, that's not right. It was the ground shaking beneath my feet. Time shifted slightly as Marietta declared her intentions. My stomach lurched as I wobbled between her time and mine. Should I go back? Can I stay here?

Why struggle now? I appeared tethered to the dark events that were unfolding around me. The clash between Mary and Marietta had no predictable end. None that I could see. Was it possible that this entity wanted to re-emerge in Heather's family? Is that possible?

Suddenly, a warm, living hand slid into mine. The honey hue often associated with the entrance of my dream walks and dream catching reappeared. I caught my breath at the sight of my husband's handsome face.

"Ash? How did you get here?" I wanted to blurt out, but it was important to remain quiet in any dream situation, and where was Rachel? Changing the past would bring about unwanted changes in the present and maybe even the future. I'd already made that mistake once. I didn't want to repeat it.

There was no time to remind him of any of that. I was no longer in the house but in the boneyard—and now so was Ashland. A chilly mist rose from the ground. So strange. The warmth of the honey hue vanished quickly and was replaced by the shimmering white fog. We were in the center of the boneyard, dead center. The shaking! It had to be proof that the Beast approached!

As if he already knew, Ashland clutched my hand, and we began to run. It was a natural instinct to run from danger, but we had to know how this would end. We needed to know, for Heather and her family and for all the lost ones who'd been murdered by this heinous spirit. Would the Beast attempt to force Heather to pick up where Marietta left off? Was the Watcher contributing to the supernatural storm that brewed here?

Yes, a storm. The air began to crackle with energy. The kind of energy that accompanied the paranormal. Something big was about to happen, about to emerge into this in-between reality. I tugged my hand back because I couldn't run. I couldn't do it. I saw Mary's face. Her tear-filled eyes and quivering lips. Mary's hidden child out there somewhere, facing darkness alone. Mary's situation tugged at my heart. What if that had been me?

I could not leave. Not yet.

Rachel? Where are you?

My husband's voice whispered my name, but then he was gone. I felt his familiar warmth vanish. Torn between two worlds, I hung in the middle. Ashland would understand. He would know why I was doing this. Everything would be okay, but I could not run from this. I needed to witness it all. I ran back to the center of the boneyard, but I lost my way. I ran far but could not reach the clearing on the other side.

The mist gathered higher. I could not see the ground at all. But as I ran, it swirled away, and I got a clearer picture. *Not my feet! Not my body!* The soft green grass felt wet, and the ground continued to rumble as if something horrible was about to erupt.

"Ashland!" I screamed as my terror level rose. He had come to rescue me, but I wanted to stay. I regretted that decision now.

"Run, Carrie Jo!" I heard his soft voice. But where had it come from? I was no longer Carrie Jo. I'd often experienced my dream catching sessions as someone else, but this had a different feel to it. My skin crawled continually, and my brain shuddered. I'd had a seizure once in my life. As a child, I fell off the merry-go-round and got a concussion, which led to the seizure. This reminded me of that. The sensation was similar in many ways.

No, CJ. Keep it together. Stay in the moment. Open your eyes and pay attention.

Strange how in these moments, my own voice warned me. Or was it my voice?

Momma? Are you here with me in the fog?

I heard footsteps walking toward me. Not Ashland's footsteps, either. I would know them anywhere, even in the dark. This was a woman's footsteps. "Rachel?" No answer came, but my visitor continued to make a beeline toward me. That weird brain shuddering continued. What was happening? Was I having a seizure? Clearly, I was not quite myself. I didn't recognize myself.

Closer, closer, the footsteps drew closer.

"Momma?" I whispered hopefully. Maybe that had been her voice I heard. Maybe. Anything is possible in the dream world or on a dream walk. Which one was this? Or was it something else altogether?

Barreling through the fog it came, the two footsteps becoming four. As the fog rolled back, I could see clearly now. The horror of Marietta, the hellhound thing, the Beast—it was not a grim but a Beast—came racing toward me. Black with scaly skin, no fur at all. Even its eyes and gums were black, but those sharp white teeth practically glowed in the dark. It did not make a sound as the ground shook beneath me. All around me were the cries of the dead. The dead beneath me, all around, warning me.

"Oh, God! Ashland!"

That was all I could say or think before I was thrown on my back, the wind knocked out of me. The Beast, twice my size, flung its shaggy head back, and a drizzle of spit poured out of the corner of its mouth as it roared. A rising moon peeked out of the clouds, as if to strengthen the creature, to witness my death. The dead were rising, their moans and groans horrible to hear. My terror continued as the ground shook beneath me, but it didn't matter.

I was certainly going to die here in this dream. Death was a surety.

The Beast placed its huge paw on my chest, and I could not regain my breath. It pulled its face closer to me. Those teeth—I could not take my eyes off them. They snapped once and then twice.

The face of the Beast began to contort, twitch and change. What was happening? The dark furry face evolved into a horrid, familiar face. This was no mindless creature! No grim or hellhound!

This was Marietta Lancaster! Somehow, she and the Beast were one. It had taken on her likeness, not Adam Crossley! She had become the thing of nightmares! Her body remained that of a large wolf, but her face morphed between the two. Was this really happening?

I am going to die. And my child. We are about to die. My baby...I am so sorry.

Mary's voice folded over mine. The two of us were one. Now I know what happened to Mary. The Beast took her. She had been the sacrifice! Mary's voice infiltrated my brain.

Murdered me. Help me. Find my baby! Evil that will not stop...

Then I saw everything. Even as I twisted beneath the Beast's paw, struggling for breath, as near to death as I'd ever come, I could see it all.

Mary would not stop talking. Someone needed to know what happened to her. And that someone was me.

Wanted me to do evil, but I would not offend God. Demanded I offer a child, but I refused and set the boy free. She pinned me to the ground with stakes and ropes. Sally cut me, made me bleed. I screamed and screamed, but nobody came. Nobody rescued me. I heard voices...

John Lamar!

He saw me, came to me. Smiled at me. At last, he would know, and he would rescue me. At last!

But he did not untie me, merely stared down at me curiously. Still smiling, but that smile was not one I recognized. So cold and calculating. Unfeeling, unloving. I had been a fool. He whispered to his mother and left me screaming and crying in the rain. Sally retreated from the Boneyard, clearly concerned about what was about to happen. It wouldn't be safe to be here.

No, John! Do not leave me! God help me!

John and Marietta walked away and disappeared into the fog...

I heard the chanting of the Native Americans; they were trying to intercede even back then. These dead were not dangerous or evil, only moaning and groaning to mourn the sacrilege that continued to take place here. They wanted to stop the evil that had taken over their sacred burial land.

But they had no one to help them. The Watcher could not rise. He could not stand against this wicked Beast. It was too strong.

Poor Mary—and now poor me. I would die too. I suddenly felt ropes wrapping around my wrists and ankles. The pounding of stakes. I was not a Lancaster, but I was a threat.

How had this happened? I could see no one except the Marietta-Creature, which thankfully stepped back while roaring over me. The fog wrapped around it, but it would not be gone for long. Finally, air filled my lungs. I took in big gasps of air. The pain in my back was real, but I was still alive. Still alive. But for how long? How was this possible? The dead weren't supposed to have this kind of power. I'd never been attacked like this on a dream walk. As soon as I could breathe good, I began to scream for Ashland and Rachel. I didn't care who heard me.

I didn't care what happened to the future.

I had to think of my baby. And my poor AJ. And Lily Bean. Tears flowed down my face as I struggled with the ropes. The ground staggered beneath me. The soil loosened, as if something were burrowing up to take me. To pull me under, just as it had taken Mary and before her Portia and before her so many others.

Oh, God! No!

"Ashland!" I screamed at the top of my lungs. "Muncie! Where are you? Please, don't let me die here. Please!"

Just like Mary had been tricked and trapped, so was I. Tricked and trapped, and soon to be dead.

This was about to be the end of Carrie Jo Stuart. Now and forever.

Chapter Fourteen—Rachel

I heard her before I saw her. It hadn't been easy to break through into the dream world. This was not a natural talent for me. Focusing and calming my mind were the hardest things for me on any given day, much less now. I screamed at the sight of my sweet friend pinned to the ground with dirty ropes. The ropes were wrapped around bones that were being used as stakes. She was clearly meant to be a sacrifice to the Beast here at Marietta. I could not stop screaming at her.

"Carrie Jo!" I hung back a moment to survey the situation.

Ashland was here; I could hear his voice. Only he wasn't by himself. A tall Native American man—no, this man was a ghost—walked beside him, and he carried a strange staff in his hand. "Ashland!" I screamed at him just as a bony hand clutched my shoulder.

Out of the corner of my eye, I could see that this hand had skin; it was skeletal and strong. A voice whispered in my ear, but I could not understand the language. I sensed I was being warned not to interfere, but how to be sure? Whatever the purpose, the hand terrified me. As if it knew this, it clutched me tighter. I whimpered in pain, afraid to turn around and look. I was unable to do anything, certainly not move.

Ashland raced toward Carrie Jo, the ghost streaking beside him. I don't think he saw the Beast at first. Ashland was on his knees beside his wife, trying to untie her from the stakes. The ground moved beneath her. Any moment, she would be lost, lost forever. Swallowed up by the undulating ground.

I had to go. I shoved the bony hand off my shoulder, but as I began to move, it was as if an invisible force made it impossible. It was as if I were running against a blast of wind. My short hair blew around my face, and my jacket flapped back. But despite the resistance, I continued to push forward. I could only move a few inches. Inch by inch, I reached for my friends. Even though I was stuck in some weird sort of slow-motion resistance, Ashland was hustling to set his wife free.

"Behind you, Ashland!" I screamed, but the sound of my own voice came back to me.

Apparently, they couldn't hear me. Could they see me?

I couldn't be sure, but my heart was breaking for her—for both of them.

The Beast charged Ashland as he untied yet another rope. Carrie Jo's hands were free now, and she was sobbing as she worked the ropes at her feet. Fortunately, she looked up and saw the creature stalking toward them.

Drenched in mud, her long dark hair matted around her, the corpse of Marietta Lancaster roared angrily. She began scratching at the air as she came closer to Carrie Jo. Even from twenty feet away, the black fingernails appeared long and dangerous.

"Mine! My sacrifice! Give it to me!" The voice gurgled as if it were stuffed with mud and hatred. "She belongs to me!"

The Watcher had disappeared from my view, but his chanting I heard perfectly. Ashland had the medicine stick in his hand. "You have no power over us, Marietta. No power over my baby!" Carrie Jo screamed her warning, and the ground beneath her shook and rumbled in response. The red dirt flew around her. This powerful entity was determined to steal her away.

And then Ashland swung his stick at Marietta but missed her completely. She moved too fast for him.

In fact, she struck him, slicing his flesh with its fingernails. I heard Ashland's muted scream, but the chanting was getting louder. She was changing again, morphing into the Beast.

The chanting grew louder and louder still. I mumbled along with the invisible ones. The Watcher was with us, not against us! The injury caused Ashland to fall to the ground, but he didn't stay down long. He was back on his feet and struck the Beast again. This time, he struck it solidly on the back.

The dead around us, invisible to me, moaned and groaned their warning pitifully. The Watcher chanted, and I found myself chanting along with him. *Was he using me? How did I know these words?*

I heard the Watcher's voice in my mind, and his words streamed from my mouth. As I spoke, the resistance that had kept me in my place began to weaken, and the skeletal hand released me. I couldn't run yet, but walking was much easier.

Ashland was fighting the Beast. It kept morphing in and out of view. One minute, it was a bizarre-looking beast with black fur; the next moment, the Beast became a rotting Marietta Lancaster!

The chanting continued as I made my way to my friends. I wanted to cry, but the tears would not come. My heart beat faster. My heart might explode if I wasn't careful. I had heart issues; I was born with them. I never told anyone about them. It was my own cross to bear, and normally it didn't bother me. The occasional skipping heartbeat.

The occasional racing pulse didn't usually trouble me, but this situation had me in a bad way. I was in danger. Truly in danger.

A sacrifice must be made.

The last one, and the curse will be broken.

The Watcher's voice was soft but insistent. I was surprised to hear him speak English directly to my mind.

"What? What do you mean? Oh, no! Carrie Jo! Ashland! I'm coming!"

There was no chance to ask more questions. Ashland was badly injured, and Carrie Jo lay flat on her back again. The Beast was on top of her; I worried about her baby. She'd get crushed if it remained on top of her.

"Get off of her! Your reign of terror is over, Marietta!"

The Beast roared at me, but I didn't have a chance to be frightened. The Watcher was in my ear again.

Get the staff. Use the staff and make the sacrifice. The last one, and the curse will be broken.

"No! Not Carrie Jo!" I argued back. I assumed the Watcher was speaking of my pregnant friend. "Ashland! Use the staff!"

Like me, Ashland had no idea how to use the staff. Not really. This situation was getting out of hand. The fog thickened again, and the air chilled substantially. I grabbed the staff. I was panting and crying—almost screaming.

I banged the staff on the ground, and to my surprise, the ground shook a little. Wow, that was amazing.

"Get her out of here, Ashland! Marietta won't be satisfied without killing her. Let's go! Help me get her up!" I stood like Gandalf from Lord of the Rings but without the magic and confidence. The chanting continued. I struck the ground again and held the staff tight. I continued to chant along with the Watcher. The chanting was all around us. Marietta had shifted again, not a Beast now. Only a rotting woman, her black mouth wide and snapping. She twisted abnormally, but there was no doubt that she planned to continue pursuing my friend. Ashland dragged Carrie Jo away as she finally clambered to her feet. Her wild brown hair hung in dirty ropes. Her long dress was dirty, and she tripped over the hem.

"Rachel! Come on! We must go back together! Please!"

Even as Marietta scowled at me, I could see part of her skull.

My sacrifice!

"Marietta, have you forgotten who you are? This isn't you, Marietta. This isn't what you wanted." I spoke to her with sympathy, but honestly, I wanted to drive this staff through her chest. But did I have the strength? Or the courage?

What the hell was I doing?

"Rachel!" Ashland yelled at me. "You can make it!"

But I couldn't make it.

I wasn't going to make it.

I knew what the Watcher meant even as I ran toward him, toward the Beast. Yes, she was a beast again. I screamed against my own fate. "No!"

The Beast paced in front of me. I couldn't cry, couldn't do anything but scream. Until I couldn't scream any longer. Ashland called me again, but I waved him away.

When I found my voice, I commanded him to run. "Take her and go!"

Maybe this was my purpose. One good deed. I needed good karma.

Angus...I regret you the most. I loved you, Angus, but we were born in the wrong time. I always knew it, but I didn't want to believe it. I dreamed about you before I met you. You were the love of my life. This life. Maybe the next one, too.

The Beast ran to me. I clutched the staff with both hands as it clamped its teeth around it. The Watcher chanted in my ear, and I repeated those words. Words I did not know but felt deeply in my soul. The staff practically vibrated in my hands.

The Beast flinched at the power being channeled through me.

"You don't have any power over this place anymore. The sacred dead banish you, Marietta Lancaster! They banish all you evil Lancasters! You do not belong here! I banish you!"

The creature became the dead woman again. She slapped me stiffly, and the scent of rotting flesh lingered on mine. I wanted to gag. The pain hurt, but it would not drive me to my knees. I would not quit.

"My sacrifice...give me..."

She began to back away from me, and the fog had returned. It would hide her; it would keep her in the dark. Would it follow Carrie Jo back to her time? I couldn't allow that! I wouldn't! I banged the staff again and felt the air shift. I could only hope that

Ashland and Carrie Jo had left, that they were safe. I had to close this portal.

I had to close it for the last time.

And that would require a sacrifice.

The Watcher stood beside me; his knowing eyes gave me some peace, but I didn't doubt that my death would hurt. I feared the pain, but surprisingly, I had no regrets. I didn't want this ending, but it was coming.

Marietta screamed angrily as she realized that the time slip had ended, that Carrie Jo was out of her reach. She stormed toward me, her tattered gown fluttering around her, her decomposing blue flesh blackening as she threatened to transform yet again.

How had all this started? I would probably never know. But I knew how it was going to end.

The Watcher chanted, and I ran for all I was worth toward her. I clutched the staff like a spear. I wasn't alone. All the dead watched, hoping for a good ending. Tears blurred my eyes as my tennis shoes tapped on the ground.

I ran toward her; the spirit of the Watcher ran with me. I lifted the shaft to chest level and sped up. Marietta screamed like a banshee; the remaining wisps of her hair swirled around her skull. She was the most horrible creature I'd ever seen, could have ever imagined, but her eyes...something in her eyes relayed to me that she wanted this.

Marietta wanted to be free, and this was the only way. It could only be me.

The wooden stick landed on her chest, but I didn't let up. I didn't stop, and neither did Marietta or the Watcher. We came together in a collapse of flesh and bones. The stench of her body sickened me, but the shock of my own death separated me from her. I heard her sob once, then twice.

And then I was alone in a bright place. Long, tall grass brushed against my legs. Blue skies above me, the sound of a creek running nearby. Was this place heaven?

No, I wasn't alone. The Watcher was here. And he was not dead, not a ghost. He was alive and well, his skin bronze and healthy. He was old and young. Alive and dead.

He was beyond time. And now, so was I.

Meena hota! Come, brave one. You have a seat at my table.

I glanced down at my body, expecting to see something bad. An open wound. A broken bone. The pain at the moment of the collision with Marietta had been excruciating, but it didn't last long. It was all over.

I wore a yellow tunic, soft blue moccasins. My dark hair was long and braided. I was *Meena hota. Wise braid.* That was who I had always been.

I couldn't cry. I could only laugh.

And everyone came to greet me. Everyone I'd ever known, and ever would, and there were so many. And he was there too. The one I'd loved forever. Not Angus. He'd only been a shadow of him. This was my own love.

Wise Braid...my heart. My soul. You are home again.

I am home. I never want to leave again.

Maybe you will. Maybe you will not. I love you.

I feel your love. All of you. I am home.

They all said it with me, "You are home."

The brightness around me surged, and I lost myself in it. Everything else faded...

Epilogue—Lily

I dumped my bookbag on the floor of my bedroom and sank onto my bed. I was exhausted from the daily physical challenges but also all the other stuff I'd been doing. Like sneaking into the woods to dream walk.

I'd only been gone for two weeks this time, but it may as well have been a lifetime. These tennis camps were tough, but I was such a better tennis player for it. Yeah, things were changing for me. How did I feel about that? I couldn't explain it, but I sensed that everything had changed.

A shadow darkened the doorway. "Hey, Bean. Need help with anything?" My uncle peeked his head inside the door but didn't come in. He waited for an invitation now before stepping into my room. That was kind of a new rule I established before I left for tennis camp.

This is my space, Unk. Please respect my space.

Today I regretted that request. I missed Uncle Ash and Aunt CJ barging into my room without knocking. Treating me like a child. Okay, not really, but I did miss being considered a kid. Their kid. But I'd still be their kid, even after the baby arrived. They weren't the kind of people to kick me to the curb. No, this feeling...it wasn't really about that. Was it?

This was about Mitchell and the feelings I had about a crush I loved and lost without even knowing about it. Not in my waking life. Life was so uncomplicated before I fell for a ghost.

And Aunt Rachel...would I ever find her?

"I'm good. I dumped my dirty laundry downstairs, and I'm about to get a bath. Hey, I thought you guys had plans tonight. Need me to babysit?" I'd stepped up since Aunt Rachel's disappearance.

Aunt Carrie Jo worried about me. She was concerned that I hadn't cried, that I wasn't grieving. That's because I knew Rachel wasn't gone forever. I didn't know what that meant, except I was not ready to let her go. Not when the door was still open. As unschooled in dream walking as I was, I continued to look for her every chance I got.

"Are you available? I thought you had plans." He leaned against the doorway and crossed his arms.

"Nothing, besides studying. Katrina and I are going to the movies tomorrow night. Have you forgotten? You're supposed to drop us off. Her big sister is picking us up," I said as I pulled my laptop out of my bookbag and put it back on my desk.

"No, I haven't forgotten. Great. I'll tell your aunt. We're having your favorite for supper."

"Uh, pizza?" I guessed without much thought.

"Yep." He grinned, as if he were quite pleased with himself.

I didn't bother telling him I didn't need that many carbs. He wouldn't understand it. Suddenly my aunt was beside him, a frown on her face. "Ash, please. No pizza. How about letting the kids order what they want? Did you tell her?"

That piqued my interest. "Ask me what? I already volunteered to babysit. That's no problem."

Aunt Carrie Jo walked into the room with a big grin. She hugged me and ruffled my curly ponytail. "We don't actually need you to babysit. We have something else planned. You've got friends coming over. In fact, some of them are here already."

I was trying to wrap my tired brain around this. "What? Why? It's not my birthday. I had my birthday at camp. And I just got home!"

"Only because I stalled your uncle for more time."

"I was wondering why on earth you wanted to go to the zoo. We've been like a dozen times," I said as I eyed Uncle Ashland.

"Surprise!" He laughed as he walked away and headed down the stairs.

"It's not your birthday, but it's the day you came into our family, Lily Stuart. It's like a birthday. It's time to celebrate. Your friends are here, so it's not just boring Uncle Ash and me. And raincheck on the babysitting." She did a thumbs-up and made a clicking sound with her tongue.

I stepped back from her arms, a goofy smile on my face. "Really? You want to celebrate my adoption day?"

"Heck yeah. I think it's a great reason to party. Ooh. Listen. Sounds like the DJ is setting up outside." Music boomed from somewhere outback.

"You got me a DJ? This is like a for real party?" My hands went to my mouth. I tried not to jump up and down like a little kid.

"Yeah, a real party, but full disclosure, Detra Ann arranged everything. You know it is going to be all kinds of extra. Put on something cute. I bought you a few things. They're hanging up in your closet."

I raced out of the room and down the hall to the French doors that led to the balcony. I couldn't believe it. How had I missed all this when I came home? There was a big white tent, a dance floor squared off with purple lights and all kinds of purple decorations. It was amazing! The sun would be going down soon, which would make it perfect. I could already see more lights coming on.

For reasons unknown, my eyes dampened with unshed tears. I wasn't supposed to cry at my own party.

Aunt Carrie Jo stood beside me. "Hey! No peeking. Go get a shower and get ready to party."

It was then that I noticed some of my school friends were strolling around the gardens. Yeah, there was Katrina, Anna, Gabby, and her sister. A few guys too. Oh, my gosh! Was that the new kid, Chris What's-His-Name?

"How did you get them here?" I asked my aunt as she slid her arm through mine.

"What do you mean? Did I bribe them? Of course not. I got a list from Katrina. She really likes you. I'm glad to see that she doesn't have such a chip on her shoulder anymore. I'm sure you had something to do with that. You've been a good influence, I think."

"You give me far too much credit, Aunt Carrie Jo. I'm no saint, you know. I make a lot of mistakes."

"Who doesn't? Don't try to be perfect. Just be you." She patted my back and urged me to hurry. The music really cranked up now.

"Aunt Carrie Jo?" I asked, poised on the edge of telling her what I'd been doing. I decided against it. I'd continue to look for Rachel on my own. It would be good for me. I was not a kid anymore. It was time to do things on my own.

"Yes?"

I hugged her neck and kissed her cheek. I didn't usually show that much affection, but this was amazingly thoughtful. "Thank you for the party. You got me. I mean, you really got me."

"You are welcome. Now get busy." She left me alone and headed downstairs to help Uncle Ashland arrange things. I don't know why they bothered. Detra Ann had things under control—she was like a drill sergeant when it came to parties and whatnot. This was going to be so much fun.

As I turned away, I caught a strange reflection in the glass. Not me, but behind me. I turned around, but there was no one there. Who could that be? I slowly turned back to the glass and was surprised to see he hadn't moved. Not an inch.

He wanted me to see him.

"Mitchell? Is that you?"

He didn't answer me, but he looked angry. Very angry. But why? A chill passed over me, and I scurried away from the balcony. I had no idea what just happened, but Mitchell wasn't the same. He warned me that if I forced him to stay, it would change him.

But I hadn't done that. Had I?

I forced the frightening and heartbreaking image from my mind and decided to get ready for my party. I didn't see him again, and by the time I was all dolled up, as Uncle Ashland would say, I'd put it all out of my mind.

Aunt Carrie Jo didn't dream anymore. AJ had shut himself down, too. Even Uncle Ash wasn't really using his gifts. Just me. Maybe that was why he was angry?

I'd think about this later. I had a life to lead. The music pumped and thumped, and my friends screamed for me as I came down the stairs in a cute purple minidress. I couldn't believe CJ would allow me to wear a mini. The look on my uncle's face revealed that he knew nothing about it.

Happy to be home, I waved at my friends and family. I had a good life. I'd think about Aunt Rachel and Mitchell later. I wouldn't abandon my search for her. Never. Not until I had the answers I needed. Not until I was sure she wasn't stuck in between times, in between dimensions.

But for now, it was time to dance.

Author's Note

First, let me apologize for stalling the release of this book. As usual, I always add too many things to my plate, too many books on my calendar. But finally, here it is, *Footsteps of Angels*. I really wanted to make this an interesting story, one that wasn't rushed or hurried.

It was so exciting to investigate with Ashland, Carrie Jo and everyone in the ever-expanding *Seven Sisters* world. Bringing in the grim tradition (which is true. by the way) and the conflict with the holy Native American ground was a challenge, but I hope I did the story justice. Imagine two entities fighting one another over the centuries over the same piece of ground? No wonder the people who called that location home had such tragedies occurring in their lives.

Until last year, I'd never heard of a grim, except when used to describe the Grim Reaper, which is not at all what I am writing about in my book. There are many grim statues commemorating buried black dogs in Mobile's Magnolia Cemetery. It is a chilling practice and one that I am glad is no longer used in the modern age. However, one must wonder, are those poor animals still watching over their masters? Are they still pacing the graveyard at night, challenging any demon or spirit that dares step too close? It is a thought that gives me shivers. I spend a lot of time in cemeteries. I am always respectful, but I am also very aware that I am never alone. Bones may be beneath me, but spirits are always around me. And they don't appreciate disrespect of any sort. If you happen to visit Magnolia Cemetery—or any cemetery, for that matter—please show the proper respect. The dead deserve it.

Marietta isn't an actual location. I based the house on Beauvoir, the last residence of Jefferson Davis. I had the pleasure of touring the home in May. What an amazingly haunted location! Let me tell you a little of what happened during our paranormal investigation. Thanks, by the way, to SPARS Paranormal for allowing me to tag along. If you get a chance, book a tour with them. I'm not affiliated with them, but I highly recommend the experience. Especially if you are new to paranormal investigation. It's a comfortable environment with lots of places to investigate from the Presidential Library to the Confederate Cemetery to the Beauvoir house itself. The property has a feel about it.

A true paranormal feeling.

When I went, there were thirty of us paranormal investigators. That's a lot, I know, but we were divided into groups of six. It was awesome. We began our work, with each group spending thirty minutes at one location on the property. At each location there was specialized equipment, including an SLS, which offered the most amazing evidence of the night.

What's strange is, I didn't know that Beauvoir had a grim on the property, but it does! Don't tell me that the paranormal world isn't helping me with my stories. As a paperback medium, I am fortunate to receive these neat little tidbits from the other side. I live for telling stories of the past. I feel an obligation to the ghosts of yesterday, to bring them back to life through my stories. I truly do feel as if they are working with me, whispering their truths in my ear.

I pray that I've gotten the story right.

Next year, we'll all be revisiting the original story, but in a new way. I am releasing the Beaumont Saga on Kindle Vella! Can you believe it? Have you ever wanted to know why Louis never married? Why Olivia was so cruel later in life? Why couldn't Christine find happiness with the man she truly loved? Look for that in the spring of 2022.

It's going to be a joy to revisit some of my favorite characters and tell their stories, too. I hope you follow along with me. Soon I am publishing *Delivered Me from Evil*, my autobiography. In my book, I share what it was like to live in a haunted house as a child and how it affected me for the rest of my life. Those first experiences led to more terrifying ones until I found myself in the battle of my life. I hope by sharing my own journey, I can help someone.

Thanks again for reading *The Bones of Marietta* and *Footsteps of Angels*. Your love and support mean the world to me.

Make sure you sign up for my mailing list so you can receive my bimonthly notes. I usually share details from my paranormal investigations and let you know what books are coming out next and what's on sale.

I'm also active on Facebook[1]. I frequently post cat memes (I am addicted to those) and dream cast information as well as other fun posts. If you'd like to email me, you can reach me at authormlbullock@gmail.com.

I wish you all the best. Until next time, my lovelies!
Monica Leigh
(M.L. Bullock)

---

1.   https://www.facebook.com/AuthorMLBullock

Don't miss out!

Visit the website below and you can sign up to receive emails whenever M.L. Bullock publishes a new book. There's no charge and no obligation.

https://books2read.com/r/B-A-CXMC-GPBCF

BOOKS 2 READ

Connecting independent readers to independent writers.

Also by M.L. Bullock

Create and Prosper
The Prolific Writer: How to Write and Create a Successful Catalog of Books

Delta Hex
The Devil's Bayou

Desert Queen Saga
The Tale of Nefret
The Falcon Rises
The Kingdom of Nefertiti
The Song of the Bee Eater

Devecheaux Antiques and Haunted Things Trilogy Series
Devecheaux Antiques and Haunted Things
A Cup of Shadows
A Voice From Her Past
A Watch Of Weeping Angels

Gulf Coast Paranormal
The Ghosts of Kali Oka Road
The Ghosts of the Crescent Theater
A Haunting on Bloodgood Row
The Legend of the Ghost Queen
A Haunting at Dixie House
The Ghost Lights of Forrest Field
The Ghost of Gabrielle Bonet
The Ghost of Harrington Farm
The Creature on Crenshaw Road
A Ghostly Ride in Gulfport
The Ghosts of Phoenix No.7
The Maelstrom of the Leaf Academy
The Ghosts of Oakleigh House
The Spirits of Brady Hall
The Gray Lady of Wilmer

Gulf Coast Paranormal Season Three
Tower of Darkness
Haunted Molly
Dead Children's Playground

Gulf Coast Paranormal Season Two
The Wayland Manor Haunting
The Beast of Limerick House
The Beast of Limerick House
A Haunting at Goliath Cave
Death Among the Roses

The Captain of Water Street
Return to the Leaf Academy

Gulf Coast Paranormal Trilogy Series
Ghosted
Haunted
Dead
Spooked
Paranormal

Haunting Passions
For the Love of Shadows
Her Haunted Heart

Idlewood
The Ghosts of Idlewood
Dreams of Idlewood
The Whispering Saint
The Haunted Child

Laurel House
Whispers

Lost Camelot
Guinevere Unconquered

The Undead Queen of Camelot

Lost Camelot Trilogy
Guinevere Forever

Marietta
The Bones of Marietta
Footsteps of Angels

Morgans Rock
The Haunting of Joanna Storm
The Hall of Shadows
The Ghost of Joanna Storm

Return to Seven Sisters
The Roses of Mobile
All the Summer Roses
Blooms Torn Asunder
A Garden of Thorns
Wreath of Roses

River Run
River Run

Scary Fall Stories
Horrible Little Things

Seven Sisters
Seven Sisters
Moonlight Falls On Seven Sisters
Shadows Stir At Seven Sisters
The Stars That Fell
The Stars We Walked Upon
The Sun Rises Over Seven Sisters
Beyond Seven Sister
Ghost on a Swing

Shabby Hearts
A Touch Of Shabby
Shabbier By The Minute
Shabby By Night
Shabby All The Way
Star Spangled Shabby

Southern Gothic
Being With Beau
Death's Last Darling
Spook House

Southland
Southland

Sugar Hill
Wife Of The Left Hand
Fire On The Ramparts
Blood By Candlelight
The Starlight Ball
His Lovely Garden

Summerleigh
The Belles of Desire, Mississippi
The Ghost Of Jeoprady Belle
The Lady In White
Loxley Belle

Supernatural Support Group
Circle of Shadows

The Mummy Queen's Revenge
Queen Mummy

Twelve to Midnight

Mary Twelves

Standalone
The Hauntings of Idlewood
Lost Camelot
The Desert Queen Collection
Haunting Passions
Ghosts on a Plane
Halloween Screams
Dead Is the Loneliest Place to Be
Ghost Story
Believer's Guide to Paranormal Ministry
Haunted Chronicles of the Leaf Academy
Haunting Paranormal
Falls the Shadow
The Mourning Heart
Marietta

Watch for more at www.mlbullock.com.

About the Author

Author M.L. Bullock enjoys the laid-back atmosphere and the spooky vibe of the Gulf Coast, especially the region's historic districts and sites. When she isn't visiting her favorite haunts in New Orleans or Old Mobile, you can find her flipping through old photographs or newspaper clippings in search of new inspiration.

Read more at www.mlbullock.com.

Milton Keynes UK
Ingram Content Group UK Ltd.
UKHW020121221024
449869UK00010B/376